THE SUMMIT

THEIR CHAMPION BOOK TWO

K.A. KNIGHT

DEDICATION

To my readers, your support and willingness to go along with my crazy is what drove me in this book. You pushed me to be a better writer, I hope I do you justice.

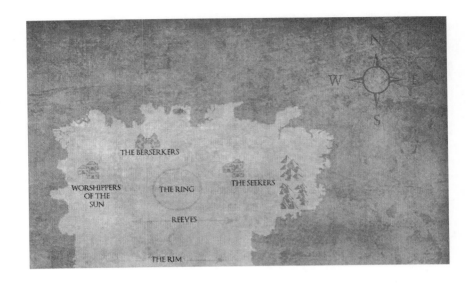

"Out of suffering have emerged the strongest souls; the most massive characters are seared with scars."

- Kahlil Gibran

CHAPTER ONE

WELCOME TO PARADISE

"What the hell is going on? How are you alive? Where are we? Where are my friends?" I demand, question after question pouring out of me as I eye my father.

He holds up his hand to stop my rapid-fire questions and walks towards me, I instinctively move back into a fighting position. Pain flashes through his bright blue eyes and he stops with an awkward smile, obviously unsure how to approach me. I bet I look like a wild animal compared to him; where he is put together and calm, my blood is racing with the need to fight. My body only highlights our differences, the scars and brands standing out against my skin in this pale room where his hair is perfect and styled, I can't even remember the last time I brushed mine. I wonder what he sees when he looks at me. Does he see his little girl or a stranger?

"I know you have questions, kiddo. I promise I will answer them. For now, know that you are safe and your...erm friends are fine. Please, just calm down." His voice is soft, the one he used to use on me when I was a scared child.

Calm down? That makes me want to stab him. The only thing stopping me is that I need his help. Is that bad? That I would be willing to kill my own father, even if he did abandon me? Shouldn't I be happier to see him?

"I want to see them," I grit out, straightening from my crouch but still watching him intently in case he moves towards me. He nods and holds his hand out. When I don't take it, he frowns, the laugh lines around his eyes and mouth pulling taut.

"Okay, why don't you get dressed and I'll take you to see them." His voice is smooth, his words slow like he's trying to corner a wild animal. Well, that's what I am after all.

Thorn falling to the ground flashes in my mind, as do Jax's eyes as he watched me hopelessly. If they are hurt—or worse, dead—I will burn this fucking place to the ground and kill everyone. There would be no holding back the monster inside me, I would succumb and be nothing more than a bloodthirsty Berserker. I should have told them how I feel, I just hope it's not too late.

Blowing out a breath, I let the death grip on my blade go, and look towards the chair where a god awful dress sits. I cringe at the thought of wearing it, but if it will get me to my men sooner...groaning, I nod. He smiles brilliantly at me like I offered him the world.

"Good, I'll wait outside while you get dressed. You can keep the knife, the grey-eyed man said you wouldn't feel safe without it. Just please don't hurt anyone." The last words are hesitant, as if he's unsure whether I would or not. It only hits home how much I have changed and how he is nothing more than a stranger to me.

Wait, grey-eyed man? Only one man I know has grey eyes, Jax. My silent demon. Even his name has my heart speeding up and joy running through me. I would endure a lot more than that dress to see him again, to touch him, kiss him.

I rush to the dress as my father leaves the room and yank it on. I grunt and growl as I wiggle into the tight material. It's silky but constrictive. Nowhere to hide any weapons at all. Why do people wear these things? If those motherfucking men of mine helped pick out this dress I'm going to put them in it, wounds or not. Then I might kiss them better. My knife glints at me from the chair and an evil smile reaches my lips. Grabbing it, I start hacking at the material, cutting the length until it's short in the front and a normalish level at the back, making it easier to move. Material goes flying everywhere as I slice through it.

When I'm satisfied, I look down at the red material. It looks too much like blood for my liking, but I grin at the rough-edged dress. It looks like it's been through the wringer and back, just like me. I'm betting Dray would love it. If I added a few swords he would die. Laughing, I freeze when I try to figure out how long we have been here. My brain trying to catch up with everything. The Summit was only days away when I left The Worshippers...

Swearing, I rush to the door. As I approach it, it opens with a whoosh, the air releasing from the room. If possible, the lights out here are brighter and guess what? More white. My father—that feels weird to say—smiles at me from the other side, but it soon turns into a frown when he gets a look at my face. He pulls his hands from his trouser pockets, and steps towards me as if to touch me. He hesitates at the last second and lets them drop, the space between us filled with tension and memories, but I have far more important things to worry about right now.

"What's wrong, princess?" His eyes search mine, obviously seeing my panic.

My heart clenches at the familiar endearment, but I have no time for a trip down memory lane. "How long have I been out?" I ask quickly.

He rubs his chin in thought, his eyes calculating and intelligent. He always was a smart man, relying on logic. I remember how he used to say my mum was the heart and he was the brain. That despite all his logic, she convinced him that love does exist. He used to come into my room and read me books on everything and anything. From science to history, I loved it all. I absorbed it all, it was just us, our time. My mum said I had his drive and thirst for knowledge, and her big heart. I grit my teeth against the memories, it's obvious seeing him again has brought up everything I have repressed.

"About a day, why?" He steps closer, but I'm too busy trying to figure out the timeline. It took us three days to get there. We spent a day at the cult. Say a half a day travelling, and a day here. Six days to be sure. That means The Summit is happening in six days. Four days until Dray starts looking for me. I have no doubt he will too. He will start with the Worshippers, burning any treaty that might be possible for the future. There will be nothing but a bloodbath in his wake. Then he will go to The Reeves. It will be a massacre, with my crazy 'soulmate' in the centre like some fallen angel. There will be nothing and no one left to help us stop Ivar. I look at my father, someone I'm supposed to trust above anyone else, and hesitate. How much do I tell him?

"Nothing, just wondered," I finish lamely, I've come too far to trust someone just because of blood. He hasn't been in my life for years. I thought he was dead for god's sake! I'm trying to ignore that thought, my whole being demanding I see my men before I question my father. Everything else can wait now that I know we still have time to get back to The Ring. He nods, but his face tells me he doesn't believe me, his eyes imploring me to trust him. When the silence stretches and it becomes obvious I won't say anything else, he deflates, his shoulders slumping and that twinkle in his eyes dimming. I refuse to feel guilty. How can he expect me to trust him when I don't even know him? I've seen too much, learnt lessons the hard way about trust.

"Come on, let's get you to your friends before they burn this place down. Or kill someone looking for you," he mutters the last, and it makes me smile. Those are my guys. Blinking, he looks at my torn up dress, obviously just seeing it, then back to my face. Wisely, he stays silent, his eyes asking what he daren't.

My father offers me his arm, the distance between us begging me to take it. But I can't, he's still a stranger to me. I start walking, and he sighs before falling in next to me.

"We have a lot to talk about, after you check on your friends, of course," he says after the silence starts to get awkward.

I nod mutely, my eyes wide as they take in wherever we are. We turn a corner and I freeze in shock, my eyes glued to one of the walls in the wide corridor. Like in the room I woke up in, there is glass from floor to ceiling. But it's the people outside that makes me freeze.

Women and children are laughing and playing in what looks like a garden. So many children, more than I can ever remember seeing. No worries, no weapons, hell there aren't even men out there. They seem genuinely happy, and their clothes! It's like before the world died. Dresses, loose pants, shirts. You name it, it looks like an advert for the early 2000's. Or a dream. A young girl runs past the window, her pigtails streaming in the wind behind her as her blue dress and white socks shine in the sunlight. Another young girl with blonde ringlets chases after her, laughing hysterically, her bright pink dress trailing behind her like a cape. Two older women, plump and clean, watch and laugh from the closest table, their smiles genuine, and their happiness almost palpable. The glass dividing us only reinforces our differences. Where they are light, I am dark. I can be happy, but I will never be that carefree. Not when I know what waits out there.

The grass is green, a vibrant colour like nothing I have seen in years, with flowers of all colours dotted here and there. Picnic tables are laid out in one corner, with a stone well in the other, a brown wooden bucket sitting on the rim. What looks like white stone, smooth and polished, encloses the garden on either side, reaching into the sky. The opposite end of the garden is covered in windows like the one I am looking out of. It looks like something frozen in time, unaffected by the devastation in the world. No worries, no cares, hell not even any dust or sand. But how can this be? And what does my father have to do with it all?

I step closer, my nose almost pressed to the glass and look up. The sun is streaming down through an open area of the ceiling, letting the grass grow and flourish. What looks like electricity runs the length of the opening in a net formation. For protection, or to act as a cage? The thought turns the scene before me sour.

"Tazzy?" comes my father's hesitant voice. I turn to see him waiting at the end of the hallway. When he looks from me to the window, he smiles and walks to my side, joining me in watching the children play.

"What the hell is this place?" I ask, my eyes drawn back to the garden. The innocence on their faces makes me feel like I am covered in blood and death, like an outsider.

"Paradise, Tazanna. It's Paradise."

The idea of Paradise is alluring, but I am not someone who belongs in a place like this. My soul is too tainted, my heart too cold. Paradise was always a rumour, a fantasy to keep hope alive, but for Paradise to exist, so must hell.

We both watch the women for a while before he goes to touch me. I jump away, my knife already palmed. Blinking, he stares at me sadly, his face turning heartbroken. The move was automatic, I'm still not used to people reaching for me or touching me. Ignoring him, I slide the blade away before straightening.

"What happened to you, Tazanna?" he whispers, his eyes glistening with unshed tears. Surely he knows the horror of the outside world, how could he expect me not to be tainted by it? To not be changed or have grown differently to survive out there? Anger flashes through me at the pity in his eyes. How dare he! He knows nothing of my life, nothing of the fight I'd had every damn day just to survive. Here he hides in this...bunker! This paradise and he has the audacity to pity me? No, I pity him. Because this won't last. Paradise will fall, and when it does nothing but death and rubble will remain, and he will have to adapt or die. He can pity me all he wants, but I am exactly the person I need to be, not only to survive in this world but thrive.

"The name's Worth," I say coldly, my mask sliding back into place. It takes longer than normal, so used to not hiding anything from my men, but when it does, I see him flinch. I look back at the women and children for a moment. What a nice life it must be with no worries, even if it is a lie. Shaking my head, I look at my father again, my eyes as cold as my heart for him.

"Take me to my friends. Then you owe me an explanation."

WE WALK IN silence for a while, him lost to his thoughts probably wondering what happened to the little girl he lost. Me? I'm checking this place out for weaknesses and escape routes, something so hardwired into me I hardly realise I'm doing it. The silence is uncomfortable, and I see him open his mouth more than once, only to close it again. A part of me feels sad that this is how we have turned out, but the other part is still angry with him.

The floor turns into tiles, and the walls remain white, which is stupid if you ask me. It will show blood way too easily, and definitely be stained by, well, everything. I catch the light of another camera. There is a camera, with the blinking red light, in the corner of every hallway. It creeps me out knowing someone is watching me, tracking my every move.

Back before everything went to shit, cameras, phones, hell technology, had taken over. People were always glued to the devices in their hands, ones which could track them, spy on them, and even be used to hurt them. The concept is so foreign to me now. How is that freedom? How do you know your privacy isn't being invaded, that people aren't listening or watching you? I guess the Wastes are good for one thing, you know when you are being spied on.

"Was that light that flared when we were fighting you?" I ask casually, my eyes constantly scanning everything as we walk. Two men walk past, their strides confident and stiff. They look like soldiers and I spot weapons strapped to each of their legs. Their eyes focus on me before flicking away, scanning everything like I am. I watch them turn the corner behind me. Are they patrolling? Why would you need patrols inside?

"Not me personally, it was a patrol who found you. They used floodlights and gas. They waited for the gas to clear then took all of you as you passed out. When you were brought back, you were put in quarantine like everyone else we encounter. I happened to be overseeing selection that day, and I saw you and well..."

"All?" I ask quickly, freezing on the spot. Surely he can't mean the Berserkers as well?

"Yes, why?" He throws me a confused look before skirting around another soldier.

"Even the Berserkers?"

"Berserkers?" He sounds it out slowly, rolling it over his tongue.

"Never mind, we can talk about that after," I mutter, but I stand up straighter, and my eyes scan everything faster, just in case. I don't imagine he would just let them walk around, and I am betting they are as confused as I am, but I can't be too careful. He nods, but he throws me weird looks as we walk.

"You must be what, twenty-two now?" he asks, as if trying to start a conversation.

"Twenty-three," I correct, uncomfortable with the small talk.

"Oh. So, erm are any of these men your...boyfriend?" He says the word like it's dirty and I wonder what his face would be like if I told him they all were. He would probably have a heart attack. I snort, but don't bother to answer.

"Tazanna, I am trying here," he says softly. Spinning, I stop in front of him and poke his chest, my face cold.

"We are strangers. I haven't seen you since I was thirteen. Ten years. Just because we share the same blood does not mean I have to give you respect or my life story. You have to earn that. My life went to hell, and I thought I had lost everyone. So excuse me if I'm not all smiles and laughter at seeing my father back from the fucking grave. We can talk after I check on my friends. But you should ask yourself, what sort of person does not come for their daughter? Who doesn't fight for her and lets her think he's dead for most of her life?" My chest heaves as I finish my rant and I realise that my anger is covering my heartbreak. How could he just walk away from me, leave me? Was is it that easy for him to give me up? I swallow down my tears, biting my tongue to stop them from falling when all I want is to demand he tell me why. The fact is, it would hurt me more to find out he didn't care enough to come after me, that is what stops me.

We face each other, my walls built up and blocking him out. How could he abandon me to that monster and be okay with that? I wish he had suffered like I did, and could understand the pain I went through. I don't know how I will ever forgive him.

"If you don't let me out of this fucking room, boy, I will slit your throat and wear you like a skin coat," comes a familiar voice, muffled, but still clear, and I've never been so happy to hear a threat in my life. It makes me smile, I spin to the door down the corridor where I heard it come from and jog to it, uncaring about my father any longer. My family is with these men. I bang on the door until someone slides it open on the other side. A small man stands there looking like I flung a turd in his face, his thin lips twisted in disgust as he takes me in from head to toe, his beady brown eyes flicking over me before returning to my face. His hair is receding and sporadic on his head, obviously pushed over to try and hide it. His ears are too small for his head, and his head is tiny in comparison to his chubby body.

"Miss, this is a restricted area. Please leave," he says it politely, his nasally voice filled with a sneer, but his face is telling me to fuck off. Would it be considered bad manners to punch him right in his ugly face?

"You have three seconds to move," Thorn's voice comes from somewhere behind him. Done with being nice and waiting around, I try to move him gently. He grabs my arm, his fingers digging into my skin as he sneers at me. Fuck this. I punch him in the face automatically. It moves him at least, as he howls and falls into the wall, his fat digits cupping his face. I slip past him, and see Maxen and Thorn facing off with two more men in black shirts. I must make a noise because both of their heads snap to me at the same time.

Thorn's face breaks out into a wide grin and Maxen looks relieved. I find myself returning their smiles, wanting to cry and hit them at the same time. I thought I'd lost them all, and now that they are in front of me I can't think about anything else but being in their arms.

"Mi Alma," Maxen says tenderly, his eyes filled with love.

Uncaring what anyone thinks, I rush around the two men and fling myself in Maxen's arms. He catches me, his arms winding around me protectively.

"I am here, Mi Alma. Fuck, I was so worried about you. They wouldn't let us see you." He growls out the last, throwing a glare over my shoulder. I dart in to kiss him quickly before dropping down and looking at the men he was facing. They look like they have pissed their pants. I don't blame them. Thorn and Maxen are double their size and height, and you only need to look at them to know they are dangerous. Maxen growls again and they jump. I hide my smile by biting my lip. I smack his chest gently as he peers at me, a soft smile on his face before I move over to Thorn. He opens his arms, that smile I love so much aimed at me, and I rush into them.

I bury my head in his chest and breathe him in, so scared I was never going to see him again when I saw him fall. I know my father told me they were okay, but I didn't believe him until I saw them for myself. My chest loosens as his arms offer me his comfort. I breathe in Thorn's scent and shiver, my eyes watering. I rub them on his chest, and he runs his hands up and down my back in comfort.

"My father's here," I whisper. His head drops to mine, his face burying in my hair.

"I know, babygirl. We will face it together."

I nod before taking a breath, moving out of his arms before I break down fully and never leave the safety of them.

"Where're Jax and Drax?" I ask them both, unwilling to move any further away from them. Maxen crosses his arms, his glare still trained on the men behind me. He's shirtless like always, but it's clear he has cleaned up a bit. My eyes drop to his muscled chest and I clench my thighs together. He looks over at me and throws me a wink before his eyes turn deadly again as he faces the threat in the room. I feel Thorn tugging on the dress and I grimace.

"In another room, they wouldn't let us see them," Thorn rumbles, thankfully not commenting on my outfit. I spin with a scowl on my face, letting my eyes go cold and deadly as I face the men. Compared to Maxen and Thorn, I must look stupid. A girl in a torn red dress glaring at them, but they must sense something because they step back.

"Take me to my friends," I grit out, debating punching them as well. Hey, it could be worse. I could stab them. The two men look at each other, seeming to hesitate. I watch as the taller one on the left swallows.

"I would listen to her if I were you. She tends to stab people who piss her off," Thorn says casually, making me grin. If the paling of the one on the left's face is anything to go by, it's a scary smile. My dress is lifted a bit at the back, Thorn obviously playing with it again, but I don't drag my eyes away.

"Now," I say slowly, making sure they understand. My father comes in at that moment, the man I punched next to him, holding his nose as he gestures wildly at me.

"Tazanna, did you hit this man?" he asks, looking at me. His eyes flicker to the guys before landing back to me.

"Yes, he's lucky I didn't gut him. Stupid prick should have moved," I snarl, done with playing nice.

My father balks, looking at me like I'm a stranger, which is ironic because I am. I don't know who or what he expected, but I'm not the same little girl who used to chase after animals and love the colour pink.

"Now, I suggest you take us to the rest of my family. I am losing my patience and me hitting some twat will be the least of your worries then."

The two men in front of me both reach for the batons at their hips. I flash them my knife as I smile mockingly at them, daring them to make a move. "If you draw them, I will slice your throats before you can get near me."

They look back at my father in indecision, clearly not willing to risk my threat.

"Tazanna, stop this!" he shouts, as he props his hands on his hips.

I lose all humanity, letting him see the monster I am. "No. You stop. First of all, you kidnapped us. Now, you have separated us and will not let us see our family. You need to think very carefully about your next actions. Do not ever order me again. You will not like my answer." My voice is cold and deadly, and the man at his side stumbles back and out the door as the two men bracket my father, clearly protecting him from me. There is a clear division in the room, and I watch as he realises how serious I am.

"Follow me," he says, his voice stern.

He spins on his heel and marches from the room. I follow after him, blowing the two men with their batons still out kisses as I pass. Sands below, this is one fucked up day.

CHAPTER TWO

THE LOST BOYS

I follow after my father silently, Thorn and Maxen at my side where they belong. Now, all we need is our other two men and we will be complete. It makes me realise how vulnerable and alone I felt without them earlier. It's crazy how things have changed since they entered my life, where I used to only ever want to be alone, now the thought scares me. We stop outside a door that looks exactly the same as all the others. My father turns to look at us, his face closed down apart from a disapproving frown pulling at his lips.

"You did not have to threaten my men to get here. I am your family, not them. I just wanted some time with you," he scolds. I don't even spare him a look, but I do answer as I walk past.

"They protected me out there, while you lived down here in your safety. I would burn this place to the ground to get to them again. They are more my family than you are, blood or no blood."

I approach the door but it doesn't open like the others, I hunch my back and grit out, "Open the door," I say, trying really hard to control my anger and panic.

"Taza–"

"Open the door, now!" I shout, everything boiling over. I am so close to exploding.

I hear a shuffle and beeping as he does something to the panel next to me, but my eyes remain locked on the door like it's my lifeline.

"There. Now Taz—"

"Don't follow us in," I warn.

Not waiting for his reply, I step closer to the door which opens automatically this time. This room is similar to the one I was held in, but has more machinery and hospital equipment dotted around. Jax rises from his brother's bedside, his head snapping to the door, the look in his eyes is dark. When he sees me, they drain of any darkness and soften, the grey swirling with so many emotions. I hiccup out a breath, and we both rush to each other. I end up in his arms, lifted into the air as we kiss desperately, our lips smashing together, getting all our fear and panic across better than any words ever could. The kiss soon turns softer, a reassurance, until he pulls away and rests his forehead on mine, and we talk silently with our eyes. I drink in his face, trying to tell him how much I missed him, how much I love him. Nodding, he kisses my forehead, a beautiful smile on his face. He gently puts me on my feet before taking my hand as we turn to Drax who is laying deadly still in the single bed.

"Is he okay?" I whisper, like how loud I talk will make a difference. My eyes stay locked on his still form. It's eerie.

"They said so, apparently he's being sedated to help reduce brain swelling," Jax says equally soft.

I drag him with me as I stop at his twin's bedside. Bending over, I sweep Drax's hair from his forehead. Leaning further down, my hand still firmly clasped in Jax's, I sweep a kiss over his forehead.

"Wake up soon, cutie," I whisper, unwilling to say everything I need to without those eyes of his open and watching me with mischief like always.

I sit on the bed next to him, watching for any movement. His personality is nowhere to be found, and he seems so much smaller without it.

"He will be okay, baby. He wouldn't dare leave you," Jax says as he stands next to me, protecting us both. I nod and lean my head on Jax's side, absorbing his strength. Maxen rounds the bed and stands on the other side, Thorn following closely behind.

"What's the plan, Worth?" Maxen's eyes flick behind me, making me look and see that my father has followed us in. I frown at the name, but a smile blossoms when I realise he is showing me how he defers to my authority, displaying respect and acknowledging who I am. I hide my smile as I look at him.

"We stay until Drax is awake, then we need to get back for The Summit before Dray goes on a murder spree."

Thorn grins. "He is starting to grow on me."

I groan and roll my eyes, just what I need.

"You're leaving?" My father's voice interrupts our little meeting, making me freeze at the reminder of everything.

"Yes. I have people depending on me." Leaning forward again, I kiss Drax's lips, uncaring that my father is watching.

"I'll be back soon, give them hell." I stand and let go of Jax's hand, needing to do this next thing on my own. I turn and face my father, calmer now that I've seen my men.

"We need to talk. Is there somewhere we can go?" There, that was polite.

He nods before looking at the men surrounding me. "Your... friends can wait here." I don't correct him, just follow him from the room with one last look back at my men.

I DON'T LOOK around this time; I just follow him as he leads me through corridor after corridor until I'm lost. He stops at a white door and inputs a key code into the panel next to it. I memorise it just in case. With a frown, I realise it is my birth date.

The room he leads me into is stunning, so different from the rest of the facility I have seen so far. A mahogany desk takes up one corner with two chairs in front of it, and a recliner behind it. Green felt covers the surface with books and what looks like maps laying on top. A floor to ceiling bookcase is on the left wall, with an old-school globe and radio next to it. To the right is a huge fireplace with a fur rug in front, and a large wingback black leather chair angled to look into the flames when lit. A chandelier hangs from the ceiling, only adding to the decadence that is this room. Where my father walks around it comfortably, I feel like a medieval warrior, bumbling and out of place. Just like I am in his life.

It's easy to compare it to Major's office. Where there I felt happy, and even safe, this makes me feel like an outsider and on edge. It makes me look at my father again, comparing him to the other father figure in my life. Where Major adapted and survived in this world, my father hid away, and stayed soft from what I can see. Major is suave, but knows darkness and brutality. My father seems to still believe we are in the old world, if the decorations are anything to go by. It reminds me of myself a little, how I was burying my head in the sand. Maybe he did the same? Tried to forget? It was probably easy in this place. No reminders, no slaves, no fighting. Instead of brutality, they have politeness and manners. It makes me wonder what my father's reactions to the horrors of my past would be.

I walk towards the desk and slump in the chair opposite it. He sits down stiffly behind it, playing with the papers on top. I watch him, seeing the nerves. I look at what he's playing with and do a double take. It's a hand drawn map of the Wastes. There are the four settlements drawn on it and an X, which I'm guessing is for our location, but everything is unnamed and some are slightly in the wrong place. Another one of what looks to be another place flashes underneath, making me frown. How did he get these? Does this mean he has been out there?

"You obviously go outside, but you don't seem to know much about the clans or what goes on outside these walls. Which reminds me, where the fuck are we?"

He flinches at my swear word before throwing me a frown. "Do we need to use such vulgar language?"

"If you have a fucking issue with my language, you sure as shit aren't going to like me as a person," I say with a bitter laugh, adding more as he calls it 'vulgar' language in there for good measure.

"Tazanna—"

"It's Worth, I told you," I grit out. He waves his hand impatiently.

"Fine, Worth. I guess your questions are a good place to start, albeit a bit vague and improperly framed." God, what a condescending asshole. Was he always like this and my childish love for my father just blinded me to it? "We do go outside, for supply runs and to map terrain. We do not, as you say, interact with the *people* out there much." He says people like a dirty word as if he would rather use another. Oblivious to my anger, he carries on. "I do not understand what you mean by clan in this context. If you are referring to the grouping of those animals, we are aware there are different kinds. We did not know they had names. We tend to avoid them at all costs, and just get in and out."

"Those *animals*," I sneer the word, mocking his use of it, "as you call them, are my friends, family, and survivors. They may not be perfect, or good enough for this place, but they are what the world is now. Brutal, unforgiving, and fucking desolate. So you might not like them, but you will show them some fucking respect, or I will leave before you can get your piece out like you so clearly want to. Where were you headed when you found us?" I ask suspiciously. He was very close to Worshippers' territory.

He watches me, searching for answers before sighing and nodding. "I apologise, the thinking down here is quite different to yours, clearly. I would be happy to be enlightened by you. To carry on, this place is a sanctuary. An old government underground bunker made to survive wars and store the best parts of humanity." He ignores my question, and I make note to ask again later.

"How did you find it?" I ask, genuinely curious.

"I did not. I awoke here two weeks after you were taken."

The mood plummets at the reminder, and my anger at him abandoning me to the Waste as a child returns.

"Taz...Worth...I would have come for you. I just got so caught up down here and I didn't know where to start..." He trails off as I stand, bracing my hands on his desk.

"Do not bullshit me. If I knew you were alive, nothing would have stopped me from coming for you. Do not lie to me, I am not a child. Admit you were scared, admit you were weak, that you were a pussy who would rather hide away and pretend none of it ever happened. At least I can understand that guy, but the lying is a no go."

He nods and gestures at my seat. I sit, my hands gripping the edge to stop me from throwing something. Of all the ways I used to imagine things going if I ever saw my father—if he was alive like I'd wished for every night—this is not it. But I am not that child, I am jaded and cold, and he is weak and using logic as a weapon. At least I'm honest about what I am. I just wish he was the man I remembered. I guess it was inevitable that he would let me down, like so many others. I don't seem able to rely on anyone but the guys.

"You're right. I was scared. I kept putting it off, making excuses until I forgot why I couldn't go after you. I even told myself you were dead, and that was for the best. It allowed me to function, and survive. Not live. I couldn't do that after I lost you both. But I survived. It might not be in the way of you and your friends, but I did."

We both go silent, lost in our own thoughts and unsure how to go from here. I would be a fool to blind myself with my anger after I demanded the truth. My men taught me that running won't change anything, and that life is too short for regrets. The least I can do is offer him something.

"Look, I don't want to push you away. No matter what, you are still my father. But you must understand I am a grown woman now, I have responsibilities and people depending on me. More than you know. My life has not been secret gardens and children playing. It changed me and I am thankful that I can keep some semblance of happiness. Arguing won't fix the past." I stop, trying to make sense of my rambling. "What I am trying to say is, if you had met me before those men in there got to me, I would have walked away and never looked back. Sands below, I would have probably attacked you and then stole everything from you to sell for booze. I am growing, learning, and it's thanks to them...my family. I can't change the past, but maybe you can be in my future. I don't know. We need to figure each other out. Unfortunately, I do not have the time. I have to get back, lives depend on it."

His face falls, but I'm betting Major would have been proud at my eloquent speech. I was honest, brutally so, I guess the guys are rubbing off on me more than I knew.

"Okay. I don't know what miracle brought you to me, but I won't look a gift horse in the mouth. I will thank God and move on." I snort, and he raises an eyebrow at me. "You do not believe in God?"

"No. I can't believe in a being that would allow such darkness, death, and pain into this world." We go silent again, our differences so glaringly obvious, so many questions spanning the space between us.

"Tell me about your life. What do you have to get back to? I would like to be a part of it, in any way I can. Maybe I can help?" He leans back, his hands behind his head as he observes me. I blow out a breath and work through my thoughts, deciding on what to tell him.

"There has been a Summit, a gathering or meeting, called between the clans. I have to be there to keep the peace."

"Why is there a meeting?" he asks, his eyes lighting up at the puzzle I'm presenting.

"Because the Wastes are descending into war again. We are trying to stop it before it's too late," I say while rubbing my head, whatever medication they gave me is obviously starting to wear off and I feel like shit.

He leans forward, his eyes imploring me to trust him. "Tell me everything."

I think about it, but he seems sincere enough, telling him things that people topside already know isn't breaking any trust. I outline the clans, using the map and give him a rundown. I glaze over my role and past, leaving out a lot just in case. I can almost hear his brain working a mile a minute, trying to figure out the missing gaps, ways to achieve my goal, and what this all means. It's strangely nice. I let some of my anger go and focus on things I can change, and he stops being an ass and is actually helpful.

"How long until this...Summit?" he asks, deep in thought.

I count the days in my head. "Six days, give or take a day."

He stands, determination in every line of his body and face, his eyes filled with a fire they didn't hold before, and as much as I don't want to admit it, they look like mine.

"Then we need to prepare you. Get all of you healthy, and see about ways we can help. It is time we became a part of this world again, maybe you are the catalyst for that."

CHAPTER THREE

TESTS AND TALKS

Everything happens so fast after that. My father talks to some soldiers and then tries to reassure me with a smile and a few soft words. I'm taken to a medical room, with all sorts of machines and technology that, to be honest, I don't have a clue about and didn't know still existed. I grit my teeth, try to play nice, and not be a bitch. I know my father is trying to help. It's the only reason I haven't stabbed the asshole examining me in his pretty boy fucking face.

"Arm out," he orders, his short sweepy brown hair falling in his eyes as he stands. He doesn't look like any doctor I remember. Tattoos, tribal lines and dots cover his neck and continue into his shirt. Letters cover each knuckle, and a rose graces the backs of each of his hands. He has piercings through his eyebrow and lip, the craziest green eyes I have ever seen, and a too perfect face. Clean shaven. It makes me feel dirty, and compared to my guys, the difference is noticeable. His black top sticks to his muscles as he moves, and the doctor's coat covers him to mid-thigh. He has on army boots and tight jeans. He's hot, but his attitude has me wanting to chop off his arm and beat him with it.

"Why?" I snarl, so bored of being poked and prodded already.

He glares at me as he shuffles a metal table to my side. "To take blood, obviously." He says it like I am a fucking idiot and I upgrade my threat to debating cutting off his balls and feeding them to him.

I drop my arm, and he grabs my wrist and turns it over. He freezes at the scars, his eyes raising to mine. He looks curious; I don't even see any revulsion there. I'm betting he's never seen someone so heavily scarred. Wait until he sees the whip marks on my back, along with my brands.

"You do these?" He tilts his head, watching my reaction, his warmth seeping into me from where he clutches my arm.

I blink at him, my face empty. "No. Some I let be done though."

That seems to throw him off, and I take great pleasure in watching him try to figure out what to say. He goes with a grunt before grabbing his needle.

"This might hurt," he warns, more like he feels he has to than he actually cares if it does.

"Don't worry, I won't move. I've had pints of my blood drained before."

He stares at me in shock again. I think this might be my new favourite game. Trying to shock the asshole doctor.

"What for?" he eventually asks, obviously deciding to believe me.

"The man who stole me from my father thought it would be fun to see the effects of blood loss on my body during extreme torture and pain," I say happily, pushing away the memories that rise with that.

He makes a noise and then swears before concentrating on trying to draw my blood.

"Done," he mutters, throwing me a look as he takes the blood over to the counter. I roll my sleeve back down. I had quickly gotten rid of that horrible dress. I demanded a shirt and pants, and they surprisingly fit quite well. The black cargo pants let me move without being easy to remove, something I learnt early on is important. It will give you the extra time to fight off your would be rapist. I am so stealing them.

"Stop playing with him, will you?" Thorn says with a smile from where he stands at the wall. I wink at him and sit up on the examining table.

"That all, doc?"

"It's doctor, or Evan. Pick one," he mutters, looking through some of his notes.

"Whatever, anything I need to be worried about, doc?"

"You really think I would have your results straight away? No, I will inform your father when I know what we are," he looks me up and down, "working with." With that, he turns back to his notes. He misses the glare I throw his way. Thorn quickly steps to my side, stopping my next threat.

"Okay, time to go," he says around a laugh as I stroke my knife, imagining using it to rearrange the asshole's perfect face.

Thorn grab my hips and pulls me from the table, his hand twining with mine as he pulls me out the door of the medical room, and into a frazzled woman who is waiting on the other side.

"Oh, there you are! Come on!" She grabs my arm, and I move quickly, slamming her into the wall with my knife at her throat. Her legs dangle mid-air as I hold her there.

"What do you want?" I growl out.

Her brown eyes widen in her plump face and her red painted mouth opens in an 'o.'

"Tazanna! Misty here is coming to cut your hair," my father calls as he jogs down the hallway towards us. I step back, letting her slump down the wall, and drop my knife. Misty stays plastered to the wall, her small plump figure flattened. She holds a hand over her chest before stepping away and fluffing her extremely large curly red hair.

"Sorry about that dear, I thought it had been mentioned," she says around a laugh. I blink at her as she goes to grab me again, only to hesitate. "Come along, time we trim that monstrosity you call hair."

Monstros—I look from my wavy hair to hers in shock. She grabs my hand and tugs me along, surprisingly strong for such a small lady. I can't stab her and I bet hitting her wouldn't work. I look at Thorn, begging him with my eyes for him to save me. He laughs, leaning against the wall as he watches me be manhandled by Misty. I narrow my eyes at him as he waves.

"Now, don't pull that face dearie, we will have you looking like a supermodel in no time, well, maybe not a supermodel but who wanted to be those skinny weirdos anyway...not that we have them anymore..." Her eyes get a faraway look, one that everyone has when they think about the past before she snaps herself back with a clap. "How about we dye it, oh, I bet you would look amazing with blue hair," she blathers on, yanking me down the hallways as she speeds away.

It's my turn for my eyes to widen, as I search desperately for an escape.

"No," I GROWL.

Misty's eyes narrow, her plump face flustered and her hair bigger than before as she points the comb at me. "Now behave, young lady," she warns, slightly out of breath as she comes at me again, ignoring my dirty look. Fucking woman even tried to take my knife off me!

I growl and grunt as she tugs and pulls at my hair. She starts muttering under her breath as she 'tackles the horror'—in her words—that is my hair. Half an hour later, she throws her now broken comb at the wall with a yell, making me laugh.

"It's time for extreme measures," she huffs, her hands on her rounded hips. She toddles away, talking to herself the whole time as I finally get a chance to look around the room we are in. After she pulled me halfway through the compound, she pushed me into a chair, which I've been in for the last half an hour or so. Instantly, she started playing and touching my hair before trying to comb it. I never knew so many creams, mousses, and I don't even know what that last one was, existed.

There is only one chair in the room, the one I am sitting in. The floor is the same as the rest of the building. Three of the walls are white, but the one I'm facing is a mix of pinks, yellows, and blues. I almost grin at the mish-mash of colours, as if someone took whatever they could find and flung it at the walls to make them less depressing. A large mirror is pointed at the chair, which let me watch what the little she-devil was doing to me the whole time. A table and storage containers sit next to the mirror.

She turns back around with an 'aha,' and when I bring my eyes back to her, I see silver flash in the lights. Instantly, I roll from the chair, crouching on the other side with my knife in my hands and a hard expression on my face as I wait for the attack that never comes.

"Oh, you poor dear. What did they do to you out there?" she cries, clutching her chest, and the...scissors there. Straightening, I start to feel foolish, but I don't show it. I simply slip back into the chair, sitting stiffly.

"You don't talk much, do you?" she asks cheerily, as she starts cutting my hair. I force myself to sit still, which is hard with a blade so close to my face.

"So, is that delicious hunk of man meat out there your

boyfriend? Let me tell you, that boy could have a nun's vag wetter than a fish in a pond."

My mouth flaps open, making me look ridiculous. I stare at the woman through the mirror in shock.

"Erm, yes?" I ask slowly.

"Yum. What about those other ones you came in with?"

"How old are you?" I ask, wincing as she tugs on my hair.

"Oh, don't you worry about that, dearie. I like them young and fit!" She laughs as my eyes widen again. I thought nothing could shock me anymore, but sands below, I was wrong.

"I mean, you know what I'm talking about. Oh my, when I saw you with them! This little thing, walking between these big hard men like a complete badass, as they watched you hungrily." She wipes her forehead "And you! I think the people here are more scared of you than they are of them!"

She talks, and talks, until my head feels like it's about to explode and I debate impaling myself on her scissors just so I have an excuse to leave.

"Done," she says proudly, standing next to me in the mirror, her face full of happiness and hope. Sands below, what has this woman done to me?! Before I can demand she rectify my hair, she pulls me out of the chair and into the hallway where Jax and Thorn are waiting.

"What do you think?" she asks excitedly, her hands outstretched to showcase my hair. I grimace, and Thorn rubs the back of his head, his mouth twitching. I narrow my eyes at him, daring him to laugh.

"She looked better before," Jax mutters.

Misty's mouth flaps open as she spins and trains her laser glare on him.

"Hmph, well you are perfect for each other. See if I care. No, thank you, Misty, no..." she mutters as she toddles off.

As soon as she rounds the corner, I pull the clip out of my hair and fling it at the wall. Bending over, I shake it out and run my fingers through it. Flipping back up, I smile at them.

"That's better," I moan, then narrow my glare on Thorn.

"You. Left. Me. To. Her." I snarl. He backs up, his hands in the air. He grins at me, his eyes filled with laughter.

"Run," I warn him. Jax shakes his head and slips past, kissing my cheek on the way.

"See you in a bit, baby. Try not to kill him."

I nod but don't take my eyes off Thorn as he spins and starts jogging away.

I stare after him, hunting him. When I get hold of him...

I let him have a head start before I chase him through the halls, my eyes on his back as he manages to stay just ahead of me. I ignore the looks we are getting, and slip and slide around people and corners, intent on getting him. Rounding a corner, I am flung into the wall. Thorn peers at me, his grin in place as he holds me there, his muscles not even straining as he pins my lower body with his.

"I've caught you, so now what shall I do with you?" he asks silky, his eyes heating as I watch.

"Thorn," I warn. He darts in and kisses me before pulling back and looking around. Spotting whatever he's looking for, he twines our hands and pulls me with him. Opening a random door, he shoves me through and follows behind me. I don't even get to turn before he spins me around, his hands on my ass, lifting me until I wrap my legs around his waist, and his mouth devours mine.

I give as good as I get, hungrily chasing him as my back meets a wall. I rub myself on him, loving the feel of him hardening between my legs. He pulls away, his eyes wild as he pants. I lean back against the wall and watch him, my nipples hardening. I lick my lips to swallow his taste, and he watches me with a pained groan.

"I need you, babygirl."

"I'm yours."

He watches me before grabbing me again and striding across the room. He drops me down to my feet, and before I can groan at losing the feel of him between my legs, he pushes me on the chest, making me fall into a table with a bang. He lifts me onto the hard surface, my legs spread wide to accommodate his size.

"Hands up," he growls. I lift my hands and he yanks my top over my head, my bra soon follows, flung over his shoulder. My nipples could cut glass right now, my desire fed by the stark hunger on his face. He looks beautiful and dangerous, and I can't wait for him to be inside me.

"Lay down and grip the table above you," he grumbles out, as he undoes my trousers, watching me as I do as I am told. I grip the edge of the table, my arms straining above me, arching my neglected chest in the air. I watch, licking my lips as he pulls my trousers and panties off. When I am lying naked and needy, he stops and runs his eyes over my prone form. His fingers follow his eyes, trailing over my skin, leaving fire in his wake. I am about to groan in frustration when his hands span my hips and dig in, squeezing in warning.

"I'm going to do to you what I have wanted to do since the moment I met you. You try to fight me and I will punish you." I arch my eyebrow as he grins at me, before lowering his mouth to my centre, his eyes on me the whole time. My head falls back with a moan as he devours my pussy like he did my mouth.

"Look at me," he demands, his voice vibrating against me. I lift my eyes, and when they meet his, he licks my pussy from top to bottom. His hands grip me tighter, holding me still, as he licks me like his favourite dessert, avoiding where I need him the most.

"Thorn," I groan out. I feel him grin against me as he sucks my clit. I nearly come off the table, but he holds me tight to his mouth as he nips and sucks until I'm screaming, riding his mouth as much as I can.

When I ride out the end of my orgasm, I lay lax against the table. He watches me from between my thighs, an evil smile on his face.

"Fuck," I pant as one of his fingers stretches me, before he adds another. He doesn't give me time to adjust before scissoring them and rubbing inside me. I can finally lift my hips and I start fucking myself on him as he watches.

"Please," I beg, my need already mounting back up, my pussy clenching around him, needing so much more. He fucks me harder, faster, still watching me, as I feel myself winding higher, so close. I cry out when his fingers leave me, feeling empty and so close to coming again.

He stands up between my parted thighs, somehow having lost his pants. His cock stands tall and proud between his legs, longer than Maxen and thicker than Drax. It's a monster, and my mouth waters and my pussy clenches.

"Thorn, either get the fuck inside me or finish me off," I demand. He laughs as he steps closer, his hands stilling my shaking legs. He rubs his cock along my pussy, making me bite my lower lip.

"Anything you want, I'm all yours." He thrusts into me on the last word, stretching me, filling me so deep I cry out and writhe beneath him. He doesn't give me time to adjust before pulling out and ramming back into me. His thrusts are brutal, hard, perfect. All I can do is hold on to the table as he fucks me.

"Fuck, baby. You're so wet, so fucking tight," he groans out. He lifts my legs until they are over his shoulders, hitting a new angle and making me moan. One of his hands holds me to him as he pummels into me, the other moves up my body, flicking my clit before moving to my breast. He twists and flicks my nipple, making me tighten around him as I pant. He grins, but it's strained and his thrusts are more erratic.

"I can't wait for you to come on me. Fuck, babygirl you are so beautiful when you let go," Thorn groans.

His hand wanders again, moving lower and I clench in antici-pation, making him growl. His hand cups my arse for a moment before running along the crack. I narrow my eyes at him as he grins. He bends over, trapping me as he fucks me deeper. I cry out as I start to reach my peak, his finger lightly rims my other hole before dipping in slightly. The pressure of his finger, coupled with his cock, has me coming with a scream, my hands rushing to his shoulders, cutting into them in my haze to keep him deep inside of me.

He thrusts in deeper than before and I feel him explode. He grunts before stilling on top of me, both of us panting and slick with sweat.

"Sands below," I gasp. His head falls into the crook of my shoulder.

"You have ruined me, babygirl," he whispers as he pants into my skin.

We both groaned when he pulled out of me, my body turning cold and empty, but it didn't last for long. He found some-thing to clean us both up with, then gently lifted me and laid us down on the floor next to the table, him on his back and me resting on his chest. Of course, he is a cuddler, I smile at the thought.

"I know about Drax and Jax, and even Maxen has told me about his past. But I don't know how you met them, will you tell me?" I ask curiously. Drawing circles on his chest where my head rests, the difference between our skin colours is amazing. We look good together. My pale creamy skin light against his dark smooth one. I should get up, we have things to prepare before we leave, but I don't want to leave his arms.

"You remember how they said I was born up here?"

I nod, my fingers still drawing circles. His hand comes up and he laces his fingers with mine, stilling my movement. Lifting my head, I rest my chin on his chest, looking into this face.

"Yes?"

Thorn leans forward and kisses me before laying his head back, his satisfied eyes on the ceiling.

"You don't have to tell me," I say softly. He squeezes me and sighs, his face stricken and his body rigid against me.

"I want to, it's just I haven't ever told anyone the full story. Even Maxen only knows parts and he's my brother." I rub my chin on his chest, trying to give him my strength and comfort. "It's strange, it's been coming back to me since we arrived in The Rim. I guess I repressed some of it after we escaped to the cities."

"Escaped?" I ask softly.

"Fuck, babygirl, I'm not telling this right. Let me try again." He takes a deep breath, his chest moving beneath me. "I was born up North and we didn't leave when it all started to go to shit. It wasn't until my father was killed by a looter that my mum decided to try and get somewhere safer with me and my sister. We made it over halfway, but my sister got sick. She was only a little girl. So tiny, I had promised my dad I would protect them both, but I couldn't. We got split up, we were near where the old coast used to be and a wave came in. The waves, the ones that never retreated. I had to fight just to stay afloat, and when I smashed into a tree and broke my ribs, I managed to climb it. I waited there for days until I realized the water wouldn't be receding. I ended up climbing down and trying to swim through it, that's where I got the scar." I lean up and stroke my finger across the wicked looking scar which runs through his left eyebrow, he closes his eyes as I do.

"I hardly ever notice it, it's just part of you. It's Thorn." He smiles at me.

"A piece of something hit me in the face. I remember I could hardly see as blood dripped down my face, but I managed to fight my way to land again. I searched for them for days, but I was getting weaker and I passed out. When I woke up, I was tied to a bit of wood and covered up. A man, he saved me. He treated my wounds and fed me, and got me to the cities. He stayed with me there, telling me how his son had died early on and he wanted to be able to save as many as he could. God, I hated him at first for taking me away. I would have kept looking for them until I died. All I saw for years when I closed my eyes was my sister's tiny little hand clutching mine as she cried, only for it to be snatched away as the water took her. It's something I have to live with, knowing I failed them. It was probably for the best I didn't find them, I think I would have curled up and died if I saw their bodies."

"You don't think they made it?" I ask softly.

"No, babygirl. It was a miracle I did, and they were ill and weak. No, for my own sanity, I can't think about them being alive."

"I'm so sorry. But you wouldn't have, you would have kept fighting. It's who you are. We are your family now. I know it can't replace the one you lost, but you have us." He smiles that breath-taking smile at me. He cups my cheek, his heat seeping into me as his eyes turn serious.

"I know, babygirl, and I am so fucking lucky. You are my every-thing, Tazanna Worth."

CHAPTER FOUR

GIVE THEM HELL

Thorn and I spent another hour together before I forced myself to get up and dressed. He helped me, his hands gentle as he dropped kisses along the way, making my heart clench. We check on Drax on the way back—when I poke my head around his door I see he's still out—before I find myself alone in the room my father assigned me. Staring around the plain white room, I spot a panel with a light flickering through a crack. Curious, I walk over to it and run my fingers along the surface.

It pops open like a door, revealing a shiny steel bathroom with a shower, toilet, sink, and mirror. Not even second-guessing myself, I strip and step into the shower. I grab the shiny knob and pray to whoever is listening that the water will be warm. When I turn and it sprays down on me in scalding hard waves, I almost come there and then. Sex is good, amazing even, but have you ever gone so long without a hot shower and then finally have one? Yeah, you know the feeling.

I take my time, letting the warm water sluice over my sore muscles. I unwrap the damp bandage while I'm in there, frowning at the black and blue bruising decorating the left side of my rib cage. Shrugging, I drop the wet material to the floor and lean my hands against the wall, my head dropping forward as the water parts my hair, obscuring my face.

I don't let myself think, instead, I concentrate on feeling the water. Wanting to remember this when I have to go back to the real world with its cold showers.

Bottles line the edge of the wall and I search through them. There are no labels, so I carefully lift one bottle and take a sniff. My nose twitches at the cloying smell and I quickly replace the lid and try the next one. Fuck, I almost groan again. It smells sweet, like strawberries and cream. I dump a handful in my palm and lather my body up good, before letting the water rinse away the soap. I wash my hair as well, using my sniff test to pick a bottle I like.

Looking through the bottles once again, I find a razor hidden behind them, a new unopened one. I look down, noticing my leg hair has grown since the last time I was able to find one. *I look like a bloody yeti!* I lather up the soap again, covering my legs, before going to town on the forest.

Half an hour later, I step out of the shower and wrap a towel around me. My legs are smooth and silky, my hair shiny and clean and I feel like a newborn. Is it weird to compare having a shower to being reborn?

When I get back into the room, I find a fresh pair of cargo trousers and a black tank top waiting for me. I quickly dress, forgoing a bra and panties. I pull on my borrowed army boots and tie them. Lastly, I pop my blade in the edge of my trousers. I really need to ask where the others are and about the Berserkers...lists form in my head as I walk to the door and wait for it to slide open. The hallway is empty, so I head in the direction I think was Drax's room. Hopefully I will find one of my men there, then I can go find my father and get answers.

I get lost a few times but I manage to find his room eventually.

The hallways are weirdly empty and it puts me on high alert, so when I find Jax sleeping at Drax's bedside, I relax a little. I don't want to disturb them, so I silently sneak in and drop a kiss on each of their heads before going back out to find someone else.

A guard in the same black uniform as the others hurries past and I chase after him.

"Hey, do you know where everyone is?" I ask, nicely for me.

He stops and shifts on his feet, his eyes darting to the hallway and back to me uncomfortably, the silence stretching.

"Okay. Let me rephrase. Take me to everyone," I demand, crossing my arms.

"I don't know if I'm supposed to," he squeaks out, making me narrow my eyes on him.

"Take me to them, before I decide to play target practise with you," I growl.

He gulps and nods, watching me in fear as I walk by his side. He slows his steps, but once he realises I can easily keep up, he speeds back up again.

"Are you really from out there?" he asks eventually.

I don't even spare him a look as we walk, instead I concentrate on not palming my knife. I miss my fucking swords. I feel naked without them.

"What's it like?" he gushes excitedly.

"Hot," I mutter, looking around as the hallway we are walking in starts opening up. Cheering reaches us and the guard speeds up, his excitement palpable in the air.

We reach an open room, larger than anything I have ever seen and packed with bodies cheering and chanting as they circle around something.

"What is this?" I demand. The guard looks from me to the crowd.

"It's how we guards blow off steam."

Not needing to hear anymore, I start to push through,

elbowing those in my way until I can see the square mats raised in the middle of the room, where my men are currently fighting.

Thorn is just putting one guy to the ground as another charges him. Maxen is fighting hand to hand with three men, a smile on his beautiful face. I ache to jump in and help, but I know they aren't in any trouble so I let them carry on.

I watch their muscles bunch and contract as they fight, the fierce expressions on their faces and their downright sexy strength. I shuffle uncomfortably, trying to relieve some of the pressure building up in me. Maxen spots me and throws me a wink before ducking a punch. My lips twitch, but I keep a calm expression as people finally start to realise I am in their midst.

My men destroy their opponents, quickly ending the fight after they spot me. The guards lay scattered on the floor as Maxen and Thorn stand in the centre, chests heaving from the fights. Watching them fight side by side has me worked up and I bite my lip to stop myself from attacking them. Not that they would mind.

Thorn leaves the ring with a triumphant smile on his face, only making my arousal spiral higher. Watching them fight is like watching art, something beautiful and deadly, and seriously hot. My guys meet up in front of me and we turn without a word, all of us ready to be out of this crowd.

"Fucking brown bastard," comes a sneer.

I stop, steel threading through my veins at the racial slur directed at my sweet Thorn, who looks back at me with a small sad head shake. Ignoring him, I turn to face the asshole. His friend is being dragged from the mats behind him, unconscious from where Thorn took him down effortlessly.

"What did you say?" I ask calmly, my voice cold and deadly like the silence engulfing me.

"You heard me, whore," he scoffs, his face twisting in hate. I hear people start to mutter between themselves as they shift uncomfortably.

"You want to take this one, Mi Alma?" Maxen asks, as he steps up to my side. I tilt my head and watch the mouthy racist prick. My smile is slow, and if the fear that flames to life in the guard's eyes is anything to go by, terrifying.

"You and me. In the ring. Now." I stride past him to the open matted area in the raised middle. I leap onto it and spread my legs in a hard stance. I watch the man who thought he was so tough wilt before noticing he is the centre of attention. He gathers some of his attitude and swaggers to me, jumping up and landing on the mat in front of me.

"Fine. I will wipe the floor with you, then make you suck my dick as your little brown bastard watches." He laughs, a few of the guards chuckle nervously with him as I arch my eyebrow and look around at the crowd. Once my eyes run over them, they soon shut up.

Turning back to the guard, I grin at him. I pull the knife from my trousers. His eyes widen as I throw it to the edge where it embeds in the mat.

"You talk too much," I say before rushing him.

I feign a punch and then sweep my leg so he goes down on the floor, hard. I don't wait for him to get up as I drop on top of him and smash his head into the cushioned ground, holding him there. I'm not playing this time, I will destroy him before everyone so they never think they can talk about my men again.

"You ever come at my men like that, talk about them, even look at them in the wrong way again and I will kill you," I warn.

I watch as he pales, realising I mean my threat and that I can follow through with it. I get up and he slowly gets to his feet. I go to turn, but at the last second, I spin and punch him square in the face.

I casually walk to the edge of the mat and retrieve my knife, sliding it into my pants. The room is silent as I hop down and a path clears through the crowd, leading right to my men who are watching me hungrily. We don't talk as we make our way through the crowd. When we reach the hallway, Maxen turns and heaves me over his shoulder and takes off at a jog down the hall, Thorn right behind him.

"Maxen–" I warn. He smacks my ass but ignores me. I grumble and glare at a grinning Thorn.

We twist and turn around corners as I try to fight back the need to hurt Maxen for putting me in a weak position. The old me would have panicked and stabbed him, but I fight against it and remind myself that he would never hurt me.

I huff as I'm put gently on my feet. Looking around I realise we are in a bedroom. I look back to my two men and arch my eyebrow.

"Strip, Mi Alma," Maxen demands, watching me. I notice he is shirtless again and my eyes get lost in the muscles of his chest.

"You first," I say with a quick smile. My jaw drops when he keeps his eyes on me and strips out of his boots and pants, leaving him bare before me.

"Your turn." He prowls towards me, stopping close so I have to crane my neck back to see him. I'm obviously not quick enough because I feel a tug, then my top floats to the ground in shreds. Swivelling my head, I spot a grinning Thorn at my side. I glare at him as he kneels down to do the same to my pants.

"Don't you dare," I warn.

"Then strip, now, or Thorn here will make sure you are left with nothing to wear," Maxen threatens.

Gritting my teeth, I shimmy out of my trousers, letting them fall to the floor.

"Fuck, Mi Alma, if I had known you were wearing nothing underneath, I would have fucked you against the wall out there," Maxen groans, his eyes drinking me in as Thorn circles to my back, so I am sandwiched between them.

"I want to be inside you so bad," he moans, his fingers reaching out like he can't help it, tweaking my nipples into hard peaks. I bite my lip and lean back on Thorn, using him to support me as Maxen runs his eyes down my body, his fingers trailing across my skin, burning it, branding it, and claiming it as his own.

Thorn kisses my shoulder, over my brand.

"I think we need to get one of these," he murmurs, leaving open mouthed kisses along my shoulder and up my neck.

"A slave brand?" I ask, my voice breathless.

"A brand to say we are yours," he whispers against my ear before biting it.

Maxen drops to his knees, his head level with my belly as he watches his friend lick a path down my neck before biting the sensitive area between it and my shoulder. I reach out and anchor myself in Maxen's long silky hair, which is pulled back in a bun. I run my hands through it, and undo the bobble before throwing it away, so it cascades around his face in a deep brown waterfall. He peers through the locks at me, his eyes filled with need. I watch him as he kisses down my belly before parting my willing legs.

He doesn't waste any time, but parts my lips and licks up my pussy, making me groan as he devours it. Thorn keeps up his kisses, both of them slowly driving me mad, until I almost scream when Maxen thrusts two fingers in me.

He sucks on my clit as he rubs inside of me, making me stiffen and my legs shake, as an orgasm rushes through me. It surprises me so much that I fall to the floor, but Maxen catches me. Before I can say anything, he spins me around.

He pulls my back to his chest as we kneel on the cold floor. Pushing my legs wider he guides himself back to my pussy. Lining his wide cock up with my wet, needy pussy. He slowly pushes in, inch by slow inch, stretching me. When he's fully seated, he stops. The angle is incredible. Maxen doesn't move as I gasp in his arms, his muscles banding around me to keep me still. I look up at Thorn as he hovers over me. He cups my chin, his hard cock nearly touching my face.

"Suck me, babygirl, while Maxen fucks that sweet pussy of yours."

Thorn's dirty mouth has me groaning as I bend forward, landing on my hands so I'm on all fours with Maxen still inside me. I feel him move to mirror Thorn, until I am trapped between them both. The position should make me feel powerless, but between them, I know I have never been so in control.

They both worship me, their hands clutching me desperately as they try to contain their lust. Plus, the idea of letting go for once has me dropping my head before looking back up and facing Thorn's hard cock and licking my lips hungrily.

I swallow him down just as Maxen starts to move. I can't do anything but hold on as they both fuck me. It's not long until I am thrown into my second orgasm, screaming around Thorn's length. He grips my hair and thrusts deeper, making me swallow him as he fucks my mouth hard and fast.

"Fuck, babygirl," he groans, trying to pull out but I hollow my cheeks and take him deeper until he hits the back of my throat. He explodes with a yell and I have no choice but to swallow him down. He pulls out of my mouth and stumbles before sitting heavily on the floor, panting as he watches me.

That's when Maxen shows me he was only playing with me before. He grips my hips in a bruising embrace and fucks me hard and fast, smashing into me as I drop my head and moan. He reaches around and thumbs my clit. I am just riding through my second orgasm when he throws me screaming into my third, coming so hard I see stars. He follows me, stilling behind me as he groans.

We both collapse in a heap on the floor, all three of us sprawled there, trying to relearn how to breathe.

"Well shit," I say around a laugh, making Maxen chuckle, then groan when it moves me.

"I didn't hurt you, Mi Alma, did I?" he asks softly, tracing the fingerprints on my hip.

"No. Don't you dare try to take it softer next time, that was amazing," I warn, narrowing my eyes at him.

"Amazing, huh?" Thorn asks. I slap his thigh and then just lay between them.

"I guess we better go check on Drax. We need to leave as soon as he is awake," I say, still not moving from between them.

They grumble, but get to their feet, both of them offering me a hand. I grin and accept both.

We head out hand in hand to check on Drax, with me managing to find a shirt along the way. I find Jax awake and watching his brother, sadness emanating from him. Letting go of Thorn and Maxen, I hug him from behind, wrapping my arms around him and resting my head on his shoulder. He sighs, and the tension leaves his body as he clutches at my arms.

"He hasn't woke up yet?" I ask, concerned.

"No," Jax mutters, his voice filled with a wealth of emotions.

"He will." I squeeze Jax and head to my other twin. Sitting on his bed, I take his hand.

"Wake up," I plead. Leaning forward, I caress his lips with mine. "Please, baby, wake up." I let out my fear that I won't ever see those eyes again, the whisper quiet so my men don't hear. "I need you."

Sitting up straight, I watch for any sign of movement. When

nothing happens, I sigh and let go of his hand, planning to go sit with Jax so we can hold each other. Drax's hand twitches and I look from it to his face.

His eyes flicker open partly, the lids heavy and swollen. His mouth parts as his croaky voice comes out, making the room go silent.

"You smell like dessert, babe."

CHAPTER FIVE

BLAST FROM THE PAST

I search until I find a buzzer near the bed. Pressing it, I grab Drax's hand and wait.

"Hi," I say with a relieved smile. He tries to wink at me, then groans.

"Damn, I feel like I went ten rounds in the ring with Maxen." He coughs on the last word, making me and Jax reach for a water glass placed next to his bed. Jax smiles and retracts his hand as I grab it and hold it to Drax, who sips through the straw.

"Why do I smell strawberries?" he asks, as he tries to sit up. Jax grabs one side and Maxen moves to grab the other as they both help him into a sitting position. When he's comfortable, Maxen claps his shoulder.

"Good to see you awake, brother. Our girl was starting to get worried, which in her case means she kicked someone's ass," Maxen says with a chuckle as Drax looks at me with a dopey smile.

"Aww, you miss me darlin'?"

I roll my eyes. I go to reply but the door opens, making my

guys and I tense before the asshole doctor who examined me walks in, with a smaller, pudgier man on his heels.

He doesn't even speak, only throws me a dirty look before moving to Drax's bedside and examining some machines. We spend the next ten minutes watching as the two doctors examine him and run more tests. Finally, they tell us he's okay, still healing but well enough to travel tomorrow. My father walks in and nods at the two men before facing me.

"Can we talk, prin-Worth?" my father asks, sounding unsure. I nod before turning to see Drax looking from him to me. I lean in and give him a quick kiss, which he tries to deepen. Laughing, I pull back.

"The guys will fill you in," I say softly, running my fingers across his face.

His eyes are serious, and his mouth pulls down in a frown as he searches my face. "You okay, babe? Whose ass do I need to kick?"

His threat makes me smile, even injured and in a hospital bed all, he is worried about is me. "No one's, I'll kick them myself. Though, if it makes you feel better, I will let you hold them down."

He grins at me, that sparkle back in his eye. One that speaks of trouble and naughty things. "Deal."

Shaking my head with a smile, I face my father, my smile dropping away as I prepare for our talk. I follow him out of the room and we walk in silence as he leads me back to his office. Once inside, I drop to the same chair as before.

"So, you in charge or something? You have an office, and they listen to you..."

He rubs his head as sits heavily in his chair. "In a way. I was voted to lead."

I nod. "What's wrong?" I demand, crossing my arms as if to ward off a blow.

He smiles sadly at me. "You always were too smart for your own good."

"Don't beat around the bush. I don't like lies or half-truths." My voice is loud in the quiet as my head runs through possible scenarios. Maybe Dray has attacked someone, maybe the Berserkers have done something.

"You can't have kids." It bursts out of him and then he winces at the harsh statement. "Doctor Sencal..." At my confused look, he carries on and corrects himself, "Evan, came and gave me your test results. It seems your womb is scarred and damaged. I'm sorry princess, whatever you have been through means you can't have children." He freezes as if expecting me to freak out.

I blow out a breath. "Okay."

"That's it?" he asks incredulously, leaning forward. "Princess, I've just told you that you can't have kids, and you say 'okay'?"

I nod, my defence up at his questioning me. "Okay. It's not like I ever thought about having them, and bringing a child into this world?" I shake my head. "Into my world, with my past and my enemies? No, I don't have anything else to say. It's harsh and true, but I'm glad that I can't bring an innocent into this world only to see them suffer." I watch as he digests my words, thinking them through. "Now, did the doctor say anything else? And why did he come to you and not me?" I demand, angry that they went behind my back. It's my body, my life. I have a right to know before a man I haven't seen in over ten years does.

"I asked him to let me know of your results. I wasn't trying to betray your trust, I just wanted to make sure you were okay," my father defends.

"Then you should have let me make up mind whether to tell you or not. This will never work if you don't show me trust, or continue to treat me like a child. I have a right to know about my own body and decide who I tell." I get up to pace, trying to burn off some of the anger.

"You're right. I'm sorry, Worth. What can I do to make it up to you?" he pleads, standing and coming around the desk to block my path. His face is open and sincere.

"The truth," I demand. He flinches but nods, gesturing to the chair. Gritting my teeth, I sit back down as he leans back against the desk in front of me.

"What do you want to know?"

"How you have a map of the Wastes if you have been hiding out down here?" It's the first question that comes to mind and one that has been bugging me.

"We have a deal with a group of survivors." He keeps eye contact as he talks, crossing his arms, almost mirroring my stance. I drop my arms with a groan.

"Who?"

"Priest, I believe his name is."

My eyes widen and he nods. "Ah, so you know him."

It's my turn to rub my head as the pain meds start to wear off again, making my head pound. "Yes. He's the leader of The Worshippers."

"A cult." At my nod, my father carries on. "We were running out of food a couple of years ago, even with the fruit and veg we grow here, so we sent out a team. I was part of that team, we ended up running into Priest on the way back to his..."

"Settlement? Church?" I provide. He nods and rubs his hands together.

"They attacked us, but Priest stepped in. We made a deal. We would treat his wives and offer medical care, in exchange for food. Through these monthly meetings, I earned some knowledge about what was happening out there, not much, but enough."

"You never tried to go anywhere else?"

He frowns. "Why would we? We have everything we need here. It's safe, secure, and we are taken care of."

"And I guess looking for your daughter was too much hassle," I mutter bitterly. The silence stretches on before he sighs heavily.

"I was a fool. A scared little man. I can't change the past. God, I wish I could. All I can offer you is my apology. How sorry I am for leaving you, for giving up on you." His eyes beg me to understand and I find myself breathing deep to push back the tears. My heart pounds against my chest as I look at him.

"All these people, how did they get here? How did they know it was here?" I ask gruffly, ignoring his last remark to return to a safe subject.

I see him flinch and a frown tugs at the corners of his lips, but he answers me anyway.

"Some were born up here in the North. A few worked here, when everything started, they came to somewhere familiar, somewhere safe. They brought their families and friends, and we took in stragglers from outside until we had here what you see now."

I struggle to think of something else to ask, my mind slow because of the headache.

"You said you brought everyone here, including the men attacking us...Can I see them?"

His hair is down past his shoulders, sectioned off in honour braids. The more hair the Berserker has, the stronger they are, and the more fights and tests they have won. His one mud brown eye stares through the glass like he can see me, the other a scarred twisted hole where his eye used to be. Plucked from his head by Ivar as a punishment. I remember it like it was yesterday, his scream staying with me even now, as blood ran in horrifying rivulets down his face.

Ivar stood over him, the man's eye clutched in his hand like some sick kind of trophy, with a vicious smile on his face. The man was wailing hopelessly, so full of agony on the ground below Ivar, clutching at his face. It was the first time in years I had smiled, living for it, loving him getting a taste of his own medicine. Of course, I didn't know then that it would warp his mind, that the pain and horror would break him until nothing existed but a crazed warrior intent only on bringing others pain.

Dreven wasn't Ivar's torturer, no that sick son of a bitch will be by his side, but Dreven here was his warrior. His fighter, because he didn't fear anything. Hell, it's like after that day, he never felt pain again. His mind was always locked on his next slave, his next fight.

He is one of the monsters I left behind, one even my mind tries to block me from remembering. My days spent in his tender care are some of the worst of my life, until all I knew was the scent of my own blood and the feeling of agony racing through my veins like a fire he controlled at whim.

My father brought me to the holding cells and I picked the first one, guess I'm just that lucky. Apparently, they captured four Berserkers with the other four already being dead. Two of those Berserkers didn't last the night due to wounds from my guys, so it leaves us with *him* and another one I haven't been in to see yet.

Staring back at me through the one-sided glass mirror is one of the men who features in my nightmares. He looks smaller without all his weapons, namely his knife. The one he named *Lijepa bol*, which means beautiful pain. The one he took great pleasure in using on me. My hand drifts automatically to the scar on my hip. The one I got when he slammed the blade into me, tearing through skin and muscle, and pinning me there like a butterfly as he approached me, the lust clear in his eyes.

My breathing picks up, clouding the glass as I try to anchor myself in the here and now. But when that same sadistic smile twists his lips, I am thrown back into one of my worst moments, a nightmare made real.

"Mewl for me pet, let me hear that sweet sound of pain."

When I refuse to let the scream lodged in my throat escape, he becomes wild, all sanity leaving his eye as he watches me. He leans down and puts his face in my long tangled hair, his rancid breath smelling like blood and beer wafting over me as he whispers in my ear. I try to strain against the bonds even though I know it is no use. I am tied spread eagle to a stone table in the dungeon, my punishment for making eye contact with him. For the defiance, he says he saw there. Ivar laughed as I was dragged from the hall in the middle of the feast, my legs trailing behind my body, hitting every stone on the way out, making my eyes water even as I kept the noises inside. Dreven lifted me by my hair and threw me down here, following after me before I could so much as try to scramble away.

Fatigue, pain, and starvation making me weak, so I couldn't even fight him off. Not that my fifteen year old body would be able to. He's double my height and has stones of muscle earned from wars on him. I was quickly bound and tied to what he calls his lover, the stone table, the position mortifying and offering me no semblance of decency. Left like an animal, only shame and dirt from not being allowed to wash in two months coating my skin. He uses my hair as a handle, pulling me to him. I swear if I survive tonight, I am cutting it all off. Never will it be used against me again, it's a weakness I can't afford.

"I was hoping you wouldn't." He stands up, towering over me before turning to his table of toys.

"What shall we play with today?" he yells, the insanity clear to hear as he talks to the toys. I focus on the light flicking from the torches dotted around the room, it bounces off the stone ceiling, the shadows twinning and twisting like a brutal dance. A tear drops

from my eye, but I refuse to let any more fall. My body is shaking and my chest is tight as I try to breathe through the panic. Maybe he will finally kill me, maybe my body will finally give in. The thought doesn't make me sad, in fact, it's a relief. At least I would finally have peace.

"Ahhhhh!" He holds up the rusty metal clamp in the light, showing it to me even as my eyes strain to focus on the dancing of the flames, trying to transport myself anywhere else. "I stole this from Kellam, let's see if it will make my pretty pet mewl for me."

I don't close my eyes, knowing it won't help with nothing to focus on except the pain, but my body braces as I strain to keep my eyes locked on the shadows above me, twirling faster now, as if to match my racing heart. Maybe I have finally gone mad, because all I want is to float up from my broken and used body, no, not my body—theirs—and join the shadows beckoning me. I will twist high above where they can't reach me, where my body doesn't exist and dance to the music of the fire.

Agony, pure unfiltered agony, rips through my right developing breast as he clamps it on my nipple, which is puckered from the cold to my horror. I bite my tongue to keep my scream in as I float away. I don't know how long I have been laying here, time slipping together as my mind blurs the pain and torture Dreven is painting across my skin like a canvas. I stopped being ashamed after the fourth toy he used, now I am angry and tired. So tired. It's like watching it happening to someone else, as if my body is numb, my soul trying to slip away even as he keeps it trapped here in a cage of horror. When he stops at the bottom of the stone table and grips my weak thighs, I know that the worst horror is coming. The room comes back with a pop as my eyes clear, and my ears stop ringing just in time for him to slip up my body, preparing himself to defile me in the most cruel and ruinous way.

Please, please let me float away again. Let me dance in the flames, my soul twisting in the shadows above, so that I do not feel it *when he pushes into my unprepared and unwilling body. So that I don't have to experience the horror of being reduced to nothing but a toy.*

I yank myself back to the present and rest my head on the glass, breathing through the memory. My body twinges in pain, as if remembering has made it rush back through me. It's the first flashback I have had in a while, but it's like the floodgates have opened. All the horrors of my past are clambering to shine in the light, to subject me to their shame and cruelty. Is it not enough that I lived through it? Now I have to remember it? It's like it knows the happiness I have been feeling, the love surrounding me, and it's determined to tinge it with darkness. To return me to the pain and flames of my former life, as if my contentment has called it from the bleakness.

"Princess?" my father asks from behind me, sounding confused. A tear slips from my eye as the man in the cells face blurs with my memories. Changing, morphing through the years of suffering spent at his hands.

"I'm broken," I whisper, it slips out before I can help it.

"What? No, you are not," he cries, his hand coming to land on my shoulder. I don't know what makes me do it, apart from that I need someone right now. I need to feel safe, I need comfort and light to fight my way through the darkness. I fling myself in his arms and sob, the tears ripping out of me unwillingly.

"Princess, god, I am so sorry. It's okay... You're okay, you're safe. I've got you, princess," he murmurs, his strong arms surrounding me, reminding me of when I was a child and found safety in his hugs.

We fall to the floor, me curled into him, my heart punching through my chest and sob after sob ripping through my shaking body. He holds me, his words mixing together. Reassurance after reassurance as he tries to hold me together. I can tell he doesn't understand, in the way that someone who hasn't experienced pain and suffering can't, but he offers me everything. He holds me as only a father can until my sobs slow, my breath hiccupping with the remaining pain.

I raise my head from his wet shoulder and gaze at his face. He looks defeated and so heartbroken, the lines on his face deeper and his frown fierce. He cups my face, his hands transferring his warmth to me, until I realise I'm ice cold.

"I've got you, my little girl. I'm right here, even if you hate me. Even if you're angry at me, I will be here for you, always, to dry your tears, and hold you when you hurt. I'm here, my princess."

We stay like that for a while, both of us lost in our own thoughts as I try to put myself back to together again in my father's arms.

CHAPTER SIX

FACING DEMONS

After my embarrassing mental breakdown, I try to distance myself from my father so he won't think I am weak. I wipe my face and slip into a bathroom to throw water on it. When it doesn't look like I just spent half an hour sobbing, I head straight into the cell of the Berserker. Straightening my spine, I walk into the room like I own it, unwilling to show any weakness to the man who is responsible for my darkened, damaged soul.

He is leaning against the far wall, taking up half the space, his stature is so big. The loose cotton pants, that they must have given him, make him look bigger. His scars and tattoos are on full display and he is shirtless. He is absolutely still, like a predator before it attacks. Only his eye moves as he follows my entrance, until I stop in the middle of the room, my hands by my side in case he tries to attack me. He moves, bursting out of stillness and making me flinch. He throws his head back and lets out his maniacal chuckle. I grit my teeth and berate myself for flinching, I remind myself of my strength and how he can't hurt me now.

His laughter stops as suddenly as it started, his one brown eye focusing on me once more.

"Pretty pet, how I missed you." His words are a growl, it sends a shiver down my spine as more memories try to resurface. "You always were so quiet, even when I was fucking you."

Everything in me goes still, I can hear him still talking, but it's a blur as a deadly rage unfurls inside me. Pushing me, driving me, until the next thing I know, I have him at my feet on the floor. I blink, not even knowing how we got here. Stumbling back a step, I watch as he spits out blood onto the pristine white floor.

"I like that fire, little pet, but it would be even better to break it." He laughs, his head raising as he watches me, a grin on his face, blood coating his teeth and lips.

I crouch down while grabbing my knife and stab the hand closest to me as he crouches on all fours. I make sure to twist while blood and air hiss from his teeth before he starts laughing again.

"I'm not going to kill you, no matter how much I want to. Instead, I am going to let you die painfully and slowly. You'll be trapped here in your insanity, your mind still here even as your body is suffering from the infection you will get in this wound. It will spread through your blood and your body to your mind. You'll die, cold, alone and afraid as the infection moves through your blood, destroying everything in its path. It's ironic really." I pull the knife out and stand as he falls back to the wall, his hand clutched to his chest. Like this, it's hard to believe he caused so much pain and suffering in my life. He sits laughing to himself as his blood drops to the floor. He looks weak and broken as his eye sparkles with a knowing look, one that tells me he believes what I said. He understands I won't let them help him. He will die alone in here and his eye fills with resignation, then determination.

With a disgusted sneer on my lips, I turn to leave when his voice stops me cold.

"You've become exactly what you hated. A monster." His voice is breathless with pain, but strong and filled with amusement.

I don't dignify him with an answer, I just step out into the hallway. Jax steps from the viewing room, his eyes cold and his face
expressionless. I don't stop walking until I am in his arms. He
doesn't ask me if I'm okay and I love him for that. He just holds me
and lets me fight through everything until I push it all back. Maybe
it makes me weak to depend on him, but I wouldn't change that,
not now. We have a war ahead of us, this could be the last time I'm
allowed to be weak.

"I need to see the other Berserker. We need answers," I
whisper into his chest, loosening the tense grip I have on his shirt.

"Later. Drax needs you and you need him." His chest rumbles
as he speaks and part of me is glad to have an excuse to get away
for a bit, even though I know I will come back later.

It's a testament to how fragile I am feeling after seeing Dreven
that I let Jax lead me away. He wraps his arm around my waist and
leads me so I can lose myself in my head for a bit. When we get to
Drax's room, he hesitates outside.

"I'm going to give you two some privacy, okay?" I go to protest
when he drops a soft kiss on my lips. "You need it, he needs it. I
will be back later." He kisses me again before leaving.

Blowing out a breath, I slip into the room. Drax is sitting up in
bed, his eyes closed. I stop, not wanting to disturb him.

"You better be here to give me a sponge bath, babe," he teases,
his voice weaker than normal.

I laugh and make my way to sit next to him on the edge of the
bed. He opens one eye and smiles softly at me.

"C'mere babe." He shuffles to the side and I slip in next to
him, laying my head on his shoulder. His chest is bare, and I find
myself running my fingers up and down it as I try to push the
image of him unconscious out of my mind.

"Maxen told me everything that happened..." He kisses the top
of my head. "Thank you for protecting me." I shrug and carry on
touching him.

"Taz, what's wrong?" he asks, his hand cupping mine. He twines our fingers together and I close my eyes for a moment before pushing out the words.

"I thought I had lost you, Drax. I thought I had lost the chance to tell you I love you." I hold my breath once the words are out there, freezing like a cannibal in headlights. Sands below, why is it easier to kill someone than to admit how you feel?

"You- you love me?" he sputters, "Don't joke, Taz." His insecurity gives me all the strength I need to get through this.

"I'm not. I love you with all my heart. I love you, and I nearly lost you." I whisper the last part my voice wavering with emotion. His arm clenches around me and he squeezes my hand. He kisses my head as his free hand rubs gently up and down my back.

"I love you too, and not even death itself could keep me from you," he promises, like saying it out loud will make it true, even though we both know either of us could die at any given moment. We have too many enemies, and not enough time.

His hand starts to turn from soft to exploring, until I am biting my lip as he moves over the curve of my ass.

"Drax, you're hurt," I warn, trying to contain the inferno of need smouldering inside of me; a need that desperately wants to feel him alive and in my arms.

"Guess you will have to do all the work." He lifts my chin up and drops a kiss on my forehead, before kissing down my cheek to my lips. "I need you, please." The vulnerability in his voice is my undoing. I kiss him back, using my lips to show him everything I want to say but can't. How scared I was, how much I missed him, the terror when I woke up. It flows out of me as our tongues tangle lazily. I pull back, ready to tell him no, that he's too hurt, but he grabs my hips and pulls me onto his lap as he leans back, looking smug. I catch myself on his chest with a glare.

"Drax—" I start, but he thrusts up, rubbing himself on me and I swallow my protests. Biting my lip, I watch as he lazily thrusts, twisting beneath me until I'm panting and trying to remember why I said no in the first place.

"I don't want any more regrets, babe. I could have died happy knowing you loved me, and now we are going back out there to face a crazed clan leader... I will fight by your side, but first, I need you," he declares, his hips moving beneath me.

I start to rock on him and his hands leave my hips to let me move. They drift higher, pulling my shirt up as they go until he pulls it over my head. It's not hurried or frenzied, and although my lust is nearly out of control, I like this softness, this caring — this promise. We quickly get undressed, helping each other, kissing in between until I am straddling him again. Him buried deep inside me until I don't know where I finish and he starts.

With my hands placed on his thighs behind me, and my head tilted back loving the full sensation, I start to ride him. We work together, the pace leisurely and tender as he doesn't fuck me, but loves me. His cock drags along my sensitive nerve endings with every thrust, making me moan, and when he hits deep inside of me, I start to shake. He grips my hips again and speeds up the pace.

"Look at me," he pleads.

I lift my head and move my hands to his shoulders, using them to pull myself up and down. He leans up and I meet him halfway for a brutal, soul changing kiss. I've never made love before, but this soft joining is how I imagined it. I like to fuck, but sometimes you need love.

When he reaches down and flicks my clit, I am gone, my pussy clenching around him, trying to milk him. His thrusts turn brutal. "I love you," he grits out before hammering home. He stills and comes with a groan, holding me hard over him, his balls pressed against me. Panting, we stare at each other. He has a soft satisfied smile on his face, which I will remember forever. I collapse on his chest and let my breath even out as I come back down to Earth.

"We are leaving tomorrow," I declare, suddenly sure it's the right course of action.

"Okay babe, you know we will follow you anywhere." He wraps his arms around me and holds me to him "What about your father?"

"I don't know. I'm still so angry at him, hurt that he could leave me out there and move on with his life. But like you said, I don't want any regrets. People don't always get a second chance with their loved ones, and I have that chance. Surely I can't just walk away, even if he could." Getting the words out there is helping, and it always seems to be Drax I talk to about my past or fears.

"You do whatever you feel is right. Blood doesn't always mean family babe, trust me, we know, but don't rush into anything because you are angry. It's a big decision, but you know we will support you, whatever you choose." I sigh and snuggle closer.

"I know, I don't know how I lived before I met you all," I mutter.

"You survived, not lived, same as us. We are learning together, it's just not an easy ride. Doesn't mean it won't work, it just takes time."

"I'm broken, Drax," I whisper, my words echoing the ones I said to my father earlier. I know I have shared some of my past with them, and they have seen my strength, but I don't think even I knew the extent of the hatred and memories clamouring inside of me.

"No, you're not. I have seen broken. You're raw. You've had a bad life, one that has shaped you, even if you don't always realise it. You're not beyond repair or lost. Just don't let the past break you now. It's the past for a reason and you survived it then, and you will survive it now. I see the ghosts in your eyes, we all do, and that look only someone who has seen true evil gets. But, baby? Your strength is endless. You fight those ghosts and we will be there to put you back together again after."

We sit in silence, me mulling over his declaration and planning for the future. It's like down here there is a little bubble, suspending reality, allowing me time to breathe and break down, but I know once I'm outside again I will have to rebuild myself and concentrate on saving the Wastes, so for now, I sit in silence and enjoy the peace. It's how Jax finds us an hour later.

CHAPTER SEVEN

THE DISHONOURED

I kiss Drax one last time and get dressed. Jax and I leave him to rest, both stopping in the hallway outside.

"You want to go and question the other Berserker?" He doesn't look at me, but at my fingers twisted in his. His voice is off as well, and I step closer, forcing him to look at me.

"Jax? Are you okay?" I ask.

"Are you mad at me for not getting to you both in time? It's okay if you are, I'm mad at myself," he rumbles.

My mouth flops open as I stare at him—sands below, he thinks I'm angry with him for not being able to save us from the Berserkers? I know he needs my answer, the distance is growing between us and I plan to make sure he fucking hears me.

"I am not mad at you. You did all you could. Why would you think I am?"

"You haven't kissed me since we got here, you've slept with all the others, but avoided me..." His jaw moves as he looks away.

Sands below, juggling four men is exhausting.

"Jax, you listen to me and you listen good. I am not mad at you, and don't you dare blame yourself. I haven't kissed you because if I do, I won't want to stop, and you needed to be with your brother and he needed you. I haven't purposely avoided being with you, it's just the way it worked out." I grab his chin and force him to look at me. "I want you. I want you so bad it's killing me. Even just after being with your brother, all I can think about is that talented tongue of yours and making you mine."

His nostrils flare and his eyes darken, before I find myself slammed into the hallway wall, Jax's darkness coming out to play.

His lips slam into mine, bruising as he keeps me pinned here, his strength astounding. I grip his shoulder and tug on his hair as I give as good as I get.

"Not here. There are cameras," I gasp as he bites my neck hard. I see fucking stars as he wraps my legs around his waist and pulls me from the wall, before moving to the next room and striding through. He doesn't even wait for the door to shut as he tosses me on the empty bed and stalks towards me, his expression fierce and his eyes dark.

I know this is going to be rough and hard, and I can't fucking wait. He snarls as he grabs my legs and yanks me to the edge of the bed, I automatically wrap my legs around his waist as he watches me hungrily.

"Kiss me," I demand. He grins, flashing pearly whites, making him look like some sort of demon, or avenging angel.

"That's not how it's going to work this time, angel." The heat and warning has my breath speeding up as he takes complete control, his darkness deepening the colour of his eyes as it sets its sight on what it wants: me.

Something flashes in his eyes, but he keeps me trapped as he surges forward and cuts my shirt down the middle. I frown, my eyes narrowing as the material splits, exposing my heaving breasts, the air making my rosy pink nipples harden. I glare at him, but the pure and utter hunger and adoration in his eyes have me panting as his eyes burn a trail across my skin.

He goes to cut my trousers and I growl. Dropping my legs, I slip forward and grab the blade that I didn't even see him produce. He lets go so I don't hurt myself, and I quickly grab his shirt and saw up the middle. It parts like butter for the blade and hangs from his shoulders in a tattered mess. He watches me as he shrugs out of it, his impressive chest moving and clenching as his muscles ripple with the movement. I knew when Jax and I came together it would be hot, heavy, and dark. He has too much pain and suffering to be soft and gentle when his control snaps. It's the total opposite to me and Drax earlier, but hot in its own way. I don't worry about hurting him or turning him off. I let out all the pain and anger from my memories coming back, and seeing *him* again, and I channel it into Jax—because he can take it, and he will love it—twisting my darkness with his own until we are one. My pussy clenches, feeling empty as he watches for what I will do next.

I run the blade lightly across his chest, leaving pink marks in my wake as I decorate him with my brand. He growls, his hands grabbing my hips, but lets me carry on. I drag the blade up his chest until it meets his neck, then across it as I feel his pulse jump. I grin as I run it over his cheek to his lips, which open slightly in a sharp inhale. His tongue darts out and licks the blade before he grabs me and pins me to the bed, my arm holding the knife smashing into the material and loosening my grip. He kisses me, harsh and fast as we fight each other for control. I hear the knife clatter to the floor as I wrap my legs around him once again. We roll as we keep our lips together, until we smash into the floor.

Even that doesn't deter us as I stand and quickly drop my trousers. I watch as he wiggles out of his and lays back, watching me.

"I need to taste you again," he groans out as he grips his cock, the end shimmering with pre-cum.

"Then come and get me." I wink as he surges up and grabs my waist, flipping me until I'm face down, his hot body pressed up against me, his cock pulsing against my ass as he leans over to whisper in my ear.

"Oh, don't worry angel, I plan on tasting all of you." He bites my shoulder, making me arch back, pushing against him as my pussy throbs.

He kisses and nips down my back, causing me to pant into the floor, knowing he will have left behind marks. Each one drives me crazy, making my lust spike to a fever pitch.

"Jax," I moan. I feel him smile against my back as he reaches my ass. He spanks me, making me yelp. He kisses it better then does the same to the other cheek.

"If you don't fucking—"

I finish my sentence with a groan as he licks up my pussy before parting my lips and devouring it like he did my mouth. He has me groaning in no time as he teases around my nub, the tip of his thumb sliding in and out of my channel but coming nowhere close to filling me. It's the best kind of torture, and I know he is trying to show me his control. I cry out as he flicks my clit, only to lick around it in maddening circles as I thrust back, trying to make him fill me.

"Jax—" I warn, but he bites down gently on my nub and I explode, crying out as my pussy clenches. I feel him crawl up my body again, his mouth touching my ear.

"So fucking sweet," he croons as his hand tangles in my hair. He yanks my head to the side and smashes our lips together. I can taste myself on him and I groan before pushing back again. He rubs his cock on my ass before pulling away slightly.

"Next time, this," he thrusts against my ass, "is mine."

I narrow my eyes in warning but he moves away, making me shiver as the heat of his body disappears. His hands cut into my hips as he yanks them in the air. He doesn't waste any time, and thrusts into me, spearing me as I scramble to hold on to something. He twists his hand in my hair again and yanks my head back, the pain and pleasure blur together as he starts to move in me. Fucking me hard and fast, as his hips slap against me.

"Fuck angel, you're so tight. So wet. So perfect." His groan has me closing my eyes and clamping around him.

"Fucking shit," he swears, his thrusts stuttering before he starts to hammer home for real. I grin as I purposely do it again. I can feel myself winding up again, his cock dragging on the bundle of nerves inside me. His hand leaves my hip and rubs my nub, and I scream as I am thrown into another orgasm, so hard and fast I can't do anything but clench around him and cry out. He slams into me twice before stilling and coming with a yell.

He collapses on to my body, and we both lay panting on the floor, him still inside of me.

"I love you," he says softly into my shoulder. My heart stutters then bursts with love as I smile against the floor.

"I love you too," I say just as softly. I turn my head and kiss him gently. His eyes are vulnerable once again, the side of him only I get to see. They fill up with love as I watch and he traces his eyes across my face.

"Whatever happens next, I will always be behind you, as will my brothers. We will fight your demons with you, angel."

I close my eyes as a soft, sad smile twists my lips. How does he always know what is happening in my head?

"Together," I breathe out, meaning it. I open my eyes as he nods and lays his forehead on mine.

"Together."

I BLOW OUT a breath, déja vu hitting me as I face the white

door to the cells. This time Jax has my back, although only from the viewing room. But it strengthens me and I slide my mask into place, the one I have used for most of my life. I step up to the door and it slides open, revealing the Berserker who is pacing his cell like a caged animal.

He snarls at me before he comes to a standstill in the middle of the room.

"You." His voice is rough. It sounds like it has been burnt out at one point, which with Ivar's men, could be true. Yet I sense no hate or malice, more like simple curiosity and maybe relief? The thought has me frowning as I watch him.

"You do not remember me?" he asks, his voice thick with a harsh accent. He doesn't step closer, instead his hand forms a symbol I know well. I watch as he taps three fingers over his heart, a sign of respect, of friendship—of Noah.

I flick my eyes back to him as he nods. "So it is you, little queen."

Now that I know he isn't going to attack me, I focus on him fully. His hair is short—obviously hacked away, his honour braid lost—and that makes me curious. A dishonoured Berserker with the general? He has the markings of the clan, but also some I don't know. His leather pants stick to his powerful thighs and his body is big. Not fat, just big, the type that will never have definition but is a pure powerhouse. He's tall as well, taller than even Maxen or Thorn. The wrinkles around his aging face betray the years, as does the grey starting at his temples. His beard is a mix of brown and grey, and is long and untrimmed. Overall, he looks rough and hardened, like a true Berserker.

"Who are you?" I demand, my stance not loosening. It only makes him grin.

"Spoken like a true queen. I am Vasilisy. Noah's uncle."

CHAPTER EIGHT

A BERSERKER'S WORD

"Noah's dead," I say coolly, watching as his eyes turn sad in memory.

"Aye, I do not blame you. He was not made for this world."

I start at his words, his words so like my own thinking that I don't know how to respond.

"But he did love you," he carries on.

It's like a hammer to my heart and I find myself looking over his shoulder so he doesn't see the emotion in my eyes.

"Why were you with Dreven?" I demand, quickly changing the subject.

"It wa' the best way to find you. Me and Noah's da split up, him searching the other side of The Ring and me this side. Dreven found me and a few other loyal men, and decimated them all. He tied them to posts, cut off their cocks and burnt them alive with it in their mouths." He spits on the floor in disgust at the memory, I wish I could say it would be the worst thing I have ever heard, but that would be a lie.

"Why didn't he kill you?" I cock my head, watching his movements carefully. Body language will tell me more than his words ever will.

"He wanted me alive. A present for our fucking king." He sneers the word king and I find myself smiling.

"Did he dishonour you?" I ask, nodding at his hair. His hand comes up self-consciously before dropping again.

"Aye. Fucking animal," he snarls.

"Well you found me, sort of, so why did you attack my men?" I bring my arms in close at the chill in the room and his eyes automatically drop to the movement, a fighter's habit.

"I didn't, I was tied to a bike when the pale ones found us." His voice is rough, and reminds me of the harsh life I lived before.

"Pale ones?" I arch my eyebrow and start to feel silly for my fighting stance, I relax and lean against the wall instead.

"Aye, they lie down here like rats. No sun, so pale ones." I bite my lip to hide my smile at the description.

"What do you want with me?" I finally ask.

"The same thing you want. To kill Ivar. Our people were once great, we were about brotherhood and family. Warriors fighting to protect, not to kill. He twisted that when his mind warped, and we were helpless to stop it. You, little queen, were the catalyst. If a slave girl at sixteen can win her freedom and fight his tyranny, so can we." He makes my life sound like a fucking musical, not the horror show it was.

"So you and his 'da', two people, are trying to bring down his whole clan?" I scoff.

"No. There are more of us, loyal brothers. Warriors who see the wrong, who hate the torture. Some you saved, some you befriended even when you didn't know." His eyes beg me to believe him.

"What the fuck are you talking about. I had no friends there," I snarl.

"No? What about Tren, who snuck you food? Or Cole, who accepted watch with you every time so that you wouldn't have to fight off your partner. Or the men who refused to take part in your torture, refused to fight you. They may not have stopped it, but they weren't accepting it either. All it took was one look in them deep soulful eyes of yours, girl, and they were lost. They say, stare too long you will see your soul, your destiny, and your death." His voice is harsh, like he is unused to staying that much but it holds steady enough. I don't say anything and he spreads his hands wide in a pleading gesture.

"You don't have to trust me, little queen, but work with me. Help me kill Ivar."

I leave the cell confused and thoughtful. I didn't agree to anything, but I didn't reject his idea either. It would be good to have a Berserker loyal, to inform me of changes, but it's a big risk, he could turn around and betray us. That symbol however, the one when I first walked in, it was a secret, one me and Noah made. I know he taught his father, who I would trust if he was here. So, for him to teach Vasilisy...

"What are you going to do?" Jax asks as he steps into the hall-way. I rub my head where yet again another headache is forming.

"I don't know yet. I need to speak to my father though, to plan for us leaving tomorrow. Why don't you go check on the others and make sure they are packed and ready to leave at first light?" It's easy to lose track of time down here, but from the sky, I would say it is night. I'm getting comfortable, and I can't afford to. That means it's time to leave.

"Okay, angel." He kisses me quickly, offering me a smug smile when I try to chase his lips, and then leaves me alone with my thoughts.

I walk slowly to my father's office, trying to sort through everything and give myself time to breathe as well. By the time I reach the door, I feel more organised and a rough plan is forming in my head. I knock and wait for the door to open. When it does, I step inside to find the fire roaring and flickering around the darkened room, with my father hunched over his desk, pouring over papers.

"I need my weapons back," I blurt out. He lifts his head and blinks at me.

"Okay?" He seems confused and I don't blame him. Biting my lip, I make my way over to the chairs near the fire, sinking into the one with the view of the door, because old habits die hard. My eyes are automatically drawn to the fire, watching as it twists and dances in the hearth.

"Tazanna?" His voice brings me back to see him watching me from the other chair. *Sands below.*

"What did you say?" I ask gruffly, keeping my eyes on him and not the flames. He looks from it to me with a question in his eyes that I don't bother answering.

"I heard you are leaving in the morning." He holds his hand up to still whatever I was going to say. "I am not asking you to stay. But I would ask you take a few of my people with you. If this Summit is really a meeting of leaders, we need representation."

I groan. Sands below, he is too smart sometimes. Obviously wording it in a way I can't deny, even though I know he is sending them to watch me.

"Fine, but I am taking the Berserker in the cell with us. I want weapons and food as well. Oh, and if your men get in my way, if they betray me, or fall behind, I will leave them for dead. Understand?" I keep my eyes cold, and my voice emotionless. He searches my eyes obviously trying to figure out if I am being honest.

"Understood." He sighs. "Tazanna, we have things to talk about. We need to work through this." He throws his hand up and gestures between us.

"We don't. Talking won't fix anything. I trust in actions, not words. But for now I need to leave, to get back before another war breaks out." I watch his face fall. "Maybe after..." I trail off unsure why I even offered that. His face breaks into a wide smile.

"After. Go, get some sleep. I will have everything prepared for your departure tomorrow morning."

I nod and stand, leaving him there alone lost in his thoughts. Every step I take is filled with regret and pain. I just hope I am making the right choice.

I GROAN WHEN I see who my father has picked to go with us. We are in a hanger on the edge of the property, filled with vehicles and a gas tanker. There, packing a bag into a jeep, is that fucking pretty boy doctor. Vasilisy is next to him, ripping into a piece of meat as he watches the men scurry around like ants. He seems amused as they give him a wide berth.

Maxen squeezes my shoulder as he walks past, the others on his heels to pack our stuff. As promised, my weapons were delivered to our room this morning, but I have yet to see my father. Maybe that's a good thing. I'm not good at goodbyes.

"Tazanna."

I wince and turn to see my father there, watching me as if my thoughts summoned him.

"Here, take this." He holds out a bit of paper to me which I accept, but raise my eyebrow in question.

"It's a map, so you can always find your way back to me." His voice breaks on the last word, and I see the strain on his face at having to lose me again. The difference this time is I am walking away, I am choosing my own path, and I know it's the right choice. I could stay here, with him and pretend I don't know what's going on out there. I could bury my head in the sand again, but I am done running. It's time I faced my past, it's time I made use of my skills and if it was the last thing I do, at least I will die trying. It's strange that I don't fear death as I feared living.

"Thank you," I say uncomfortably, putting it in my pack. The others near him retreat to give us space to say goodbye.

"Dad–"

"Prince–"

We look at each other and share a small smile, more emotion in that then we could ever convey with words.

"I'm going to miss you. I know I don't have to right to say that, but I will, you will always be my little girl, Tazzy. But I am so proud of you, for what you have become. You're a lot like your mother and I know when she set her mind to it, she didn't walk away or give up and I respect that. I just hope one day that path will bring you back to me." Tears drip from his eyes as he grabs the back of my head gently and lays a soft kiss on my forehead.

"I love you, princess," he whispers against my skin, before turning and striding back to his people. My heart clenches at the familiar words.

"Goodbye, Dad," I whisper to his hunched, retreating back. When I can't stand to watch him anymore, when the pain and guilt become too much, I turn and face my men. Who are waiting with smiles and open arms at the car. One look at them is all the reassurance I need.

My time here has been nice, a retreat, an escape from reality to let me heal both physically and mentally, but it's time to return to the real world, my world filled with blood and death, the things I do best. If I learnt anything here, it's that paradise doesn't have to be a place, it can be people, and with my men at my back, I know what that means for the first time.

CHAPTER NINE

TRAPPED

The steel bunker door rolls up with a siren and a flashing orange light at each corner. The door, which is more like a building, stretches from floor to ceiling and is a mixture of steel and concrete. An old-world method to protect against radiation and nuclear bombs, and I guess they had the right idea—just the wrong way the world would end. The big black truck from pre-scorch days is a tight squeeze with all my men, but they refused to be separated, which I can't say I am sad about. My father insisted on letting us take the vehicle, weapons, and food. I explained it would make us a bigger target, but when he argued the point that it would make it faster to get back to the Summit, I could hardly refuse. So, now I'm waiting for the sand to be revealed beyond the door to paradise.

I thought I would be sad to leave, but I guess once you live a certain way you get used to it. The glare of the sun hits us first, making me grin. Once I can see the open sand-covered stretch of land, something in my chest loosens, and I instantly become more primal. Dr. Perfect Face, my new name for him, insisted on driving and now he throws me a look through the rearview mirror as if seeing the glee in my eyes.

"You ready to head into the Wastes?" he asks everyone.

"More ready than you are," I taunt.

His hands are tight on the wheel and his eyes tense, I'm betting he has never been out of the bunker. Does it make me a bad person to enjoy his discomfort?

Vasilisy smiles at me from the car next to us, filled with a few guards. We drive out, side by side heading to The Summit. I grab the shades out of my bag and kick my feet up on Dr. Perfect's seat and tilt my head to watch the scenery go by. The sand blurs together as we drive until I find myself nodding off.

"Think she wull mak' it thro' this one?"

Through the slit in my ballooning eyes, I see the Berserker turn to look at me, it was a bad fight. Real bad, no better than the first time, except this time I managed to stay conscious long enough for Ivar to beat me. Now, his little minions are driving me back to the castle in their pikers. Modded out versions of old vehicles. This one being a bus. My broken body was carelessly tossed on to one of the only seats remaining; the rest of the bus was stripped and filled with weapons. The side was even cut out to install flamethrowers and pikes.

"Who knows, tough bitch though, I will give her that." He says before turning back around.

"Aye. Wonder how many fights she will live thro'?" He flicks me another look, filled with pity before dragging his eyes back to the road and the waning light.

"Or how long until Ivar kills her." His friend scoffs from beside him.

The flippant way they are discussing my death has me focusing on the landscape out of the window. The rough, ripped seat I am on pushes into my cheek as I curl up and face the big piece of glass. I watch the world pass by as they take me back to my cage.

I must fall asleep because the next thing I know my hair is pulled, used as a handle. I whimper as I am yanked up and thrown into the open area of the bus, the man who isn't driving standing over me leering.

"Looks like we are camping for the night, slave. Why don't you keep us entertained?"

My eyes fall from him to meet the driver's. He quickly looks away, obviously unable to watch me be tortured. I make sure to keep my eyes on him the whole time, if I have to live through it. If he won't do anything to stop it, then he damn well has to live with that choice and at least live through it with me.

I can feel someone's hand in mine, squeezing and offering me comfort, and I know it must be Jax, I smile and go to close my eyes again when I spot something through the window. Frowning, I blink to clear the nightmare and sleep away.

I watch as a wall of wind and sand crawls towards us, covering the land and broken buildings. Until the orange blots out the sky, Dr. Perfect Face keeps looking from the road to his side window as he tries to out drive it. Sand storms are common, there's only one way to deal with them. Get the fuck out of their way and lay low.

"FUCK!" he yells.

A sand twister forms in front of us, reaching at least a hundred metres high and ten metres wide. We swerve and drive in the opposite direction as the sandstorm starts to catch up with us. I spot a building up ahead.

"We need to get off the road," I say casually, using the knife to clean my nails. Dr. Perfect Face throws me a glare as he white knuckles the steering wheel. The front window is now completely covered, and we can't see in front of us. We are driving blind.

"Pull over, we can wait it out in here. Or there was a building not too far."

He finally listens to me and yanks the wheel and stops the car. The sand completely covers us, but I can just about spot the outline of the building in front of us. I pull up my neck scarves and hood before reaching between my legs and grabbing my bags. I shimmy forward in my seat and strap on my swords before facing the guys. The material covering my nose and mouth hides my smile, but I wink before slipping out of the car door. I hear swearing as they scramble to pack up and come after me, but I don't bother waiting, I stride through the wind, my face to the floor and my hand outstretched until it meets the outside of the building. Running it along, I grin when I hit a door, it would seem luck is on our side. I shove it, but it doesn't budge. *Sands below.*

Stepping back, I kick it and the steel groans before slamming inwards, announcing our presence to anyone inside. When nothing comes sprinting out of the darkness, I take shelter in the doorway and wait for the others. One by one, they trickle in until all that's left is the Doc. When I don't see him, I frown.

"Fuck," I groan.

Shaking my head, I brave the sand and shimmy along the wall. I see him twisting and turning, obviously, lost not far from where we are. I grab his arm, as he lets out a shout before I yank him inside. Slamming the door to stop the raging winds and sand, I breathe a sigh of relief before turning around.

"Looks like we are camping here tonight."

THE BUILDING INSIDE isn't as destroyed as most places in the Wastes. It seems we have lucked out. It looks like an old warehouse, with massive high up old yellowed windows that only have cracks and not holes. The floor is unforgiving concrete and unused dead machinery covers half of the floor. But there is a break room, hidden away in the back. Not big enough for every-one, but I don't give a shit about everyone. It adds a layer of protection between me and them. The door is crooked and looks like it's about to fall down, but the two dusty sofas inside are calling my name. Striding through, and uncaring about the debate of sleeping arrangements, I drop my bag on the floor in the break room and strip off my jacket and scarf dropping them on top. Drax follows me in and collapses on the red dirty sofa next to me, obviously still a little weak from his wounds. Even laid sprawled, he looks hot as hell, with one leg propped up and one arm behind his head as he watches me. I manage to drag my eyes away long enough to take in where we are. The room is probably just big enough to fit me and my men, with windows covering one wall.

Dr. Perfect Face stops outside one of the windows to the break room and cocks his eyebrow, with a grin I pull down the blinds and block out his face. Drax laughs as he stomps around to the door and glares at me.

"Debriefing in five." He scowls before turning and stomping away. I groan and look at Drax. He pats his chest with a mischie-vous twinkle in his eye.

"I know what we can do in five minutes."

Laughing, I walk over to him, my boots leaving footprints in the dirt and dust on the floor. I stop just before him and bend over, putting a hand on either side of his head.

"Only five minutes? I'm disappointed." I tug on his lip with my teeth before straightening and turning around. Vasilisy stands at the door looking very concerned.

"What is debrief? Does it mean he wishes to undress me? I will beat him with his own arm," he growls, banging on his chest with a triumphant look in his eyes. Closing my eyes, I groan in frustration, sands below, it's going to be a long trip.

"No, it doesn't mean that." I walk towards him and crane my

neck back to see him. "Now come on, let's get this the fuck over with so I can get some sleep."

"Yes, little queen." He steps to the side and follows me to the middle of the room where the others are gathered. It makes me nervous to have him at my back, but I don't show it. Instead, I manoeuvre around until I can lean on one of the machines so that no one can sneak up on me. Maxen comes to stand on one side of me and Jax on the other. I watch everything as the others mill around, my stillness and gaze seems to unnerve them if the looks they are throwing my way are anything to go by.

Vasilisy sits on the ground near my feet and pulls out his honour dagger. Ignoring everyone, he starts to pick his teeth with it, disgust fills the faces of the paradise men and I can't help but laugh. They aren't cut out for the world out here, it's going to get them killed, and I don't plan on being there when it does. After all, they don't have my loyalty, and I don't give a shit about anyone in here but my men.

Maxen drops his arm around my shoulder and kisses my head. I smile up at him and lean into his side, my other hand grabbing Jax's and twining my fingers with his.

"Okay, so we should plan for tomorrow and set up roles for tonight..." I tune out the guard who has made himself in charge. Instead, I close my eyes and let stillness overcome me, helping me push back the memories that came to me today.

"Are you listening to me? I'm sorry, are we boring you or do you simply not understand what we are talking about?" The sneer makes the room go silent and I slowly open my eyes to see the guard glaring at me. Maxen tenses and Jax squeezes my hand as I watch the guard. I know my eyes are cold, still locked in my stillness, but he doesn't seem to care or understand the warning in them.

"Well, which is it?" He scowls, the condensation dripping from his words.

"Shall I kill him for, you little queen, and offer his head as trib-
ute?" Vasilisy asks casually.

"If I want him dead, I will kill him myself," I reply, watching as
the guard's scowl deepens, but I see the flicker off fear in his eyes
before he masks it.

"Now listen up bitch, just because your daddy thinks he rules,
doesn't mean you get to do whatever the fuck you want. You will
shut up, listen, and be a good little girl, so I can do my job and get
you and these other savages to your shithole."

I cock my eyebrow and straighten my pose, it makes him flinch,
and I hide my smile. For all his bravado, he is scared of me. I walk
towards him and stop when our feet touch.

"Now it's your turn to listen and listen closely because that is
the only slur you will get out of your fucking mouth before I cut
out your tongue and wear it as a necklace. I don't give a fuck what
power you think you had down below. Out here, you are nothing
but feral fodder. This world is mine. I know how to survive, how to
fight, and how to run. You are nothing but a child throwing a
tantrum. So you better learn some respect and fast, or I will leave
you to the cannibals." Each word darkens his face with anger, but
ignoring him and showing the ultimate disrespect, I turn my back
on him and face the others.

"The fact is, none of you know how to survive out here and
unless you start to learn, and fast, you are going to die out here.
Now, we will have watch at every door and window, switching
every three and we leave at daybreak. You will not give away our
position with loud noises or lots of light, and you will man the fuck
up, or I will leave you all behind tomorrow, I do not have time for
dead weight."

With that I walk away, leaving the stunned silence and Vasilisy's laughter following after me. I make my way around the building, searching for possible entrances, and testing the strength of
the windows. Rubbing the dirt and age away from one of the

windows, I look outside. The sand is still blocking everything, with twisters occurring now and then. I look around for anything else I might have missed.

A metal staircase is hidden at the back of the room leading to a walkway above, I follow it around and find a door I didn't spot before marked as a fire escape. I nudge it open, covering my eyes in case the storm is right there. When the door isn't flung away from me, I peek outside. My eyes widen as I step through the door. A metal railing runs around the square space, with windows just before it, blocking out the wind and sand. The brick of the walls seals it in on the other two sides. A metal garden chair is on the floor, rusted and mangled. I step further out and peer out of the window, it is a perfect vantage point if it wasn't for the storm.

Dragging my eyes away, I turn around to leave, only to come face to face with the guard. He steps through the door and lets it shut behind him with a bang.

"You ever question me in front of my men again and I will put you in your place." His face is red and his chest heaving.

"And what place would that be?" I ask curiously, stepping back and letting my hands dangle by my side.

"You are nothing but a savage whore!" he roars, spittle flying from his mouth. I've met his kind before, the ones who think they're gods, that no one is above them—especially woman. He sees us as nothing more than a place to stick his dick. Even now, I can see his eyes drop to my chest before meeting mine. I'm going to enjoy putting him in his place, maybe I will make him my bitch.

Sighing, I start to unstrap my weapons as I speak. "Because I enjoy sex and pleasure that makes me a whore? When a man fucks who he wants and takes what he needs he is called a hero, and warrior." Finished, I bend over keeping my eyes on his and place them on the floor.

He grins. "You should have kept them," he taunts.

I shrug and crack my neck from side to side. "I'm not going to need them."

He moves without speaking, swinging his fist at me. I dodge and bounce on the tips of my toes grinning at him as the adrenaline rushes through me, my blood lust rising with it. "See, I don't think you realise how I came to be a free woman in the Wastes." He swings again and I dodge. I start to circle him as he tries to hit me. "I won my way here, fought like a mad woman, like a Berserker." He growls and rushes me, but I move out of the way, slipping around him like a dancer in The Rim. "I didn't care about dying, I only focused on the next moment, on staying alive. I learnt how to handle myself around men, especially men like you." He yells wordlessly and tries to uppercut me, I laugh as I twist away dancing around the small area.

"You are nothing compared to the warriors I faced. You are pampered." I slip in and kick his legs out from under him. "Slow." I wait for him to get to his knees before bringing my knee up and smashing it into his nose. "Weak." Using the toe of my boot, I nudge him over as he screams and holds his face.

The door slams open and Dr. Perfect Face, my men, and Vasilisy are crowding into the doorway. I throw them a wink and walk around the guard on the floor, I grab my weapons and walk to the door. "Anyone else hungry?" I ask to the sounds of blood being spit out behind me. Dr. Perfect Face who is the first one at the door gives me a smile, which throws me of for a second, before his usual bored and irritated face returns and he looks at the man behind me. "Someone get me my bag."

CHAPTER TEN

BARELY HUMAN

After my lesson, I go back to our break room, and me and my men eat our rations. We laugh and joke, with Maxen telling them all about me and the guard. I decide to take first watch and kiss them all goodnight before heading back to the vantage point. I make sure to keep my weapons strapped on, in case any of the guards, who throw me dirty looks as I walk past them, try anything.

I slump against the wall, my eyes drawn to the windows and the dying swirls of sand. It looks like by morning the dust will have settled again. The door opens next to me, and I have my dagger in my hand before they can step through. Thorn looks around before spotting me, he sees the blade and smiles. I smile back and slip it away as he joins me on the floor. His whole body touching mine, we sit that close. Out of all my men, Thorn is the one I have spent the least amount of time with. Only here and there have we had private conversations, but after Paradise, I feel like we are a lot closer. But in some ways, he is still a mystery to me. A man so big, he towers over everyone, yet with the gentlest heart I have ever met. His past is as messed up as mine, and I wish I could help him forget, and forgive himself.

"Tell me about your brother?" Thorn asks, his arm wrapping around my shoulder and pulling me close.

"Why?" I mumble.

"Because even though it hurts, he deserves to be remembered," he says softly.

My heart clenches and pain spreads through my chest. Tears build up at the back of my eyes, but I refuse to let them fall.

"He was my best friend. He was older than me, so I used to follow him around everywhere. Yet, even when his friends made fun of him for letting me play with them, he didn't care." I cut off and breathe, concentrating on the dust swirling in the distance. "He protected me always. There was this boy in his year, who used to pick on me. He pushed me, so I punched him. The kid went running back to his mum crying, who turned up at our house. I knew I would be in trouble, so I hid behind my brother." A sad smile twists my lips as I remember him reaching back and grabbing my hand. His eyes so fierce, so determined to protect me even at his age. "He took the blame, said he had done it." I shake my head with a pained laugh. "He was grounded for two weeks. He snuck into my room that night to read to me, I always did have trouble sleeping. I asked him why." I breathe in and it hiccups as my eyes burn and my throat closes. "He told me it was his duty as big brother to always protect me, and that he always would." I finish brokenly, my heart falling apart at the old memory, one I didn't even know I could recall.

"He sounds like an amazing person," Thorn says, pulling me closer. I drop my head onto his shoulder and let the pain run through me even as I smile at the memory.

"He was."

It goes quiet for a bit as we watch the twisting of the air and sand in front of us. "What about your sister?" I ask after a while.

"She was so little. So full of life, god she drove my mum crazy with her attitude. But no matter how much she was winding me up, I loved her. She was my weakness, my sister with the smile that could make even the biggest man cave." He breathes in against me, as his body shakes. "I should have protected her," he whispers brokenly, and I turn to see tears tracking down his face.

"You did everything you could. You told me even though it hurts she deserves to be remembered, well you deserve to forgive yourself even though it hurts." He tightens his arm on me. "What was her name?" I ask, pushing him to see past his grief.

"Petal." He lets out a laugh. "See the pattern? My mum was obsessed with flowers, so Thorn and Petal. She was so beautiful, she had this big curly hair that would not be tamed. These two dimples and deep brown eyes that you got lost in."

My heart stutters and the more he talks the more I freeze up as a memory flings me into the past, even as he carries on talking.

"Chocolate," she says with a smile, her head tipped to the side to face me. Her swirly brown hair poking through the bars. The stone cell she is in is opposite mine. Another punishment for me, and her as well. Her dirty, once white, now brown cotton dress barely covers her legs as she holds them to her chest for warmth. There's a blood stain on her side, but I don't ask. We both know talking about it doesn't help.

Two torches bracket her cell, reflecting off the damp cold stone. At least we have light this time; last time he left me down here in the dark with nothing but my pain and hunger for days. You spend so long in the dark, being out of it feels wrong. Even now, I sit to the shadowed side of the cell bars, my face slightly hidden as we watch each other. My stomach throbs in hunger and I pull my legs to my chest, mirroring her. I can't remember the last time I ate anything, and my bones are beginning to stick out now. Yanking on my own dirty tunic, I try to cover as much of my bare legs as possible. The rip from Ivar earlier tears a little more making me close my eyes in pain at the reminder of what happened to me.

"Ice cream," I whisper, trying to breathe through my shame.

"Apples," she says through a soft laugh, her voice melodic and helping me concentrate on our conversation. It's our way of staying sane. She's younger than me and has been here only a couple of months, but in that time, she has been through the same hell I have. I don't reply, and I hear her sigh. It took her a whole month to get me to talk at all.

"Thank you for protecting me again today," she says, gripping the bars. I shrug and focus on the flames, a coping mechanism of mine. It's not like I saved her life, just took the beating meant for her, much to Ivar's delight. He asked me why as I lay curled in a broken ball on his floor. I didn't bother telling him it's because I know it will break her. Even now, I can see the strain in her eyes. They have dimmed as well, the hope leaving them tired. It's the same look I see in my eyes every day, but there is a difference between us. She can't endure, I have seen that for myself. It sends a sharp stabbing pain through my chest because I know before long, she will die. If not by her own hand, by theirs once she is nothing more than a shell—after all, she is useless to them. I have seen it happen time and time again, slaves come and go. Their minds breaking from the torture, just another body for his men to dispose of after. Yet, I am still here. I wish I knew why, but I refuse to let that bastard have the last laugh. He would love it if he finally broke me.

I never let myself get too close to the other slaves, it only brings more pain, but something about this little girl made me reach out. Made me change my rules, and I know Ivar has spotted it. I just don't know how he plans to use it against me.

"What's your real name?" she asks, breaking into my thoughts. I turn to face her once again, my bruised and raw cheek pushing against the stone behind me. I grit my teeth against the pain of

moving, my body is locking up. My muscles sore and abused, but at least the pain blocks the hunger for a while.

"Tazanna." The word sounds foreign, and my voice croaks from not being used but her brilliant smile makes it all worth it. It's breathtaking, like the sun rising in the morning.

"Nice to meet you, Tazanna, I'm Petal." She keeps her smile until I find myself offering her one back. The feeling of it stretching my lips foreign to me. Footsteps sound as someone descends the stairs. Her smile falls away and her eyes turn panicked as she grips the bars harder, her face going white.

"Don't fight them, they like it," I whisper hurriedly. It's my turn to grip the bars as she seems to be miles away, stuck in her panic. "Petal. Promise me," I demand. She blinks before nodding at me, a tear dripping down her little face.

The man stops between our cells and I drag my eyes away from her, letting them go cold and vacant. Ivar's right-hand man, Dreven, appears between our cells.

"Well, ladies. Ivar has a deal. One of you is mine tonight, while the other is safe. Pick. You have thirty seconds." He grins, and almost giggles as he watches Petal hungrily. I know he hasn't had her yet, he loves breaking in a new slave. I watch as she trembles, her mind obviously screaming at her.

"Me. I will go with you," I say, I don't know why. I have never volunteered to save another before. It's not what the slaves do. You look out for yourself, all the others would have thrown me at him, some did, but I can't let him touch her.

He frowns before shrugging, that same crazy smile returning.

"I have some new toys, pet." He walks to my cell and starts to unlock it. I catch Petal's eyes as tears stream down her face. She mouths 'thank you' and I nod.

I come back to myself to find Thorn crouching before me, his hands on my knees as he shakes me desperately.

I watch him with wide tear filled eyes, and remember what happened last time, and my promise for truth. I search his concerned eyes and know if I don't tell him, he will never forgive me.

"I knew her," I choke out.

"Wh-what?" he croaks.

"She was Ivar's pet. He brought her in a couple of years after me. Thorn... I'm so sorry." I try to reach out, but he drops his hands and falls to his ass before me.

"She dead?" he asks, his eyes locked on mine. I bite my lip and his eyes harden. "Worth, is my sister dead?"

I close my eyes in pain "Yes," I whisper.

I open my eyes to see him flinch, like a bullet tore into him as he sucks in a breath.

"How?" he demands.

I shake my head and he grabs my cheeks. "I want to know how!" he shouts, the anguish etched across his handsome face.

I lick my dry chapped lips and swallow harshly. "A stab wound. She dropped a drink on one of his men. He stabbed her in her stomach. I–" I hold in my sob, my memories fighting to resurface. "I held her as she died. I sang to her and told her everything would be okay. I made sure she wasn't alone, that she wasn't scared. I held her even when she was gone, until they dragged me away from her kicking and screaming." I remember the night, the one where I learnt how depraved and evil Ivar really is. How much hurt and pain can be imparted, not physically, but mentally.

"I'm sorry. I tried to save her, I did. I promise you! Please don't hate me, Thorn. Please," I beg, the tears finally falling. He looks away from me, his face a mask of bitterness, pain, and even self-loathing. No doubt he is blaming himself for not going back for her. But if anyone is to blame, it's me.

"I don't hate you. I never could, but I need some time." He

stands up and with every step he takes away from me, it's a blow to my racing heart.

"I love you," I whisper. I know he hears me because he flinches, but he doesn't bother to turn around. Just slips inside, leaving me alone with my pain and regret.

CHAPTER ELEVEN

BLEAK AND BEAUTIFUL

I don't crawl between Jax and Drax where they have clearly left an open spot for me, I don't deserve their comfort. Instead, I curl up in the corner on top of my coat, my back to everyone. I can't see Thorn, but I know he must be somewhere around here, the thought that he couldn't even be in the same room as me has the tears falling again; the pain shooting through me until I have to hold in a whimper by biting my arm. Slowly, as everyone else is asleep, I cry out my pain and rebuild myself once again. I let the pain and horror turn to hate and anger. It spurs me on, it follows me even into sleep, and I know for certain what I will do before I die. I will kill Ivar.

My sleep is restless, a mirage of horrors from my past running through my head like a fucked up film, the door that usually keeps them locked away from me stands thrown open, and I don't know how to shut it. Eventually, I give up trying to sleep, I slip out of the break room where all my men except Thorn are sleeping. I pick my way through the others slumbering in the main room and ascend the metal staircase, slipping out of the door into the vantage point again. I find Dr. Perfect Face—I really should bother to remember his name sometime—leaning against the windows.

"The sand storm died?" I ask. He jumps and spins to face me with a scowl. I smirk at having got the drop on him and move to the windows to look out. The sand has settled, and I can see out into the Wastes now, even see the cars with a layer of dust on them not too far out. I feel him throwing looks at me, but I scan the horizon for any issues.

"What?" I eventually ask, breaking the tense silence.

"Why did you attack Derick?" he asks, and I sense no malice, only true curiosity.

"Huh, so that's the pricks name?" I sigh, and lean against the railing and face him. "Because he attacked me, he felt challenged by me. If I hadn't of won, we both know what he would have done to me." He turns to face me and nods. "What, not going to try and deny it? To protect your friend?" I sneer.

"He's not my friend, and what you said is the truth." I raise my eyebrow at that, but he carries on talking. "What's it like out here? I mean really like? I haven't been out since they rescued me a couple of years ago, and before that, I lived in a little house with no one and nothing around."

"It's..." I try to think of a way to describe it. "It's like the films you used to see on TV about war zones but more primal. It's brutal, and everyone and everything is trying to kill you, so when you find something good, you hold on to it as hard as you can."

"Those men, they your something good?" I sense no judgment; his face remains curious.

"They are the only good thing I have ever known," I admit truthfully. Done with sharing, I straighten. "Better wake your people, we need to pack up and leave."

I leave him there and descend back downstairs as people start to rouse, I ignore them, still feeling a bit sore from last night. Striding to the door, I pull it open and slip out, and let the silence soothe me. Stepping away from the building, I take in where we are, trying to pinpoint our location. The sun is just starting to rise, breaking over the horizon and bringing blistering heat with it. Walking a little away from the building I pee, and as I am buttoning my trousers, I hear a scream. Snapping my head up, I look around and frown when I don't see anything. A scream comes again, from somewhere far into the Wastes. I break into a sprint and slam open the door to the building.

"We are leaving. Now!" I yell. Maxen stumbles out of the break room with my remaining weapons and possessions.

"What's wrong, Mi Alma?" he asks, his eyes alert as he scans around.

"Cannibals. We need to leave before they get here." He nods and jogs off to help people pack. We are out the door in five minutes, no time wasted as we jump into the vehicles and speed off. I am tense the whole time, looking through the back window until the building fades into the distance with Maxen gripping my thigh.

"Are we safe?" he asks, tense next to me.

"For now," I reply.

THE DAY IS long and being stuck in a truck with big men makes it sweaty. It makes me miss my bike, I wonder what ever happened to. Probably lost on the road. We stop again for the night, with only a day's worth of travel to The Ring. This time, we aren't as lucky to find a building, we camp behind an old road sign. Thorn hasn't spoken to me all day, and I can feel the distance between us. The others keep throwing me looks, but I ignore them and decide to clean my weapons instead. I keep my back to the camp, uneasy about being out in the open with this many people, and the fire they insisted on lighting. It feels too much like tempting fate.

Maxen sits down next to me and begins to clean his own sword.

"Has a Summit ever been called before?" His voice soothes me as always, and I feel my shoulders dropping, the tension in my belly unfurling.

"Probably, I only remember one, when I was a slave. Ivar attended and chained me to his chair." The truth flows out so easily now, and no shame fills my words. My past is just that, my past, a horror I survived, and I refuse to feel ashamed of that—especially around Maxen. He falters for only a moment, his hands stilling with the cloth on his blade before resuming.

"What was it called for?"

I look back at my sword. "Territory lines, Berserkers were claiming more from both Worshippers and Seekers. It didn't end well, after a night of arguing and more death than I could count, they settled it in The Ring."

Murmurs reach us from the people behind us, but I don't turn around.

"I don't know what has happened with Thorn. It is his and your business, if either of you want to tell us you are welcome to, but if not that's fine too. Either way, it does not affect how the rest of us feel. "

His words stop me, he always knows what I need to hear. "He is your brother, your family..."

"And you are my heart. I could never choose between you, and he would not make me. I still see the love he has for you, he just needs some time. He is like that, if something is upsetting or hard, he retreats to think about it so he doesn't say or do something he will regret. It doesn't mean he doesn't care, in fact, it is the opposite, it means he cares a great deal."

I stop cleaning and look at him. "Thank you. I needed to hear that."

"Anytime, Mi Alma. Whatever you need, I am here. I will never leave you, I will never betray you. It would be impossible, I might as well cut out my own heart. It only beats for you."

A tension and stress I didn't know I was carrying melts away. I guess my father's appearance and betrayal, along with the argument with Thorn, has hit me more than I thought. I had started to distance myself from them so that they couldn't hurt me. But that's no way to live.

"I love you, Maxen. I know it might not always seem like I do, I don't know how to give or receive affection. I am going to mess up, I'm going to test us and pull away. Promise me you won't ever let me."

Dropping his sword, he scoops me up like I weigh nothing and wraps me in his arms, his forehead on mine. "Never, Tazanna. I am never letting you go, for as long as I live on this Earth, you are mine."

He kisses me gently, sealing his words. The kiss starts to slowly heat up, our tongues tangling as he grips me harder. He pulls back to nip at my lip, only to devour my mouth again. By the time the first scream reaches me, it's too late.

Jumping off Maxen's lap, I grab my swords, one in each hand and watch in shock at the deformed beings that materialise from the darkness, on all sides. In various stages of undress, their bodies more animal than human, they let out a scream that has terror racing down my spine. I have only met a cannibal once, it was hurt and had been left behind by its pack. It was still one of the hardest fights of my life, and surrounding us now, crouched to the floor and flashing their teeth at us, their eyes alight with pleasure, must be at least twenty of them.

Creatures that were human once and turned to eating their own kind to survive. The meat changed them, the first notable signs being the shakes, which grows to difficulty walking, poor coordination, and finally dementia and mood swings. They quite literally forget how to be human, and the ones surrounding us now are so far gone, they would rip into us in seconds. They wouldn't even try to use weapons, just their teeth and hands.

The one closest to me is on all fours. Its hair is hanging down in a straggling mess as its blue eyes peer at me through it. Its mouth is stained with blood, and its teeth blackened and decayed. Its nails are long like claws, and shaped into points and other than some holey, dirty pants which look like they are about to fall off, it is naked. It watches me as I grip the sword and wait for them to make a move. Bursting into movement, almost too quick to see, the pack launches through the air at us, almost as one.

I roll under the leap of one and gut the one behind it, spinning I skewer the one flying through the air at me. Rolling over it, I use my momentum to free my sword and spin to face the next one. I hear the screams of the others, and the sound of fighting. But the noise of skin and muscle ripping and chomping also reaches me. Keeping my eyes alert, I search until I find the source, I have to quickly swallow bile as one of the guards from Paradise wails in terror as four cannibals rip him to shreds. I go to save him, but I know it's too late when one lands on his stomach and rips it open and starts to eat the insides.

Sands below, I thought I had seen all the horror this world had to offer—I was wrong.

CHAPTER TWELVE

THE BLAME

Something lands on my back and I spin, throwing it off. The creature crouches in front of me, hissing before jumping at me again. I slide behind it and grab its hair, pulling it back and using my sword, I hack through its neck. Blood splatters on me as I turn, only to be knocked to the ground. My sword drops out of my hand to the ground near me.

The creature starts biting, trying to get to my unprotected throat. Gritting my teeth, I lock my arm in front of me and almost scream when it bites through my flesh. Scrambling through the dirt with my other hand looking for my sword, I start to panic when blood runs down my arm and drips on my face.

The creature's eyes go wide before blood and brains rain down on me, its corpse slumping on my chest. Groaning, I push it off and roll, so I am crouching next to it, my arm still locked in its mouth in a death grip. Using my free hand, I open its mouth and rip my other arm out, wincing as agony tears through me.

With no time to waste, I jump up and turn to see Jax with my sword outstretched to me. I nod quickly and grab it, putting my back to his as we fight through the chaos.

By the time I realise there are no more cannibals to fight, I'm panting and leaning on my sword, which I had stabbed into the Earth. Bodies litter the ground, including some of our own.

"What was that?! Why didn't you warn us?! This is your fault!" Derrick screams as he comes towards me. Flinging insult after insult at me until he is right in my face. Done with his shit, I grab my knife and hold it to his balls. Unlike Dray, his eyes go wide as his mouth flaps open helplessly until a little panicked squeak comes out.

"I tried to warn you. You wouldn't listen, these lives are on your hands. You ever, and I mean ever, come at me like that again and I will rip your little cock off and shove it so far up your arse you won't be able to get it out." I twist my blade against his tiny cock. "Understand?" I demand as he arches on his tiptoes trying to relieve the pressure.

"Yes!" he cries out.

I let go and he stumbles back, looking at me with wide fear filled eyes.

"I am not who you should fear out here." I turn my back on him and face the others. "From now on, you listen to me. You follow my orders to the fucking letter or I will kill you myself. If you want to live long enough to make it back home, I suggest you start learning how to defend yourself!" I shout. Shocked faces watch me, some injured, some covered in blood but all the exact same. They have seen the horrors this world had to offer, realised the nightmares exist, and now they are looking at me to save them from this darkness. They just don't know I exist in it too.

"My Queen!" Vasilisy calls before falling to the ground in front of me, his sword in the dirt before him and his head touching the steel. It's my turn to freeze in shock. What he is doing is the highest of honours and trust, reserved for the leader of the Berserkers. A true warrior. He is offering me his life—his sword.

"Get up. I am not him. I will fight by your side, but you will never live on your knees with me," I plead, looking for a way out.

He raises his head. "I know. That is why I follow you, little queen."

"Well, well, well. I thought we would let the eaters finish most of you off before we came to collect what's ours," comes a yell from next to us, echoing through the darkness.

Spinning, I groan at the three Berserkers grinning at the edge of our camp. *Really, can't we catch a break?* The bigger guy at the front, with the longer braids and bright red hair, watches me hungrily. It's obvious he knows who I am and if the evil glint in his eye is anything to go by, this is not going to go well.

"How about a game?" he sneers at me, the words echoing in my head as he rushes toward me. I try to fight the pull, but the memory is too strong, the last thing I see is the wicked smile of the Berserker bearing down on me.

"How about a little game, pet?"

My breathing picks up as Ivar's voice brings me back around. My head hurts from the punch, which knocked me out, but I manage to crack open my eyes—only to wish I never had.

Five girls of all ages, not including me, are tied to the ceiling in a line. My hands are bolted to the chair, and Ivar stands in the middle of us grinning. Looking along the line, I spot at least two new slaves, one is a child, younger than me. She must be no older than twelve, and an older lady, at least fifty years old, Petal, and Tenessa who is a middle aged woman. She has been with Ivar for a week now, and last but not least. Criena—the bitch herself.

"Ah, she's finally awake so we can play!" he cries, rubbing his hands together.

I see the other girls' eyes bulge in panic as they fight the restrains, the chains clinking and slithering along the floor like a snake.

Ivar steps into my field of vision, his crazed smile parting his square face. He was handsome once, that is clear to see, but along the way, he got hurt. A fire ravaged the left side of his face and broke something inside of him - twisting his soul until nothing but the monster before me was left. You can still see his handsome features, his corn blue eyes and long lashes, high arched cheekbones, and plump lips. His brown hair is tinted with age and reaches his lower back in honour braids, the longest of the Berserkers, and on top sits a metal crown, spiked and grey medieval like the man himself.

He wears no shirt, his wide powerful chest on display with his Berserker brand right in the middle. His leather pants creak as he moves, mixing with the sound of his many weapons hitting together.

"I have a new game, aren't you curious?"

I don't bother answering him, instead, I look straight ahead and try to calm the panic shaking through my skinny body. He carries on like it doesn't matter than I am not participating, and to him it doesn't. He will see the fear in my body, and in my eyes where I can't hide it and he will feed off of it. Even now I see his eyes fill with glee.

"It's a simple game, pet. I will ask if you would rather me do something to you or them." He kneels in front of me, his hand landing on my bruised knee and twisting, making me bite my tongue to hold in my cry.

"Would you like an example?" he whispers, twisting my knee more. When he abruptly let's go and stands, I sag in the chair I am sitting in, the pain already wracking my body. This is the third day in a row I have been left to his tender care, I don't know how much more I can take.

"So, I would say... Pet, do I cut your clothes off... or one of these slaves?" I watch the young girl start to sob as the new older lady cries out. I swallow hard and watch him. He shakes and slaps his head before muttering to himself. Eventually, he turns to face me again. "That was an example of course—now let's play for real!" His voice booms around the room, only overshadowed by the young

girls crying. I know it will get her hurt, so I try to catch her eye to no avail. I watch, almost in slow motion, as he turns to her with a frown.

"Yes!" I shout. He turns and blinks at me. "Let's play," I say, my voice shaking.

He booms out a laugh and wags his finger. "So eager, my little pet. Okay. Should I stab you through the thigh orrr..." He turns and runs his eyes over his slaves. "Or her." He points at the little girl like I knew he would. I close my eyes in resignation.

"Me," I say softly.

"What was that? I didn't hear you!" he shouts making me jump.

"Me! I said me!" I scream, a tear trailing down my cheek as he laughs and turns to a table I didn't notice.

Grabbing a knife he walks towards me, licking his lips the whole time. He stops in front of me, the sharp blade in my face.

"This is going to hurt pet," he warns, before slamming the knife into my left thigh.

"Taz!" comes a panicked voice, I try to fight my way through the darkness latching on to it like a lifeline but it's not enough. The darkness drags me back to its depths of horror and pain.

"Now, pet. Should I try my new toy on you or Petal?"

I can barely lift my head, focusing on the blood dripping from me to the floor. Agony is all I can feel and I wish I was numb—maybe this time he will finally go too far.

I cry out when he yanks my hair and pulls my head up, grinning at me with my blood covering his face and mouth, even his teeth are stained with it. He holds pliers in his hand and I can't bring myself to care anymore. I would take all the pain, how could I not? I tried to tell him a couple of turns ago to use one of his toys on one of the slaves. But I couldn't do it, the words lodged in my throat. If I cross that line, take that step, I am nothing more than the monster he wants me to become, born of blood and pain. That's *what this is, after all, another tactic to break me, to tame me, and make me his.*

"Me," I croak.

I must pass out sometime between the second and third finger-nail being pulled because I wake up with a gasp as cold water is thrown over me.

"I think we will mix it up a bit. Ce. Your turn. Shall I hold your head underwater for two minutes or my little pet here?"

I look through my drenched hair and meet her eyes as she smiles at me. "Her," *she decides. I see Petal fight and spit at her as Ivar laughs.*

"See, my pet. Never look out for anyone but yourself, they won't thank you for it and they sure as shit won't return it. I am all you have." *He undoes my chains but I am too weak to move, to fight. He drags my limp body across the stone floor, the blood and water trailing in my wake. Ivar throws me over a bucket of ice cold water, and I only just manage to catch myself with my hands on the rim. He grabs my hair again, ready to submerge me.*

Hate runs through me, but so does defiance. I lift my head, purposely pulling on my hair in his hand until I meet his eyes. "You can break my body time and time again, but you will never break my spirit. My soul. You will never have me. I will never be yours."

Anger darkens his face and I laugh, blood flying from my split lip as he pushes me face first into the awaiting water.

Pain explodes in my face making me stumble back to myself and with wide eyes to face the red-haired Berserker who just smashed the pommel of his sword into my face. I fumble and grab my sword, but I can see it is too late. I let my demons get the better of me, and now I am going to pay for it. I watch in dawning horror as the sword pommel comes at my face again, it makes contact and flings me to the ground as I try to stay conscious. The Berserker stands over me, triumph and malice on his face.

"Some champion you are," he sneers before bringing his sword down again. I manage to block it with my own this time, but I am weak from the hits I took and my head is ringing. Gritting my teeth, I brace my back on the ground to try and stop its descent when the Berserker above me is thrown to the side and away from me. Maxen stands before me, chest heaving and eyes alight with bloodlust. Blinking, I look around to see the other two Berserkers already dead and a Seeker Assassin dressed in all black standing above one with a dagger in his hand. I don't have time to question it as the others head my way.

Thorn growls when he sees my face and moves around me to help me into a sitting position, as Drax and Jax look at me in anger.

I prop myself up using Thorn's chest as Jax crouches in front of me, Drax moves to his back watching everything and anything.

"It's not always about winning Taz, it's about getting back up. Time and time again," Jax says, watching me as if he can see the hate I have for myself. By letting my memories overwhelm me I gave those men a chance to hurt not only me, but also my men.

"Where's Maxen?" I ask, then realise that might hurt his feelings, but he just smiles and leans forward to kiss me.

"Protecting what is his," he says before moving to my side, so I can see my warrior, my rock.

I watch in sick fascination as Maxen roars at the man who touched me. Fury, unlike I have ever seen from my gentle giant, is stamped on his face. The man on the floor screams as Maxen uses his short sword on him. The screaming stops abruptly and Maxen turns, blood covering his face, which to be honest turns me on a little bit, before walking up to me. His sword in one hand and the head of the man in the other. The head is covered in blood, and those eyes which not too long ago were filled with malice, are now empty and unseeing. Maxen stops before me, towering over me like an avenging angel. The head like some kind of sacrifice.

"This is yours. He hurt your head, so I took his." I blink as he drops the head at my feet, which rolls and hits my boots. I guess I should be horrified, but I end up smiling at him. He kneels near me, his finger hovering over what I am guessing is a swelling from the sword used to hit me.

"You might be the strongest, badass bitch I know, but everyone fails sometimes. You're not perfect Tazanna Worth, you have demons I can't dream of. But I will always be by your side fighting them with you. Anyone hurts you, I hurt them. Like you would for us. So, get that self-pitying look out of your eyes, it's not you and I hate it. So what you froze? So what he beat you? All that matters is, he is dead, food for the vultures while you are still alive."

His words boost my confidence, and he is right. Self-pity isn't my thing, it's useless and I have no time for it out here. Looking over the men gathered around me, I know that they will always be there to protect me when I can't protect myself.

"Let me look?" Comes Dr. Perfect Face's voice from somewhere behind Maxen. I keep my eyes locked on his as he leans in.

"I am quick to anger, Mi Alma. Remember that, we might share you between my brothers, but that does not mean I will share you with anyone else. I see the way he looks at you, don't make me have to kill him." With that he stands and turns to the side, watching our backs.

Drax laughs from my other side, making me groan. "Men," I mutter, making Thorn's chest shake with laughter. I can't say I have seen them jealous before, is it wrong it made me want to jump him then and there?

"Sorry to break up the party, but I need to speak to The Champion," comes a cocky voice from behind the wall of men.

Unwilling to meet the assassin on my knees, I let Jax pull me to my feet as Dr. Perfect Face roots around in his bag near me, muttering about silly women with swords.

"Dray sent you?" I question, making sure to keep my hands near my blades. He is an assassin after all. They might work better for sneak attacks, but they do know how to fight. The scar, the exact same as Dray's, stretches across his face as he smiles, watching my fighting stance.

"Yes." The clipped word has me raising my eyebrows, and I thought I wasn't a talker. When I continue to stare at him, his lips twitch again.

"I see why our fearless leader is so taken with you. He dispatched his best men to different corners of the Wastes in search of you."

I frown. "I am not yet late for his deadline."

He nods. "Priest arrived at The Summit, when you did not, Dray started to send his men out."

"The leaders are all there?" I wince as my head throbs, but try to concentrate on the conversation.

"Yes." His voice is cold and bored. "It is time for The Summit."

CHAPTER THIRTEEN

THE ASSASSIN'S RESPECT

"Who is there from The Rim?" I ask, as we climb into the cars once again, the assassin with us this time so I have to sit on someone's knee. I choose Thorn's, needing to feel close to him and know that he doesn't hate me. I breathe a sigh of relief when he wraps his arms around me.

"Some crazy old lady," he grumbles, and I can hear the frustration in his voice. It makes me laugh; Nan definitely has that effect on people. Though I can't say I expected her to make the journey.

"And Priest and Reeves are there?" I ask as he turns to look at me from the front seat.

"Yes, Priest refuses to do anything without and I quote '*the destined one.*'" He throws me one last look and turns around, slumping in his seat and pretending to sleep. I know he is aware of everything going on, and would kill anyone who approached him. It's a tactic I have used a time or two before to get people to fuck off.

I snuggle back into Thorn's body, not the least bit ashamed of using him. I turn my face into his chest as he buries his in my hair. "Sorry I've been distant, babygirl, I just," he blows out a breath, "needed some time." I nod and let him hold me, not willing to admit how scared I was that he would hate me, and I wouldn't blame him. I didn't save his sister, I was there for her death—I might not have done the deed myself, but her blood is on my hands.

"Do you remember your family?" Petal whispers into the dark. Footsteps sound outside the door and we both freeze, not daring to move. I know at some point Ivar will come and get me, to let his 'pet' sleep in her place where she belongs—on the floor in his room. Right now, we are in the slave quarters, the other two are currently entertaining the men in the hall and I can't bring myself to care, except to be thankful it's not me or Petal. Somehow, she is starting to get under my skin, and I give more shits than I should if she lives or dies.

I learnt my lesson early on—look out only for yourself. But I can't seem to, my soul rebels at watching the other girls being punished, an anger I didn't know I had clawing to the surface and begging to be set free. To burn this place to the ground and stand like a phoenix in its ashes.

When the footsteps fade away, I shift on the stone cold floor and turn to face where I think she is in the dark. The empty stone room is our prison, our room, our refuge. We were moved from the cell when he realised we could never escape.

"Do you?" she asks again quieter this time, but still loud in the room.

"Yes," I whisper as my father's terrified eyes flash in my mind, making me close mine in pain, I gave up thinking he will come for us, especially since Ivar told me in excruciating detail how he killed him. A hand touches me in the dark, making me jump and my eyes snap open. Petal's hand squeezes mine before holding on tight.

"I do too. I guess we are each other's family now," she whispers, trying to offer me comfort, but all it does is cause my heart to drop and my head to hurt. She won't survive; I can just tell. She's too

strong, too defiant, and yet, weak at the same time. They break her body and soon they will break her soul, even as she spits at them and rebels. She is fire, where I am ice. I wish I could be like her, I wish I could fight and rage, but I know it will not change anything. So instead, I bottle it all up, like a pit burning deep inside, and one day I will let it out, and it will cover this world like the fire that ended it.

I squeeze my eyes shut harder, trying to block out the memories. I need to be strong, I need to be fierce, I need to be the fire that burns that bastard to the ground. I wish I could blame my father for bringing up all these old memories, but facing Ivar again is going to bring them up anyway, at least I can try and get a handle on them now.

Get to The Summit, convince the clans, kill Ivar. Get to The Summit, convince the clans, kill Ivar. Get to The Summit, convince the clans, kill Ivar.

I repeat it like a mantra in my head as we travel through the Wastes, we will be at The Ring by nightfall, and I need to be the warrior they all know—I need to be The Champion, but right now in Thorn's arms I let myself send a promise to the girl I couldn't save, a promise to fight—a promise of vengeance.

"What was she like?" he whispers. I bite my lip and try to think of what to say.

"She was a fighter, she was so fierce. Kind of like you, she had this fire in her eyes that I never knew was possible. She rubbed off on me more than she would ever know. She... I." Blowing out a breath I carry on, "She tried to be my friend, tried to get to me fight. When she died, it set something in me free, made me realise that not fighting wasn't a way to live."

He's quiet and I worry I was too blunt. I didn't tell him about the bad shit but I also didn't sugarcoat it. Then eventually he breathes out on a shudder against me. "Thank you for telling me, babygirl."

"Touching, truly is, but can you two suck each other off somewhere else?" the assassin grumbles from the front, making me smile.

"How about I cut your dick off and stuff it in your mouth, then you can suck yourself off?" I say loudly. I raise my head and watch as he chuckles in the front seat.

"Oh yeah, you are perfect for Dray."

We stop a couple of hours later to stretch our legs, riding our bikes was never as bad as riding in a cramped car with five massive warriors. I step out of the car to the sand and quickly grab my shades from my bag. I strap on my swords as well, because have you ever tried to sit in a car with two swords, eight daggers, a whip, and a crossbow? Some are new toys from my father, and I am weirdly excited to use them.

The sun shines down making me sweat instantly. I have become pampered, the air con on the car and in Paradise making me unused to the heat again. I can feel my skin burning, making me frown. The car doors slam open as the others get out and I force myself to lean against the hot metal of the car and wait. The assassin comes to lean next to me.

"You know much about Seekers?" he asks, as he lights up a cigarette and watches the others. Maxen and Jax throw me a look asking if I am okay and I nod, they turn away and help the others.

"Some." He tries to pass me the cigarette and I shake my head.

"Okay, so I am just going to lay it out there, if you are going to help Dray with this crazy ass plan of his, then you are going to need to know how to act with us. I know you know how to deal with the Berserkers, Reeves, and you even seem to have impressed Priest. But you will need more for us, we are secretive, strong, and downright terrifying if you mess with us. We will not respect you simply because Dray does, or because everyone else does. Your titles mean nothing to us, you have to earn them."

"You know Dray personally?" I murmur.

"Yeah, I'm his right-hand man, they call me The Shadow. You will not get my real name unless you earn it."

"Does Dray have another name?" I ask curiously.

"Girly, you know nothing. He's the avenger, the protector, the fighter. I would be dead if it weren't for him, and so would a lot of others." He throws me a dirty look and turns away again.

"His father," I add, I feel him look at me in shock, the first real expression to cross his face.

"Huh, he told you about him?" He stares at me like I'm interesting him for once.

I shrug, my eyes still locked on my men.

"His father was a bastard, he wasn't fit to rule. He thought just because he could, he should. He tortured our people, ravaged our lands and raised his child to be unforgiving, harsh, cruel, and cold. Dray killing him set our people free, and now they would follow him to hell and back. I know what everyone calls him, says about him. It's all true," the assassin replies, speaking more than he has before. I meet his eyes as he turns to me again. "He is not a soft man, he's a bastard. A cruel motherfucker who will kill anyone who hurts what is his and he has claimed you as his own. You are never going to be free of him. My advice? Don't try to run, he wouldn't let you."

"Do you see me running?" I get into his face, my eyes cold and deadly, I can't ignore the slurs thrown my way. I don't give a shit if he's Dray's right-hand man, the fucking shadow or death itself. "I am like him. Anyone hurts what's mine and I will make them beg for death. I don't give a shit if you don't like me, don't respect me, but you try to kill me or mine, and I will teach you why I earned that respect, boy."

He grins, like I didn't just threaten him, and I see a smidgen of respect creep into his eyes. "You are going to need that strength for what is coming." I cock my eyebrow at him as he looks away into the Wastes. "War. I can feel it."

With that he straightens, snuffs out his cigarette, letting it fall to the floor, and disappears. When I look around, I can't even spot him, fucking assassin.

Jax wanders to my side, framing me with his arm on top of the car. "You okay?" he asks. I nod and sigh before leaning into him just a bit.

"I thought I got through all the pissing contests years ago, I forgot how annoying they are and it's only going to get worse with all of the clans in one place," I grumble.

"Want to test your strength?" he asks, and I see a flash of lust in his eyes, the demons peeking out behind it.

"What did you have in mind?" I question, with a quirk of my lips.

He grabs my hand and tugs me around the car. I spot the building next to us as he pulls me towards it. I grin as he kicks open the door, the dust and age bursting out into the air.

I follow him inside the building, covering my nose at the stale odour that hits me. Light streams in between the boards on the building, and I'm guessing this used to be a shop of some kind. Clothes half torn up or covered in dirt are scattered everywhere, railings overturned, a cash machine laying on the floor open with the money still inside. It's depressing to say the least.

I don't get to look around for long before Jax is spinning me and smashing his mouth to mine. I groan as he nips my bottom lip, before plundering my mouth with his tongue. Reaching up, I grab on to his hair as his hands drop to my ass and yank me until I am against him. The door opening has me pulling back from the kiss, slightly out of breath, to see Drax at the doorway; Jax ignores him and starts kissing down my neck.

"Well, were you going to have some fun without me?" Drax grins as he takes us both in. Without waiting for a reply, he lets the door shut behind him and strolls towards me, his eyes locked on where his twin's hands cup my ass. Coming up behind me, he drops his face to the other side of my neck and whispers against my ear. "I'm all better now, so how about I show you..." I groan as Jax lifts his head.

He arches his eyebrow at his brother, his lips slightly puffy and his eyes alight. They have some sort of silent conversation before Jax looks back at me, that smile he saves just for me on his face. "What do you say, think you're strong enough?" he taunts, making me narrow my eyes before I spin and yank on his twin's head to slam my lips to his.

Drax's kiss is more refined than Jax's needy one, he takes his time and builds me up to a fever pitch with strong sure strokes of his tongue. My hands drop to his shirt and bury underneath, tracing his muscles, as Jax pushes up against my back.

Drax pulls away and I twist to kiss Jax. I groan into Jax's mouth when his brother bites my earlobe. "Are you sure you can handle us both?" he whispers before licking up my ear. "Not that we would let you walk away. I want inside that pussy and you can teach my brother exactly how amazing that mouth of yours is."

The dirty words only make me crazier and I bite down on Jax's bottom lip, he growls and thrusts against me.

I move away to look at Drax. "On the floor," I demand. His eyes darken, and he winds his hand through my hair and yanks my head back, the pain mixing with pleasure.

"That's not how it's going to work babe, my brother here might let you order him around, but you are going to be a good girl and suck his dick as I fuck you from behind." He grins as I narrow my eyes at him chafing the control, but I can see the seriousness. He won't let me be in charge and unless I want someone walking in on us, we don't have time to argue.

"On all fours," he demands.

Gritting my teeth, I do as I am told, stripping in the process until I am naked and needy, waiting for whatever he will do.

On my hands and knees, I almost get back up, but Drax's wet warm mouth lands on my pussy, making me groan and hang my head as Jax steps in front of me, his cock proud and erect as he starts to rub his hand up and down it.

I push back against Drax's face and he rewards me by slipping not one, but two fingers into my needy pussy. I explode so fast I see stars. Before I know it, Jax's cock is nudging my lips, and I open happily and suck him down. I hollow out my cheeks before pulling back and licking the pre-cum from the top. He groans as I hum around him, which quickly turns to a moan as Drax thrusts into me with no warning, stretching me. His hands grip my hips as he sets the pace, every time he thrusts I suck and he drives us all.

Pants and the sound of flesh hitting flesh fills the abandoned shop as we twist against each other until I scream around Jax's cock, and Drax groans and stills behind me. Jax yells and thrusts deeper than ever into my throat as he explodes.

Jax gently pulls out and I collapse into him as Drax mirrors his brother. They both slump to the floor, me propped between them.

"Well, fuck," I say breathlessly.

CHAPTER FOURTEEN

MEMORY LANE

"We better get moving, we don't want to be hanging around in the dark. Not with this many people," I say gently.

They both groan but start moving to get dressed, grabbing clothes from the pile we are laying on. I watch them for a minute, just appreciating their beauty. When Drax catches me looking he winks, and I roll my eyes before slipping into my clothes and weapons.

Dressed once again, we go to make our way out of the shop when Jax stops at a small glass stand near the counter. Bending over I hear him rummaging about, Drax rolls his eyes and slips out the door, the sunlight streams through lighting up the dark space. Hesitating, I let the door shut and make my way over to Jax.

"What have you found?" I ask, standing next to him, trying to peer over his shoulder. Silently he extracts something from the broken glass and turns to me. His face is expressionless like always, but his eyes are nervous. Something I am not used to seeing in him.

"Jax?" I hesitate.

He stretches out his hand which is curled into a fist, slowly he opens it to reveal one of the most beautiful necklaces I have ever seen. A tree, with leaves and branches twisting into a silver circle, hangs from a long silver chain that sparkles even among the rabble and destruction.

"It's the tree of life, it seems fitting for you baby," he whispers, waiting for my reaction.

Blinking, I look from him to the necklace, stunned. "You want me to have it?" I ask slowly.

Now, some might not find this romantic. After all, he did just find it. But to find that beauty amongst everything else, to think about me enough to give me such a beautiful present, is something I have never experienced. Hell, Dray was the first person to give me something and that was a bloody sword. It makes sense that my deep, emotional twin would find a diamond amongst rocks for me.

Slowly, I turn around, baring my neck to him and with it, showing him my trust. The feel of him at my back should have me wound tight and have me ready to pounce, but I trust him. So, I relax my shoulders as his breath hits my sensitive nape.

"I could kill a thousand Berserkers for you, I could lay their heads at your feet for what they did to you, but it will never be enough to remind you of how deep you are buried in my soul. You are not my light in the darkness Taz, you are the fire in the dark that keeps me warm and reminds me of why I fight. I hope that even at the darkest of times, even when you can't feel me behind you, this necklace will remind you of why you fight."

Swallowing hard, I close my eyes as he kisses the back of my neck before laying the cold metal around it and closing the clasp. Turning to face him, I let my eyes do the talking for me. He smiles at me before I reach up and drag his head down, so I can kiss him with everything I have.

We break away slowly, our breath mixing together. The door smashes open, popping our little bubble.

"Time to go, Mi Alma," Maxen says from the doorway, I nod but kiss Jax one more time.

I let him watch as I rebuild my defences to face the others, he takes it all in before whispering, "Thank you."

Turning away before I do something stupid, I step to where Maxen waits at the door.

"Nice necklace." Maxen picks up the metal, his fingers stroking my skin. "Suits you." He grins at me and I smile back.

"Time to lead your people." He drops the necklace and holds the door open for me. Striding through I pull down my shades to face the waiting crowd.

WE GET BACK on the road, the assassin slumping back into his seat again. I keep my eyes peeled and look out of the window. An uneasy feeling is settling in the pit of my stomach, and I don't know why. Maybe because we are going into the fucking lion's den with only the word of peace to protect us. The men that are gathered there are hard and fucking killers. I have killed their men in The Ring, slaughtered them in the Wastes, and now I have to face them with that blood on my hands. But we have no other choice, like the assassin said. War is coming. I can almost feel it vibrate the sands with the need for blood. Ivar has been hanging over my head for a long time and I knew one day he would try and snatch not only me, but power from the other clans. It's in his bones, destruction is all he knows.

The Summit seemed like a nice idea at first, but if what Vasilisy says is true, if the Berserkers are turning on their king, then we might just stand a chance. If we don't kill each other first.

This journey feels like the last time I rode to the pit as a slave, but nope, I have something much worse to lose than my life. Hope.

That's what my men are, plus the possibility that I might finally get my revenge.

I meet the assassin's eyes in the rearview mirror, I don't know what he sees but he offers me a feral smile, which throws me back into another memory.

I watch in horror as Petal's limp body is thrown to the ferals. They tear it apart as the men laugh and drink, the noise they make... the noise of the blood spurting and the bone and skin tearing has bile rising up my throat as tears fill my eyes.

That poor girl, even in death she doesn't get any dignity, no peace, just pain and suffering. At least she isn't here to feel it or see it, but there is something so wrong about her body being defiled like that, even if her soul isn't present. She should be laid to rest, finally getting closure, but instead, Ivar has one last torture to impede, and it isn't for her. No, it's for me. Showing me what will become of me even if I escape him in this life and into the next. Death will not bring me peace or lack of pain, I will die like I lived. Bloody, raw, and entertainment for his men.

With the sounds of them defiling her body, a fire like never before starts to burn in the deepest section of my heart, the agony and hate of it starts to crawl slowly through my blood so that eventually I am like the flames I always escaped into. I raise my head slowly, the tears drying in tracks down my dirty, blood covered face. I let everything else float away, leaving that fire. Ivar meets my eyes with a feral smile, but falters at whatever he sees there. Because I am going to use this fire, I am going to burn him and his sick fucking men up until all that they can hear is the sounds of dying men and agony, as they beg for forgiveness that I will never grant them.

I let him know with my eyes, with the defiance etched into every bone in my body that he will pay for what he has done. With Petal's death, I lose my innocence, and in my young body, a true Berserker is born. A monster that I plan on using.

Gritting my teeth, I pull myself back, but it reminds me of who I have become. Of why I fight, my memories are horrors that no one should have to witness but they are the reason I am this way. They tug and scream at me, an ever-present reminder. No, they will never be anything but horrors, but what do monsters thrive off of after all?

CHAPTER FIFTEEN

THE BERSERKER'S WAR SONG

The day passes in a blur, each mile making me more and more restless. I am not one to be cooped up with other people, not even my men for this long. Maybe it's because I know with each mile, we are coming closer to The Ring and The Summit. It feels like all of my life has been leading up to this. I just hope I can make the leaders of the other clans listen.

Vasilisy starts to hum from the seat next to me. His head is tipped back, and his eyes closed, his legs kicked up against the seat in front of him, much to Doc's chagrin. Frowning, I try to think of why the tune seems familiar even as he gets louder.

Watching him, I see his mouth part before a powerful, heart wrenching voice flows out. I can't help but stare, entranced by his words and expression, his face changes with every word like he is living the tale he is weaving.

"The winds may rage, and the sands may burn. Danger surrounds us at every turn. My land I fight, my men they scream. For the world, I will bleed."

"Bleed, bleed for the cause. This dusty land will be my fall, with swords which clash and mouths that scream. For the world, I will bleed," I whisper. It isn't until my eyes meet his that I notice he has stopped singing and is humming along to my voice.

"Yes, my little queen, for the world, you will bleed."

We stare at each other, and movement in the front seat interrupts the silence.

"There is something in the road," Doc says softly. Turning away I look at what he is talking about, and there in the middle of the road with a flamethrower aimed our way, stands a stranger.

"Stop, let's see what they do," I command, Doc grunts but breaks until we stop just before the person... who I can now see is a woman. By the looks of it, a fucking angry one.

Short spikey brown hair points up from her head in all directions, while mud covers her face and baggy clothing fits loosely on her frame, all meant to make her look like a man, but she is definitely a woman, even if her muscles bulge and her stance is strong. Her lips are plump and long brown lashes surround deep intense brown eyes. Her cheekbones are high and sharp, and her jaw is pointed. She is pretty, in a masculine way.

Taking a shot, I slide out of the car and round the side of the vehicle, using the bonnet as protection so I can easily jump away if her itchy trigger finger slips. I don't want to be burnt alive, no thank you.

"Nice thrower. Homemade?" I ask casually, leaning against the war car.

Her eyes shift from the car to me before tightening slightly on the device. I arch my eyebrow at her and tut.

"Well, that's not very nice, here I am trying to make polite conversation even as you rudely hold a weapon at us," I point out.

Frowning, the nozzle dips slightly. "Who are you?" She pitches her voice deeper making me grin.

"You might fool some idiots out there, but I know you are a woman," I point out, as I shield my eyes and look up at the sun to judge the time. I don't blame her for trying though, it's a dangerous world out there for women.

"I am not playing at being a man or to fool those dick swinging idiots. I was born a female, but I am a male," she shouts, jerking the thrower at me again as anger etches on to her face, I am betting it's an old anger too.

I look at her, taking in her appearance. "Okay. So, what do you want?"

The weapon is obviously getting heavy and he has to choose to drop it or shoot, wisely he drops it even as the blade I palmed automatically itches in my hand, wanting to be used.

"Okay, just like that?" he asks incredulously. I am betting he has had to fight his whole life to be seen for who he really is. It must be hard, knowing you are something that no one will accept.

"Yep. I don't give a shit if you have a vagina or a dick, all I care about is why you are pointing that at my car. I am not a forgiving person, so I suggest you decide real quick."

He scans my face before hoisting the weapon onto his back. "I need the car. They took my girl." Anger flares in his deep brown eyes, making me grin harder. I like him, I like his flamethrower more though.

"Well, I would hate to be them right now. 'Fraid this car is taken though," I drawl. "So, what do we do now?" I tap my chin with my blade that he obviously didn't even notice if his startled look and sudden step back are anything to go by. "I could kill you, I could disarm and leave you here, or I could take you with us." I tilt my head in consideration, eyeing him once again.

"I don't want trouble, I just need to get Cherry back," he says, keeping his hands out to his sides. Cherry? Sands below, sighing I drop the blade.

"Cherry? Girl from The Rim? Big tits, bigger attitude?" I ask with a disappointed pout. I was really hoping for some action. To stretch my legs, maybe release some tension before I'm forced to talk politics.

"You know her?" he growls, taking a step forward protectively. Cute.

"I worked the bounties at The Rim. Don't worry, I never touched your girl." His shoulders slump at that before rounding out again, a fresh determination replacing the jealousy in his eyes. "Who took her?" I don't know why I care, but Cherry was always nice to me, even helped me out once or twice.

"Scavs, dirty bastards broke into the house we were holed up in while I was out hunting. Dragged her out fighting and left me a message in blood."

Whistling, I nod. "Whatcha do to piss them off enough to leave you a message?"

"Told em' I had a bigger dick than they ever would." He grins, and I throw back my head and laugh.

"Yeah, that would have done it." I wipe all traces of the smile from my face and his drops quickly. Obviously sensing the predator in me.

"Name's Dagny. Either give me a lift or fuck off," Dagny says, obviously wondering whether to take his bet on the next sorry bastard to journey down this road, which might not be for the next couple of days and by then we both know Cherry will be dead. Fuck. When the hell did I become such a bleeding heart?

"I like you," I declare. Sighing at my own stupidity I jerk my head at the cars behind me. "Sands below, pick a car kid and get in."

DAGNY KICKED OUT the assassin, well tried to. Only when I gave him the nod did he slip out and into the car behind us. Now Dagny sits in the front seat directing Evan to where the scavs who took Cherry are.

"Are we really going to go looking for a fucking fight all because some chick can't protect herself," Evan grumbles, making Dagny tense.

Leaning back in the middle seat I nod my head. "Yup, gonna fight out some tension before we get to The Ring. Plus, Cherry was cool, so shut your trap pretty boy or I will shut it for you," I threaten half-heartedly. He scowls even as his hands tighten on the wheel, but he does shut the fuck up.

"Here I thought I would have to wait until The Summit was over to start regaining my honour," Vasilisy purrs from beside me as he bounces giddily in the seat next to me.

We share a grin as I wind the new whip around my arm and lean forward to sling the crossbow on my back, I need to remember to get Drax to teach me to shoot properly.

"You are all fucking crazy, you know that right?" Evan yells, looking at us in the mirror.

"Stop being such a pussy, a fight is good for the soul," Thorn rumbles next to me. Maxen is sprawled in the boot fast asleep and the others are in the other car, keeping an eye on the guards for me.

Vasilisy grunts. "We splitting them evenly, little queen, or are we seeing who can kill more?"

I pretend to think about it as Evan gapes in horror at us. "Hmm, I think we should let Dagny burn at least one of the little bastards with his toy, but the rest are a free for all."

Evan sputters even as Vasilisy hums his agreement. "I can agree to that. May the best Berserker win."

"They should be just up ahead." Dagny jerks his chin at the road.

Nodding, I grab my sword. "Okay, pull over Doc, we don't want to let them know we are coming."

Slowly, he pulls over to the side and turns to face me, his face ashen. "We don't have to do this, we could walk away."

"And why would I do that? We look out for each other, or we are no better than the cannibals. Plus, I can try out my new toys." Winking at him I turn to Thorn who smiles at me with blood lust flaring in his eyes

"Time to have some fun, big guy."

We slip out of the car and I stretch, cracking my neck as the other car comes to a stop next to us. Quickly my men surround me with now alert looking Maxen at my back.

"Drax, you hang back and pick off any runners. Jax you are with me. Maxen and Thorn together, and Vasilisy and Dagny," I declare.

"The others?" Maxen rumbles.

"They are a liability. Half go left, the others go right. Circle around, I want none to escape."

The excitement on my face is mirrored on my guys' as we slip silently across the heated sand. Up ahead are the remains of a building. The stone crumbled and broken. It offers no coverage and if I were the scavs I would camp behind it rather than in it. So, we circle the building. My men with me.

Once I reach the corner, I peer around to see the scavs right where I thought they would be. I do a quick count and duck back around to face the others.

"Ten in the camp, probably two on patrol. Cherry is tied to an old well in the middle. They have swords and shooters but no guns. Hit 'em fast and hard."

They all nod at me and I duck back around the corner, careful to not let the scavs notice me yet. I spot Vasilisy doing the same at the other corner and I hold up my fingers in a countdown.

When I reach one, we all burst from behind the building,

Vasilisy letting out an animalistic roar that startles all the scavs as they desperately grab weapons.

Arrows fly past us as Drax picks some of them off from his vantage spot outside of the camp. Leaping over packs with both swords in the air, I land on a scav, skewering him as he screams.

Using the momentum I roll away, dragging my sword out of his body and leaving a trail of blood behind. I roll to my knees in time to block a swing from an axe descending from a ginger scav, his mouth open in a silent scream. Using both swords in a crossed position, I push the axe up until he is forced to retreat. Getting to my feet I wait for him to come at me again, and he doesn't disappoint. Yelling, he heaves the axe back, but the weapon is too big for him and slows him down, allowing me time to drop my swords and grab two small knives, sliding, I cut him in a figure eight shape. Panting, I spin and throw both knives, one at a scav trying to sneak up on me and one at a scav fighting Vasilisy.

Grinning when he looks disgruntled, I hold up my hand with four fingers. Jumping back up I grab my swords and look around at the carnage. Blood is staining the sand as scavs die with tears and snot dripping down their faces. Only one is left and he is standing with a knife to Cherry's sobbing throat as Dagny paces before him.

Only one body is littered near Vasilisy, the other four surround my men, making me heat up at how fucking amazing they are.

"You even accidently cut her, and I will cut off your toes one by one," Dagny calls to the scav. Strolling towards them, I stop at a safe distance and start cleaning my blades.

"I would listen to him, he's a little crazy and that's his woman," I say casually, as I sheathe my swords.

The scav looks around as everyone surrounds my back. His panic is palpable and sweat drips down his face. An idea comes into my head and I have to bite my lip to hide my evil smile, even as my hand inches to where the whip is wound around my arm. I wait until he looks at Maxen and I move as quickly as I can.

Flicking the whip out, I knock the blade from his hand and cause him to stumble back.

Dagny uses this opening and rushes forward, cocking his fist back and punching him. Cherry cries and flings herself at him. A chest pushes against my back and I lean into it automatically. With his arm around Cherry, Dagny walks towards me.

"Thank you," Dagny says. I nod and he cups Cherry's face. "You're okay. I will always come for you," he says softly, the love clear to see on his face. I go to shout a warning as the man who Dagny punched starts to get up, but Vasilisy is already there, swinging an axe and chopping through the man's neck. Cherry screams and huddles closer to Dagny.

With blood still dripping down the axe, Vasilisy grins at me and holds up two fingers. I snort out a laugh and turn to the lovebirds.

"Need a lift anywhere?" I ask.

Looking around Dagny turns back to me. "No, thanks for your help, but we will take one of the bikes." Turning back to Cherry he cups her tear and makeup stained face and brings their lips together. Feeling weird watching them, I turn to my men.

"Let's leave them to it. Oh–" turning to Vasilisy I wink, "I win."

CHAPTER SIXTEEN

New Friends and Old Enemies

Feeling pleased with myself, we quickly head back to the cars and jump in. We have had enough distractions, we need to get back on the road and to The Summit before Dray goes mental. The assassin pops back up and slouches in his spot in the front of the car.

"Nice of you to help us," I say, rolling my eyes. He doesn't even bother looking at me as he answers.

"I was curious how you would handle it."

Sands below, he's a fucking asshat.

"I'll admit, I can understand the fascination. You're a good fighter, and an even better one for a woman, but you are sentimental and that makes you weak." He yawns mid-sentence.

My eyes narrow on him and before he can react, I have a knife at his throat. "Do not ever mistake my kindness for weakness. I would just have soon slit their throats if they came at me or hurt my men. Just like I will do for you, Dray's man or not," I warn, my voice deadly.

Grinning at the shock in his eyes from me getting the drop on him, I lean back between Maxen and Thorn. "I will forget you said anything."

"What, not going to run to Dray to say I was being mean?" he mocks, but I sense a genuine curiosity underneath.

"If I have a problem, I solve it myself. Same goes if I need to teach someone a lesson."

He says nothing more but the tension in the car is high, and when I drop my hand on Maxen's thigh I can feel the steel underneath and the anger radiating from his body, almost vibrating.

We spend the rest of the journey in silence and before I know it, I spot The Ring up ahead. I direct Doc to park and then sit for a moment to compose myself. Heaving a sigh, I slip from the car on Thorn's heels. Maxen grabs my hand at the last minute and kisses my knuckles.

"You got this, Mi Alma, and we got your back." He winks, and slips out his door. In shock, I turn my hand over to see he slipped me a tiny metal spike that looks decorative, but when I prick the end, blood wells on my finger. Smiling, I slip it into my hair and close the car door.

With my men spread out behind me, I stroll to The Ring like I have no care in the world. Cars, bikes, and other transports litter the front entrance like a jigsaw puzzle, and the guards have doubled and it's obvious they are nervous. The tension rides the air with so many warriors and leaders in the house. When I reach the gates, I look up and prepare myself for The Summit.

Sands below, I hope we don't kill each other before we kill Ivar.

THE GUARDS LET me in with no hesitation this time, but they

do offer Doc and his men a wary look. They scream outsider and by their wide-eyed shocked looks, it is obvious they don't belong here. Just another issue to add to my long list to deal with.

Walking through the gates like I own them, I let the guards and hangers from other clans see I am not afraid. Weakness here would be fatal and used against me quicker than my knife. Making my way through the zoo with my men, Dr. Perfect Face's men, and not to mention the assassin in tow, creates quite the stir. Scavs and roadies stop what they are doing to watch and when the assassin drops back a step to let me walk first, a sign of respect, some even openly gape. When I look into his eyes, I see the calculation, and I know he didn't step back out of actual respect for me, more respect for his leader. Not that it bothers me, he just showed the whole Summit he fears me, which will make them hesitate, and coupled with my reputation it might mean we don't get attacked...as much.

By the time we make it to the building—which holds Major's office and the meeting rooms I am guessing The Summit will be held in—nearly every free scav/roadie or assassin is trailing us like some fucking puppies with nothing better to do. At the top of the stairs are two of Major's enforcers, blocking the doorway like fucking royalty is hiding inside. I don't let myself hesitate, telling myself I belong here, I stride up the stone steps and when they don't stop me, I slip through the two big wooden doors. My men follow me, and I let Dr Perfect Face and his men in before the doors shut behind me with a resounding bang.

"It's about fucking time, it was starting to get boring," comes a deep honeyed voice from behind me.

Turning, I meet the cold eyes of Dray, my soulmate as he told me. He has his usual swords strapped across his chest and if possible, his scar on his face stands out more. There's always something so lethal, so predatory about him. Like a wild animal ready to pounce, and if the lust and anger in his eyes are anything to go by, he actually might. I don't know what the fuck is going on between us, but even I can see he has come dressed to kill today and not in a fashion sense. Nearly every inch of his body is covered in blades and he strokes them absentmindedly like you would a cock.

I stand stock still as he prowls towards me, but I do drop my legs wide just in case he decides to attack. Like I said, you never know. I don't think he would kill me, not really, but I am probably the only person that he won't kill.

"What took you so long?" he asks as he stops before me, ignoring everyone else like they don't matter, and to him I guess they don't.

Shrugging, I grin at him and play down what happened. "Ran into some trouble with pale faces." The word slips out and I hear Vasilisy laugh behind me as Dr Perfect Face grunts.

"Do I need to kill any of these people?" He reaches out a scarred finger and runs it across my face in a caress like we are discussing what to eat, not who to kill.

"If I wanted them dead, I would kill them myself," I remind him, as his finger stops at my lips. I watch the anger in his eyes morph into bloodlust and I know he is thinking about the last time we were alone together. I fight the need to fidget even as desire blooms in my chest, one day the two of us are going to implode, and I am not sure either of us would come out of that alive.

"True, why the Berserker? Keeping slaves?" He steps closer and whispers the last part to me as his bottom half pushes into mine. The cool steel of his blades seeps through my clothes and into my skin, even as I feel the proof of his need pushing against me.

"Not my style, he does serve a purpose though. Would it not be better if I am addressing the whole Summit rather than just you?" I ask, and blinking I realise my hand is against his bare chest. The steady thumping of his heart pulsating through my hand.

"Always so full of secrets, fine. The others have been waiting, though not patiently."

"Dra–" The last of the sentence finishes in a muffled shout as Dray—who was in front of me one second basically eye fucking me—disappears and suddenly has the man who dared talk pinned against the wall.

I can't help but lick my lips at the display. He is effortlessly holding the assassin by his throat meters above the ground. The sight of his back bulging and the feral barely leashed violence thrumming through him turns me on in the strangest fucking way, I have just given up trying to fight it. Not that I will ever let him know that!

"Dr-dray," the assassin manages to gasp out, I don't see him struggle though, more like he is just trying to remind him of who he is. Rolling my eyes, I decide to step in, really a mad move on my part but it's not like we have a lot of time to play dick measuring games, even if those games do have me all hot and bothered, and imagining him pinning me to a wall like that.

Approaching him like I would a cannibal, I circle to the side, if I had bothered to touch his back he would have attacked me too, and rightly so. You never sneak up on a wild animal.

"Dray," I demand. He ignores me, but I do see his lips twitch.

Leaning against the wall next to the dying assassin, I play bored and look at him. "Really? I came all this way and you are going to make me stand here as you kill this asshole?"

His cold eyes flick to mine, as he seems to forget about the assassin suffocating in his hands. "Am I boring you?" he asks, his voice even lower than normal and I see his wildness dancing in his eyes. I need to tread carefully.

"No, but it got your attention didn't it? Now, as much as I would love to watch you choke him to death, and I mean really, I would. We have things to do and I don't imagine you are going to let me walk into the lion's den without you at my back, are you?"

With his eyes still on me, he drops the assassin to the floor where he crumbles gasping for air, his face turning back to a normal colour. I arch my eyebrow at Dray and he grins at me, that evil fucking smile. "He interrupted my time with you, he won't do that again," he says casually.

"Who tames the beast, shall walk with grace and bravery," comes a loud booming voice from behind Dray, one that I recognise well, even if I didn't recognise the crazy in it. Priest.

Stepping away from the wall, Dray falls into my side ready to protect me if necessary, although I am betting he would see what I chose to do first.

"Priest." I nod at the man who is standing in the middle of the corridor. He looks small compared to all the big, crazed warriors in here, especially my men who, throughout Dray and I's fight, have been quiet but now they step up to my back. Offering their support, and if I need it, their weapons.

His short black, wavy hair is still styled to perfection and he's clean shaven. He has his priest's robes on but I spot some blood splattered near the collar, which seems to make the threat of him so much worse. For something to be out of place with him, it must have been bad. I look from him to Dray; the differences are crazy. You can almost feel the power and deadly intent leaking from Dray, and his body is a weapon... Priest? He's controlled, small, and perfect. Yet, I can still feel something out of place with him and those eyes still give me the creeps.

That calculating gleam in his gaze has me standing taller, and when his smooth cultured voice comes again, everyone pays attention. "I see you made it back alive, I am betting we have much to talk about."

"You could say that," I grit out, my anger at him for knowing my father returning. A man in a hooded robe steps up behind him. He is easily double Priest's height and weight, compared to this mountain Priest looks like a child.

"My lord," his voice is rough and damaged, but Priest holds up his hand to silence him. The man instantly steps back and bows his head, and not for the first time I wonder how he has this much power over his people. They fear him, but they also worship him. Why?

"I can feel your anger, Champion. I did tell you to be careful on the roads, did I not?" he says idly, and when he looks down and spots the blood on his shirt he grimaces. Holding out a hand to his man, he waits patiently as the man offers over a cloth. When he dabs at the blood, which is fresh, and smears it, he makes a disgruntled noise and glares at the offending spot. If I was that drop, I would be running the other way from this crazy train of a man. Holding up the stained cloth between two fingers with a disgusted look, he waits for the man to take it before looking back at me.

"Now, why don't you tell me why you have a look in your eyes that says you would very much like to hurt me?" he asks casually, but underneath that is a warning, one that has Dray and my men moving not closer, but further apart. So, we have room to fight if need be.

"The man, the one who saved your wife, the one you tried to warn me about. You knew, you knew he was hiding down there. You knew Paradise was real," I say quietly, my tone deadly. It's not what I really want to say, but I can't go around declaring he is my father or people would try to use him to get to me, or the other way around. No, my anger is there but I can't admit to why without starting another war, one that I won't have a chance of fighting.

"I see, I also see his men here with you now. It all seemed to work out for the best, did it not?" Priest says, arching a perfectly shaped black brow at me.

Grinding my teeth together, I crack my neck from side to side trying my hardest not to jump at him and try to shake the crazy out of him. The mountain at his back must sense the threat because he steps around Priest to face me.

"No," Priest declares, holding his hand up to stop the man.

The man hesitates but when my hand drops to my knife, just in case, he roars and throws his hood back. Revealing a mangled and scarred face. I don't get chance to check him out before he is flying at me, righteous anger twisting his monstrous face and his fist aimed at my head.

I react instantly, my knife flying through the air and imbedding in his stomach. When it only slows him down for an instant, I grab my whip and coil it ready. I sense my men getting ready to join the fray and I hold my hand up, mimicking Priest.

"No, he's mine," I shout before ducking under the punch and sliding across the floor until I am behind him. Kicking off the floor, I jump onto his back and wrap the whip around him. He tries to buck me off, spinning wildly with me attached. Using his elbow, he hits back making me grunt, but I stay locked around him as he starts to get winded, his thick neck contorting against the black leather whip until he falls to his knees. Jumping off his back, I plant my feet firmly and use the floor to hoist the whip harder. It doesn't escape my notice that both me and Dray have tried to choke someone out in the last ten minutes.

"Enough. The Summit has been called, peace will be upheld here," Major's voice booms as he strides into the corridor and our little impromptu meeting. When he sees me with a whip wrapped around the no longer hooded man, he throws me an exasperated look. Twisting the whip, I knock the man out and drop him to the floor, offering Major an innocent look as Priest starts to laugh hysterically. The laughter cuts out as suddenly as it started and leaves an uncomfortable chill in the air.

"No peace was broken, we were simply airing some unfortunate issues which arose. There is no ill will between me and the Champion, isn't that right?" Priest asks, and they both look to me waiting for the answer.

Gritting my teeth, I nod, after all if I want him to fight with us, I can't go around issuing challenges, and it's not like he knew that was my father even if he did know something was off. Stepping back, I look around to see Dray cleaning his knife against the wall as if he hadn't cared who would win. Maxen, Thorn, Drax, and Jax are standing close, but not too close, their fists clenched, obviously wanting to kill the man.

"Plus, my man was at fault. I told him no, he did not listen." That is aimed at the man who is slowly coming to at my feet. The anger in his voice has us all stepping back as he approaches the mountain of a man.

"Michael. Kneel," he demands, his voice echoing around the corridor.

Dray steps to my side again as I wait, my curiosity piqued with what Priest will do. He leans into me and whispering loudly says, "I like the whip, you can use that on me anytime."

Rolling my eyes, I tie it back to my waist. "Crazy bastard," I mutter, and I hear him laugh.

"Then tell me you didn't just imagine using it on me," he replies in a whisper, making me shiver. I mean, I should be concentrating on what is happening in front of me, but with Dray whispering dirty thoughts, which yes, I did imagine, it's hard.

Using the toe of his shoe, Priest raises the man's head. I get my first good look at him and he is just as monstrous as I first thought. Scar after scar crisscrosses his face, some on top of each other until his eyebrows, nose and mouth are all distorted. It looks like someone took a fence to his face, but I can see the scars are old and whitening, with only a few laid-on top still pink and fresh.

"Michael, you dare defy me?" Priest demands, his eyes flashing dangerously.

"My lord," he gasps painfully, panic in every word.

"I said no!" Priest screams, his chest heaving with every breath. He reaches up and runs his hand through his hair, shaking it back in to place perfectly. "You know the price for your insolence," he finishes, his voice deadly.

The man nods, his breaths gasping out still, now in panic and not in his effort to breath. I watch—I can't seem to look away—it feels like I am getting a sneak peek look into the private world of The Worshippers. Didn't I just say I wondered how he kept his men in line? Watching now, I realise it is not just pure unadulterated worship, but fear. It is the screaming of the man kneeled at his feet. This small man wields and plays with terror like I play with knives, and that makes him dangerous. No, not dangerous, deadly. Sands below, I am glad he is on our side.

Priest hands him his knife, one that I didn't even see him produce and in amusement watches as the man takes the blade. Meeting Priest's eyes, he holds it to his forehead.

"Priest, forgive me for I have sinned," he yells as he drags the knife through his skin. I hear someone behind me gag and someone laugh, but I can't look away as the red blood splashes on his skin. Holding the knife back to his temple again as the blood drips to the floor he carries on. "Priest, forgive me for I am merely a sheep to your wolf." Screaming raggedly, the sound reverberating around and making a horrifying noise he drags the knife through his skin again.

I hear someone get sick as the smell of copper hits the air and you can taste the blood on your tongue. "Priest, forgive me. I am not worthy," he whispers brokenly, as he slashes his own face one more time. Blood pools around him and he has to close his eyes as it drips everywhere. With a clatter, the knife drops to the floor, blood covering the blade. The man yells wordlessly as he holds his own face together.

Priest stands above him, his face calm and empty. Like he sees this daily, and he probably does if the existing scars are anything to go by. "Stand my child, for you are forgiven. What was given, is now received."

The man at his feet weeps and crawls towards him until he kisses the shoe in front of him. "Thank you, my lord," he whispers.

"Well fuck," I hear Drax whisper behind me and I nod. Yep, that pretty much sums this up.

I thought I had seen all the crazy this world had to offer, clearly, I had never met Priest. He makes me look like a kid.

"Err-okay." Major coughs and offers me a wide-eyed look, as if to say what the fuck. "Shall we go back to the room? The others are getting restless." I nod and look at Priest who straightens his sleeves and offers us an 'after you' wave of his hand.

I don't let him walk at my back, not now that I know what he can do. Instead, I walk by his side with my men behind me.

"Oh, and Michael?" he calls as we walk away.

"Yes, my lord?" Michael answers.

"Clean up that mess before you join us." Turning, he walks away and I join him.

Sands below, The Summit has not even started yet, and the blood is flowing.

Major leads us into a different corridor, with only a brown door at the end. No one speaks, but I feel a few hands brush against me, offering me their strength.

Stopping in front of it he throws me a look. "You ready?" he asks.

I nod, and he opens the door wide and utter chaos spills out.

CHAPTER SEVENTEEN

THE SUMMIT

"Ya fucking call me that again, you fat old bastard and I'll shoot ya!"

Blinking, I take in the scene before me, Nan in all her pearl and cardigan wearing glory, has a shotgun double the size of her aimed at Reeves. The man has an arched eyebrow, but I can see the fear dancing in his eyes. He's twice the size of Nan, with a little more weight around the waist. His hair is solid grey and his eyes a deep brown. Wrinkles stand out on his tanned cheek and only confirm that he is older than most in this room. Nan stands there, her frail chest heaving but her stance steady and strong, and a serious anticipation etched on her face.

"Come on then, you fat bastard!" she screams at him again, poking his chest with the gun. Reeves holds his hands in the air, signalling peace and also stopping the scavs and roadies from his clan from inching forward, and causing Nan to pull on her itchy trigger finger. I spot a few of Dray's Seekers lingering around the edge of the room, seeming to blend in with the woodwork in here. Major also has a few, and Nan has three men at her back, obviously who she brought from The Rim.

The room is big, a long rectangle with a large wooden table taking up most of the room. Old world paintings line the wooden walls and there are only two large windows in here, one to the left and one to the right. Six large leather chairs are pushed around the table, with one at the head, obviously where Major was sitting. Figures the cheeky bastard would put himself in prime position, just another calculated move to prove his dominance and stake his territory. The room is filled with stifled violence and it feels like a bomb is about to go off, everyone is waiting for the action to start, their bodies tense and thrumming with anticipation. Rolling my eyes, I step in further, Priest steps back to the wall with his eyes locked on me, waiting to see what I will do. Mumbling under my breath, I take in the old lady and man locked in a death stare, someone needs to defuse this before a war starts here, and Ivar has no one left in his way.

"Really, Nan? I leave for two minutes and you gon' shoot the place up? I think Major likes this room," I say casually, my voice breaking through the staring contest. All eyes swing to me and my congregation of men behind me. Nan's eyes dance with amusement before she masks it and pokes Reeves in the chest again.

"Aye, this fucking fat prick is tryin ta tell me how ta rule ma place!" she yells, her accent more pronounced than ever, and Reeves sighs.

"All I said was, you should kill them." His deep voice rumbles out of him, calm and collected, though I see his hands itching with the need to pull a weapon.

Sands below, I hate politics.

"Drop the gun," I demand.

She swivels it around to me, a dare in her eyes. "Ya trying ta tell me what to do, girly?"

Making a quick decision, I stride up to her and knock the gun away, not a good idea but the only one I could think of. "You know better than to point that at me, you think I give a shit if you kill each other? Go ahead, it means Ivar will have your land and people that much easier." The room goes quiet and I watch as Nan deflates, dropping the gun so it points to the floor.

"Ya right girly, we here for a reason. I wouldn't want to break the treaty." She nods and turns to look back at Reeves. "We good. But you ever talk like that to me again and I will blow you to the next fucking room." With that she waddles back to her chair and sits down heavily. I have to bite my lip to hold in my smile, but when I see everyone is still looking at me, I quickly wipe it away and gesture for everyone to resume their places.

Priest slides past me, whispering more crazy as he goes. "And they follow her, even in death."

He takes his seat next to Nan, and Major squeezes my arm before sliding to my side. "Everyone is here, let The Summit begin."

I nod and go around the table to stand in a corner with my back to a wall when Major stops me with a hand on my arm. I look at him and he grins. "Your seat, Champion." I follow his gesture to see he means the seat at the head of the table. My eyes widen and swing back to him, I wanted to fade into the background, not play centre stage. When he notices my look, he drops his voice. "They are right, this won't work without you. You know Ivar better than most, you know the laws. This is your Summit."

With that he walks to the chair on the left of mine, dramatically pausing before sitting down. I hear people gasp, for Major to give up his chair means he thinks I am above him. That I rule him. Unwilling to show him any more disrespect in his house, I stride to the chair and sit down, all eyes locked on me. I sit straight and confident, not showing them any weakness.

"Interesting," Reeves mutters and I narrow my eyes at him.

I watch as Dray holds my eyes and sashays until he sprawls in the chair to my right, showing his support and respect also.

Fucking hell, did I mention how much I hate politics? Even where to sit is a fucking mind game.

My men quickly enter and fan out behind me. When the leaders spot Vasilisy, they roar and slam back from the table, all shouting to be heard over one another as the Berserker grins madly at them.

"Come on then, ya twats!" he yells as the warriors leap at him.

Slamming my head against the table and knocking myself out sounds like a good idea right about now, twice now weapons have been drawn and within the first three minutes. How the hell are we supposed to get through a whole meeting, never mind a war?

"Enough!" I scream, standing up and smashing my fists on the table to get their attention. Everyone freezes like naughty school children, even as Dray chuckles next to me.

"Enough," I say again, sweeping my eyes across the room.

"He's a Berserker!" Reeves shouts while someone else yells, "Traitor!"

I watch as Dray stiffens.

"Enough, he is here as my guest and he will be the reason we can bring down Ivar, so if you would be so fucking kind as to remove the axe from his neck?" I ask, well more like demand. The warriors slink away from him, but everyone is on edge.

"A guest? Girly, what have ya done?" Nan asks, looking at me like I am the crazy one.

"He renounced Ivar, he has paid his price and has saved my life. You might not trust him, fuck, you don't even have to like him but if anyone, and I mean anyone," I sweep my eyes again to meet all of theirs, "kills him, then the treaty is broken, and your life is forfeit." Grumbles sound through the room and I narrow my eyes, bringing my whip down next to me on the table. "Is that understood?" I demand. I hear a few 'yeses' and see a few nods. I relax slightly until I hear "Fuck it," and a scav bursts into action from my left, aiming at Vasilisy who is still glaring at an assassin creeping closer to him. Not thinking, I unravel the whip and launch it through the air until it wraps around the scav's neck.

Yanking it, he flies onto the table, his face turning pink and panic stretches across his features as he faces down my anger. Leaving him there, I glare at Reeves.

"Does this one speak for you?" I ask in a deadly voice.

He stands, making sure to move slowly. "Champion, he does not." He glares at the man before looking back to me.

"He broke the treaty, brought arms to my guest," I yell the last, as the man gasps for breath as I tighten the whip around his throat. "You know the law," I finish, and when Reeves nods, I release the whip and pull it back to myself, coiling it up around my arm just in case.

Reeves looks at the man sadly as he gasps and slides from the end of the table to the floor, holding his neck as unwilling tears drip from his eyes. "Sirla, what did you do?" he asks the man.

"Re–" The man coughs before carrying on, "Threat, to you. Had... to... protect." He finishes in a hacking cough.

I can see the understanding and sadness in Reeves' eyes, even as his face hardens and his hands flex. "You know the laws, no matter the reason." His voice carries through the room, his decision ringing clear. Not that there was one. If he does not punish his man for breaking the law, then he too is breaking the law, and a direct push from the leader of the meeting. A game, yet another in which we must all play carefully. He is out of moves and by the look in his eyes he knows it. He has no choice.

"Forgive me," he whispers as the scav looks at the floor, holding his throat as he coughs for air. I watch as the gun is raised and the trigger pulled, and I feel nothing. The man's body falls to the floor lifeless, and I watch it do so, his blood adding to the ones already on my hand. I might not have pulled the trigger, but I sure as shit gave the order. Reeves looks at me, and I await his reaction. When he nods, I let out a breath I didn't realise I was holding.

I should feel guilty, I should feel sad. A life was just snuffed out, but it was necessary and in war there are casualties.

"Let The Summit begin." I knock the end of the whip on the table as everyone sits back down in their seats.

"He's a fuckin' coward!" Nan yells, glaring at Reeves and Priest who just lean back in their chairs. Reeves looks pissed but Priest just looks blank like always.

Before it can come to blows I lean forward and draw their attention, I have been doing that for the last hour, they clash on nearly every word with only me to smooth over the differences between the clan leaders. "What he is, is crazy. Let's not beat around the bush. His mind is warped, but he has an army behind him. It makes him a deadly threat."

Priest nods and smiles at me. "Thee who faces the demons, will come out stronger for thy have seen the face of evil and chose the path of light."

Everyone goes quiet before I hear Nan mutter, "And ya thought Ivar was crazy."

I have to stifle my laugh by grabbing a drink of water from the cup in front of me. Priest's head slowly turns to face Nan and he wipes all expression from his face. "Madness is only the beginning."

Major grunts. "None of this matters, we must come up with a plan and furthermore, a truce."

Reeves flies to his feet, dramatically bashing his meaty fists down on the table making the cups jump. "Why must we be involved at all?! This is not our fight, I will not send my men to death for one girl. I say we let Ivar have her."

With his words, the room erupts in chaos, but I continue to keep watching. I'm glad he got straight to the point, he is right, why should they fight? I go to stand when out of the corner of my eye I see Dray already beat me to it. "No one will be giving Worth to him or I will cut off their cocks and wear them as a necklace."

Reeves's face turns red as he starts to wind up for a fight. I can see Nan grinning, obviously enjoying this and Major looks tired. Standing slowly I face them all. "You are right, you could give me to Ivar. It might calm him, for a while, but we all know as soon as he kills me or gets bored of me, he will be back to his ways. He will never settle for staying still, he wants to expand. He believes the Berserkers are the best of the clans and he won't stop until no one stands in his way. I was with him for years, I know the way his brain works, and he spoke often of leading this world into a new time. That means killing all of you. So yes, you could hand me over now and buy yourself some time, but then you are only signing your own death warrants. He is coming and he will kill us all. We need to work together or nothing will be left in the Wastes but dust."

Two hours later, I call a break and the leaders start to file out, obviously intent on getting some fresh air—I wish I could join them. Instead, I need to talk to Major, get some advice, and a crash course on Summit rules. He notices my look and nods before sitting back down, waving his men to the door. They nod and leave; the only other person left is Nan who is downing a drink of whiskey like it's a lifeline.

Sands below, when was the last time I had a drink? I stare longingly at the cup and a snort comes from behind me before Maxen rounds the table, grabs a glass and pours me one, leaving it in front of me and slouching in the now free chair next to mine. My other men take that as an invitation and go and find a seat, all but Drax.

He kicks back my chair and waits. I throw him and look, and he hikes his thumb in the air, gesturing for me to stand. I do as I am told, and he slumps in the chair before grabbing my hip and pulling me into his lap. Rolling my eyes, I get comfy and face a grinning Nan.

"Don't fucking start," I warn, narrowing my eyes.

"Ah girly, I wouldn't say a thing," she jokes, pushing the whiskey bottle to the middle, so we can all reach. Major doesn't grab a glass but everyone else does.

"You look tired," she adds, and I nod. "Aye, when this is all through, ya need to go back to ya old job. A lot less madness." I arch my eyebrow, really? My last job was so much easier than trying to save the world? No fucking shit lady.

"Dunnie give me tha look, girly. Anyway, I need ya to come back and take care of them city boys." She spits the last and I freeze with the drink halfway to my mouth, dropping it back to the table with a bang. I lean forward, making Drax groan quietly.

"City boys?" I demand, and she waves her hand in the air.

"That's what I fuckin said didn't I? Fucking boys came from

tha cities and started causing chaos in my place. Threatened my men and even the whores, some people left, and others are laying low."

"Why are they here? That can't be good," I say, grinding my teeth.

"Aye, first we sort that prick out tho'."

I nod and offer her a smile. She toasts me with her glass and I do the same before knocking back my drink. She shuffles to her feet, grabbing her shotgun on the way. "I'm goin' to piss off that bastard again, see if I can't shoot him." With that she shuffles out the door leaving me worried about what I might find when we reconvene.

Thorn reaches out this time and fills my glass, pushing it towards me with a soft smile. I smile back and play with the glass, trying to think everything through. We haven't really got anywhere, just more squabbling than anything, and the way they are pushing me I know I need some advice from Major. I turn to ask him when his voice comes out quiet, soft, and filled with pain.

"I had a daughter." I freeze and swing my eyes to him to see him looking at the table.

"I know," I say equally as soft.

"Her name was Cara." I don't interrupt, I have asked him so many times about his past and he never opened up, so I have to wonder why he is now. "She was twelve when everything happened, it was her birthday. I was supposed to have been there." He rubs his nose with his hand before reaching for a glass. Maxen fills one and passes it over without a word. I throw him a grateful look, which he returns with a soft smile.

"Her mother and I had split up when she was five. I wasn't a great husband, but I loved Cara more than anything in the world. She was my little girl, my angel, my chance at being a better person, at giving someone a better life than I had. I worked hard, day and night to make sure that happened. To make sure she never went hungry like I did, or had to wear threadbare second-hand clothes, that she could have anything she wanted. I never realised all she wanted was me and that no amount of presents could make up for me not being in her life as much."

He takes a deep breath and throws back the whiskey. Maxen reaches out and instantly refills it for him, we all can hear his pain and we all have our own stories. Sometimes you need to get them off your chest, so the best thing you can do for someone is just listen and be there.

"Her mum remarried, he was a good guy. Boring, an accountant, but good. He loved my daughter and never showed me anything but kindness, even when I was an asshole to him. I saw the way my daughter's eyes lit up when he was around, and I hated it. They had become the perfect family. I started not seeing her as much, until I was only a stranger that sent her gifts. I worked my way to the top, I was a lawyer. I became CEO, I got distracted by the money and the lifestyle. I took bribes, I framed innocent people... anything to make the next deal and money." His voice cracks and tears swim in his eyes as he raises them to mine. "But I loved her, she was my light. The thing I did it all for, I stained my soul, so she wouldn't ever have to... and look what it got me. That money didn't help in the end, it didn't save her," he finishes.

"What happened?" I ask, leaning back and letting Drax offer me some comfort.

"She died. When it all started going to shit, I got in my ridiculously expensive car and drove like a mad man, my only thought of getting to her. I knew where she would be, I had received an invite to her birthday party. Her mum told me all she wanted this year was for me to be there, not a present. Just me." He starts to play with his glass as he talks, and I find myself entrapped in his heartbreak.

"I got there an hour later, my car broke down halfway and I

had to fight my way through the chaos and panic, but I got there. This stupid restaurant with balloons outside. The door had been broken in the rush for people to leave, and a body littered the car park as if someone had run him over to get away, as if they could outdrive this thing."

"Major, you don't have to–" He cuts me off with a look and I snap my mouth shut.

"When I got inside, I saw her. She looked so beautiful. She had on a black dress and converse high tops. I bet it drove her mum mad, but she was always different. All the other girls wanted dresses and Barbies, she wanted trucks and trousers. I loved her for it." He throws back his drink again and pushes it to Maxen, who fills it and shoves it back. "There my little girl was, her mum sat beside her, her little face blank and numb, eyes empty as her mum rocked back and forth. She had lost a shoe, that's all I kept thinking. I tumbled to my daughter's side and fell to the floor where she laid, so still. I remember shaking her, screaming at her mum, but nothing worked. She was dead, my little girl was dead, wooden beam from the ceiling had fallen down with the quakes and crushed her. I slapped her mum, I screamed and raged as she sobbed. She told me that stupid bastard had left her, them, in the panic and she didn't know what to do. She screamed at me that I should have been there. She pounded on my chest with her fists until she slid back to the floor in a heap."

I can imagine it in my head, his words that vivid, and my heart hurts for the man I considered a father.

"It wasn't fast, I wish I could say that it didn't hurt. Everyone loves to hear that, but I knew the truth. She suffered, it was painful and long and no one saved her, even as she begged her mum for me. She was so young. Sometimes I wonder if it was for the best, what kind of life would she have lived in this world now? Would she be cold and heartless like her old man, would she have made it? I don't know, so maybe it's for the best." His voice breaks as tears drip steadily down his face.

"What happened to her mum?" I ask, needing to know.

"She killed herself." He throws the drink back again. "While I watched, she picked up a steak knife and slit her own throat. I held her for as long as I could, staunching the blood, but it pumped through my hands. When I came back to, her cold lifeless body was in my arms. I said goodbye, I kissed them both and laid them side by side before burning the place down. I didn't care if it would have got me in trouble, I could not stand the thought of leaving them there. Then I wandered, uncaring whether I lived or died... but I did. I lived, I always figured there was a reason why, Cara was obsessed with meanings and all that spiritual crap. She told me once that I would know why I was in this life one day and I guess she was right." His eyes meet mine, honest, open, and so full of pain and suffering that it rips my chest open. How can he hide all that, how can he function with all that in his chest?

"I survived for you, kid. So, I could save you, so I could help you. So, you could save whatever is left of this world, so you could have the life my daughter never had. I lived so you could, and I thank my little girl every day for giving me that hope."

Tears drop from my eyes mirroring his, but I don't stop them even as Drax's arms tighten around me. "I might not do anything amazing, I will never make up for my past, but I can help you. I can do that for her."

It goes quiet as we all linger in his story and words. I always wanted to know and now that I do, I can't help but love him more. He might not think he deserves to be forgiven or loved, but I do.

Blowing out a breath I knock back my drink. "Okay, crash course in rules."

He snorts out a desperate sounding laugh but nods. "Yes, let's help you stop the end of the world."

I smile at him and he grins back, his eyes lightening and his tears drying up as he starts to outline everything I will need to know to keep me alive, and this Summit on track. I watch him as he talks, my heart aching for him. Now that I know what he lost, I can't help but wonder what I would do—what I would become if I had gone through the same. Probably something a lot worse than him.

CHAPTER EIGHTEEN

NEWS FROM HOME

"So we have agreed, waiting and seeing what Ivar will do is stupid. It puts us at a disadvantage and leaves us unprepared for the attacks he is obviously planning," I say slowly, summing up what we have finally agreed on so far. I take measure as all the leaders reluctantly nod. At least we have agreed on one thing, now we need to figure out a plan of action.

"So Champion, what do we do about it?" Reeves asks, reclining in his chair and munching on some food he found.

"We need to make a plan, one that involves all the clans. It won't work if we attack him on his own territory. He has too many protections in place, mines, and booby traps, not to mention warriors. We would be at a disadvantage again. We need to draw him out into the open, surround him, and then kill him. Cut off the head of the snake, and the rest will follow," I say and I see Major grin at me.

"How da we get him in tha open, girly?" Nan asks, but a tightening around her eyes suggests she already knows.

"We use me as bait, give him the one thing he wants more than anything in the world. He won't be able to resist." I hear my men move but I throw them a glance and they nod, we can discuss it later, but it is the best course of action and I need to get them to see that. Surprisingly, Dray doesn't protest, instead his hand lands on my leg under the table and starts feeling me up. Crazy bastard. Not that I kick him away.

"That's all well and good, but what do the rest of us do? What if it's a trap? We are taking the risk and pinning all our hopes on a slave girl!" Reeves shouts, but I see Priest nod slowly and even Nan sighs.

"He's right girly, we need a better plan." She doesn't apologize but she watches me grimly. Sands below, this is never going to work.

I lean my head back with a sigh as they all start arguing again.

FOR THE HUNDREDTH time in the last four hours, I want to kill everyone. I under anticipated just how hard it would be to get five leaders to see eye to eye on a single subject. Nan is agreeing with me, as is Major, but Reeves is just disagreeing with me to be contrary and probably as payback for his man's life. Priest is only adding in his crazy to stir it up and everyone is getting restless. Sands below, by the time we all agree, it will be too late. There will be no Wasteland left to save. Rubbing my head in exhaustion I try to think of a plan, it's clear we are not going to agree today. Emotions are running too high and everyone is tiring.

"Call a recess until tomorrow," Major whispers to me, his eyes still on the squabbling leaders.

"Huh?" I ask, dropping my hand from my head. I know some of the laws and rules when it comes to Summits, thanks to Major, but I didn't have time to look them all up and it is becoming more and more clear as the meeting goes on... I am out of my depth.

"A recess, a break, until tomorrow, it is allowed to be called twice. It will give us time to regroup," he murmurs when he realises no one cares what we are talking about.

"I can do that?" I ask, watching as Nan throws her hands in the air and leans over to yell in Reeves's face.

"Yes, this is going nowhere. If we regroup tomorrow, hopefully emotions will have settled, and we will have more of a plan of attack," he adds. I nod and turn back to the table, grateful again that he is by my side.

"That and they will have fucked, fought, and drank down their aggression," I add with a sly smile.

"That too," Major says with a laugh.

"I'm calling a recess," I say, only to be ignored as they continue to argue with each other. Rolling my eyes, I go to yell when Maxen steps forward. I turn to eye him, but he is looking at everyone else.

Putting his fingers in his mouth he lets out a sharp short whistle, everyone shuts up and turns to us. With a nod, he steps back again, and I turn back to the leaders, remembering to thank him later.

"We are calling a recess, we will meet back here in the morning." I see some relieved faces and still squabbling, Nan and Reeves walk from the room side by side. Priest offers me a nod before standing and righting his robes.

With one last look at me, he leaves as well. Dropping my head back against the chair I groan, long and loud.

"This is fucking hopeless," I declare, feeling sorry for myself for one second.

"It could be worse, little queen," Vasilisy says and I open one of my eyes to see him grinning down at me, he looks strange upside down.

"How?" I ask, curious.

He shrugs, "They could all be killing each other."

I blink as a laugh tumbles out of me.

"True." I sigh. My eyes snap open when fingers land on each side of my forehead and start rubbing. Looking up at Thorn I smile softly. I let out a low moan as he rubs away the tension and headache The Summit has caused.

"You will get through to them, Mi Alma," Maxen adds.

"How?" I ask.

"If you can get through to us, if you can earn the respect of all the clans, if you can survive the unsurvivable, you can bring them together. You just need to be you," Jax adds. Thinking through his words, I look at the wise brother, he can still be so quiet that sometimes I forget how smart he is.

"You mean I am not being me?" I say slowly, reading between the lines.

"Yes and no. You are playing to them, trying to keep the rules, but that's not you. You are notorious for breaking them, so why would this be different?" With that bombshell, he smiles at me and leans back against the wall.

"He's right. This diplomatic approach isn't working, as crazy as it might be, you need to be you. Guns blazing and mouth cursing, show them what they are fighting for. Show them what they are fighting against," Major says, reaching across and squeezing my arm before standing. "I am going to make sure those animals don't destroy my ring." He smiles at me before straightening his suit and leaving the room, leaving me with my men.

"Maxen, can you take the others to the housing? I need to think," I say softly, letting him know I am not trying to get rid of him, I simply need my space and I can feel the looks boring into me.

"Of course, Mi Alma, we will meet you there." He drops a kiss on my lips before herding everyone out. I can feel my men hesitate, but I don't open my eyes. "I won't be long," I add and feel kisses dropped onto my head as they make their way out of the room. When the door shuts behind them I can breathe easier again. Peace at last.

"If you wanted to be alone with me, all you had to do is ask," comes Dray's voice from right next to me.

My eyes snap open in shock to see him next to me still. I thought he had left earlier, he was that quiet. Looking around the room I see it is just me and him.

I look back at him stupidly. "What are you still doing here?"

He grins, slouching back and rubbing his hand down his bare chest. "We need to talk about you disappearing. It won't happen again," he finishes, all casual like.

Gritting my teeth, I am betting my eyes are spitting fire. "It's not like it was a fucking choice! You crazy motherfucker..." I finish, holding on to the table as the anger that only Dray can stoke in me roars to life.

He shrugs, still calm, but I can see the anger and lust burning bright in his eyes. "I don't care, I told you what would happen. Do it again and I will leave a bloodbath in my wake to get to you, and when I do, you will wish you had never left in the first place." With that, he closes his eyes while I sit with my mouth flapping open and closed.

I don't even know what to say, how do you respond to crazy? But it pisses me off, only adding to the shit day I have had, all the emotions blurring together until they explode.

I don't know what happens but one second, I am thinking about castrating him and the next second our lips are smashed together. I must have thrown myself across the table because my fist is raised. He holds it in his grip before he yanks me onto his lap as we fight each other for control with our tongues and lips. Biting his plump lower one, I pull on it until he groans. The anger and lust blooming in my chest twine together until I don't know whether to fuck him or fight him. He pushes me hard, until my back slams into the edge of the table, I know it will leave a bruise but the fact he doesn't care, or handle me gently, finally lets me break through the last barrier. Growling like a cannibal, I fling myself at him, he catches me at the last second, but the chair goes tumbling backwards until we meet the floor.

I dart in and bite his neck before rolling off him. With a snarl he follows me, slamming me back into the carpet and yanking my hands above my head. I hate the feeling, especially when I see the triumph in his eyes, glaring as his head lowers, I look around. When I spot my whip lying near my hands, I reach up with my fingertips. I just grasp the edge as he bites down hard into my neck, I let out a little scream and I know it's going to fucking scar. Fucking bastard, dog fucking— Bringing up the whip I wrap it around one of his hands before wrapping it around the table leg, then I yank. I roll at the same time as he pulls against the restraint.

"You did say I could use it on you," I tease, blood trickling down my neck as I pant breathlessly. He snarls, pulling against the restraint like an animal, all signs of humanity and control fleeing his eyes. Why does the thought excite me so much? I am about to see the real Dray. With a shout, he pulls and the whip uncoils from the table. I freeze as a smile contorts his face, down on all fours he looks like a fucking animal. So why is my blood pumping and heart racing? He leaps at me and I scramble backwards to try and avoid him, more for the sake of it rather than being scared. I manage to nearly get away, but he grabs a hold of my feet and yanks. My shirt rides up as the carpet rubs against my back, burning as I am dragged under him.

Grinning down at me, I take a cheap shot while he is distracted. Wrapping my legs around his waist I see his eyes flare, and when I wrap my arms around his neck, I wink. He goes to kiss me again, but I quickly push up and twist until he is on the bottom. He doesn't waste any time but reaches up and cuts through my top. Glaring down at him, I pull off the ruined shirt.

"That's better," he coos, his cold hands reaching up and covering my breasts. I see his blade shine in the light as he tries to cut away my bra and I twist away, but not fast enough. I watch, my anger growing, as it falls down my shoulders and joins my ruined shirt on the floor. He lays back with his blade in his hand looking fucking happy with himself.

I decide to give him a taste of his own medicine, crawling back onto him I slam our lips together, one hand reaching for the blade at my waist while I distract him. I can't help but grin against his lips as I cut through his pants. I have to lean back to make sure I don't cut him as I saw through the top bits. He looks down and then back to me. "You could have just asked," he says casually.

Breathing hard we watch each other. Fuck it. I throw the knife and I hear it imbed in the wall as we meet each other in the middle. He sweeps in, claiming my mouth as I fumble with his trousers. He lifts his hips, and I have to lift up so he can shimmy them down. I don't bother trying to take the blade off him, I doubt he would let me have the time.

His hands drop to my hips and he pulls away slightly. "Off or I will cut them," he warns, tugging on my trousers.

Narrowing my eyes, I quickly stand and shuck them off, including my panties. I yelp as he drags me back down and rolls me under him. It's not soft or sweet and he doesn't ask me if I am sure like my other guys, he knows if I wasn't, I would just get rid of him myself. I can see the knowledge in his eyes as his hand drops between my legs and buries in my waiting wet pussy. I groan as his other hand comes up and tweaks my nipple. The blood is still running freely from my neck and it drips onto my breast. I watch as he rubs his fingers in it then rubs it around my nipple, it's crude, filthy, and I fucking love it.

His fingers ram into me as his thumb rubs my clit, I lift my hips, so fucking needy for everything he gives me.

"I knew you would be mine, but I never thought I would be

yours," he murmurs as he drops his mouth to my skin, leaving open-mouthed kisses until he sucks my nipple, blood and all.

Arching my back, I start to ride his fingers, and when he rubs inside of me, I almost scream. He is as good with his hands as he is with his blades, but I need more. I need Dray, I almost feel like he is holding back now, and I won't have that. Reluctantly, I pull away and while he sits back confused, I pounce on him. I see that same bloodlust enter his eyes as I grab his blade from across his chest. I can see he is about to fight me again, so I place it against his neck in warning. Sitting up, I line up his cock and lower myself onto him making us both groan, especially when something cold nudges my bundle of nerves inside. My eyes widen, and he grins at me, that crazy light dancing in his eyes.

"Like that, soulmate? I pierced my cock for you, I noticed your obsession with steel." He rams up as the steel he was just talking about rubs me inside, making me moan even as I shake my head.

"You pierced your cock because I like knives?" I ask slowly, stopping his movements by bracing my legs on the floor.

He looks at me as if that is obvious and I just gape at him. I shouldn't be surprised but, sands below, that is a new level of crazy even for Dray.

"Did it hurt?" I ask curiously, tilting my head to the side.

He shrugs, "I liked it."

Of fucking course he did, I bet the fucking dirty bastard got off on it. He grins as if he can hear my thoughts. "Yes, I did touch myself after. I closed my eyes and remembered that time I caught you here with that boy of yours." He twists his hips as he talks, rubbing inside, making me squirm.

"I want to see." I gasp, trying to control my breathing. I sit back, and he slides out of me, leaving an empty needy feeling, but it is all worth it when I spot the steel bar piercing through the head of his cock. Bloody crazy bastard even had it shaped like a knife.

"I would do a lot worse for you," he admits with no shame

before grabbing my hips and helping me slip back over him. He enters me again. I realise during that whole conversation I held the blade to this throat and he didn't even flinch. It sort of feels like a layer of protection, that I need it there to control his beast.

I brace one hand on his chest, the other with the knife against his throat, as I slowly start to move. I ride him with my knife pressed against his vulnerable neck, almost drawing blood. He's like a wild animal beneath me, his eyes filled with predatory hunger and the blade only seems to spur him on as he moves against it. I fuck him like that, me holding him, taming him with my knife. He moves his head forward and I snatch the knife away, so I don't cut him, it's all the opening he needs because he flips me before picking me up and throwing me, my back landing hard against the table as he towers over me. He shows me the blade in his hand before he runs it down my body. It reminds me of my first time with Jax, but where that was duelling for control, his is pure animal lust. Our blood lust and desire for each other mingling and bringing out our primal side. Seeing him standing naked over me with cuts along him and blood welling at his neck, my knife in his hand and an insane smile on his face, has me moaning and almost coming then and there. The cold blade hovers over my pussy before he uses the non-serrated side and gently rubs it on me. I cry out and try not to move so he doesn't cut me, sex with Dray is like the man himself—dangerous, but oh so good.

My eyes widen and my chest heaves as he pulls the knife away, and keeping eye contact with me, he brings it up to his mouth. His tongue darts out from his swollen lips and he drags it along the flat side of the blade, licking the blood and sex away.

"Fuck, little warrior, you taste like the best fight you can imagine."

Dropping the knife on the table he buries his face in my pussy, his tongue spearing through my folds as his fingers slam into me again. He has me screaming in no time, my pussy clenching around his fingers. Pulling away, he steps back and watches me as he sucks all the juices from them, making me groan.

"Dray..." I moan, and he grins.

"Say it," he demands, dropping his hands to my thighs.

"Say what?" I sulk, trying to pull him to me.

"Say you are mine," he demands, his cool eyes watching me, waiting for an answer.

"No." I swallow hard but grin anyway, if he wants me to say it, he will have a fight on his hands.

Wrapping his hands around my throat he squeezes. "Say it," he growls.

I keep that same sarcastic smile on my face as he lines himself up and slams into me. My eyes nearly roll back in my head, but he squeezes and shakes me until I look at him.

"Say it," he grits out.

"No," I gasp.

He lets go of my neck and slams into me again, smashing our hips together as he buries in as far as he can go.

"Make me," I taunt.

"Oh, I will soulmate," he growls, pulling out before slamming back into me again. Wrapping my legs around him, I hold on as he fucks me hard and fast, brutal and unyielding like the man himself.

The table creaks under our weight as he fucks me into oblivion, our hips slamming together each time. His hands are everywhere, touching, caressing, nipping. It's too much and I explode with a yell. He carries on smashing into me until I lean up and kiss his lips, he shudders and pulls his mouth away to let out a long moan as he comes.

Panting, we stare at each other. We crossed a line, one we can't come back from. I have always tried to keep him at arm's length because I know he has the power to destroy me, but I can see in his eyes that I also have the power to destroy him. It works both ways, you can only cut as deep as you cut yourself.

"I am yours," I whisper, and I watch his eyes flare in shock. "But you are also mine," I finish, feeling territorial. He grins at me, blood smeared around his face and on his chest. Looking down I see I am also covered in blood, but at least we didn't kill each other. Peering over his shoulder I see the room didn't fare so well though, broken bits of chair scatter the floor, as does blood and clothing. A knife is embedded in the wall and I hate to think about what the table looks like.

The door smashes open and we both snap our heads around, already moving to reach for weapons when we spot one panicked, out of breath Seeker. He pales when he spots us still together.

"Sorry!" the man yells, trying to back away as a naked Dray stalks towards him. I watch the ungodly fear bloom in the man's eyes as he tries to stutter out a message, his eyes pointedly staying away from me.

"There's been an attack, people are dead," he stammers out. Dray falters before carrying on stalking him.

"Where?"

"The Seekers... your land," he gasps as his back meets the wall, cowering before him. I watch as Dray freezes, his body deathly still.

"Who?" he demands.

The man whimpers as Dray unleashes himself.

"Who dares attack me?!" he screams.

The man lets out a cry and I watch as he pisses himself.

"Be–be–berserker!" he manages to get out. I freeze before jumping up and pulling on my trousers and weapons. Swearing at my lack of shirt I grab the two ripped halves of mine and tie it together to at least cover myself. When I am done, I still see Dray rooted in the same spot, his back heaving from his breathing, his hands clenching and unclenching. Careful not to startle him, I go to his side. I don't even spare the other man a look as I dismiss him.

"Go, tell Major and all the leaders."

The last words are not even out of my mouth before he is sprinting from the room like the beasts of hell are on his tail. I walk around to face Dray. His face is closed down and cold.

"Dray?" I say softly. I see his jaw clench, but he doesn't answer me. Fuck this, we don't have time.

I slap him square across the face, his head swings to me with a snarl, ready to kill, but I don't back down. He slams me back into the wall and I keep my calm mask on, arching my eyebrow at him as he growls in my face.

"We need to warn the others, and then we need to go to Seeker land...your land." I leave no room for questioning and he nods, some of his sanity returning to his eyes. If I didn't know he loved his people before, I do now.

"Then we kill them all," he pushes out through gritted teeth.

I nod. "Then we kill them all," I repeat certain, now more than ever, that death is the only way. He growls out something else before smashing our lips together again, biting my lip hard and leaving me panting and needy again. Fuck, what have I unleashed?

WAR PARTY

Everything moves fast after that. Dray finds trousers from somewhere, and I follow him out of the building to see the Seekers he has brought with him amassing on the steps, the stink of desperation, anger and need for blood humming through their group.

Major jogs around the corner with my men at his back, he takes in the awaiting Seekers before joining us on the steps.

"You okay, kid?" he asks, thumbing the blood at my neck.

I nod and turn away, not giving my back to the eyes staring at me. Nan saunters around the corner with a rumpled looking Reeves behind her.

When everyone is present, I step up next to Dray. He gives me a searching look before turning to his people. Holding his hand up he settles them down, they don't even move, their eyes are locked on their leader, waiting for orders. Looking around at the men present, I know some of them will have family back home, some will be wondering what is left to go back to. Yet they wait, trusting Dray with their lives.

"There was an attack. I do not know how bad, I do not know

how many are dead. What I do know is every single person who laid a hand on a Seeker will die before the week is through." The crowd cheers and stomps their feet as he carries on. "We will have their blood after we bury our dead." Screams come from the crowd as Dray quiets again.

Blowing out a breath, I address his men. "The Summit is postponed. We will journey to Seeker land, we will help you clear your lands and mourn your people. Then we kill them all. Ivar must die!" I finish, my last words for the other leader's present. Cheers start up as I feel Dray look at me.

"You coming with me, soulmate?" he asks.

"We stick together, we will need each other's strength before this war is through," I reply, looking around at the warriors, their faces etched with anger and ready for war. I have a feeling this is only just the beginning.

WE PACK UP quickly, everyone's thoughts on what we might find when we reach Seeker territory. I have never been before, but I know it will be even more dangerous now.

"You know he will have left warriors behind, little queen. Spies and killers," Vasilisy inserts as he stares at two weapons before adding both to his rapidly filling bag.

"I know." I shove another knife in my bag as I look around for anything I have missed.

"They will all be looking for you," he says.

Sighing, I stare down at my bag. "I know, let them come. I am tired of hiding." Turning around I run into a hard chest. Drax glances down at me, a fierce look in his eyes.

"And if she can't kill them, we will," he tells Vasilisy without looking at him. I hear movement and a bag being thrown out of the door.

"I will give you some time alone, eh." I hear the Berserker say before he shuts the door behind him.

Sighing again, I lean my face into Drax's awaiting chest. I know all my men know what happened between me and Dray, yet they don't seem bothered. Not that it's important right now, with a Berserker threat looming.

"Am I right to go?" I ask, unsure for once.

"Yes. Dray is one of yours, he needs you. His people need you, and you will show them the wrath of the Champion and prove the Berserker threat is real, so when you get back, the other leaders will agree." I blink at his logic, a surprised laugh escaping me.

"I didn't even think of that," I add.

"I know, you were too busy trying to think of everything else." He leans forward and drops a gentle kiss on my lips. It feels like forever since I got some time with my men, just running from one thing to another. "I see the shadows in your eyes baby, everything else can wait."

"He's right," Thorn says, coming up behind me and wrapping his arms around me. Jax and Maxen are readying the bikes, so I let my two other men hold me for a moment.

"You're not mad?" I ask eventually, it's weak and needy, but fuck it, I would rather know.

"No," Drax says with a smile.

"Why?" I ask generally curious.

"We told you before, he was already one of your men. You just didn't know it. Plus, that bastard is crazy, he will protect you as fiercely as we will, and I reckon not even Ivar will want to tangle with an enraged Seeker," Thorn answers.

A smile forms on my lips at that, he is right in a way. Ivar always had respect for the Seekers and tried to stay out of trouble with them, frowning I wonder why he attacked them out of all the clans. Maybe because they are closer, or maybe because they are the strongest? No, it doesn't feel right, it feels personal, like he is trying to hit me, weaken me...but the only way he would know to hit the Seekers to do that was if we had a traitor.

"I can hear the wheels in your head turning, what is it?" Thorn asks, his arms tightening.

It can't be, who would betray me, us? Who would be stupid enough to go against the Seekers? The obvious choice would be Vasilisy, but I saw the shock in his eyes at the attack's announcement and I can feel the hate pouring off him when it comes to Ivar. No, I trust him, maybe a stupid move, but my gut is telling me it's true.

There were only a few other people who knew about The Summit, namely the people here... and my father.

My face contorts in anger, surely, he wouldn't? But even as I think that, I know that if it came to saving his people or giving away something he deems insignificant, like a piece of information, he would do it in a heartbeat. But he should know how damning words can be and wouldn't he want to try and protect me? Didn't he say he wishes he could protect me or was that all pretty lies?

I can't be sure, but all I know is that I need to watch my back and trust no one but my men.

"I think we have a traitor," I say as my brain whirs and a plan forms.

I feel them stiffen. "You think one of us?" they growl in unison.

Blinking stupidly, I bring myself back to the here and now, and rerun my words through my head, wincing when I realise how bad they sounded. "No, never. But someone tipped off Ivar, we can't be sure who. I want you both to watch everyone like hawks. Trust no one but each other...I couldn't bear to lose you," I finish softly.

"You never will," Thorn declares, his promise rattling through the air, making my chest tight. I want to warn him not to promise things he can't keep, after all, war means death.

ONCE WE GET back into the main part of The Ring, it's clear panic and unease are in the air. I don't spot anyone I know, so I head to the front gate with Thorn and Drax taking up protective positions behind me, their eyes sharp and hands on their weapons. Even my hand drops to my blade and rubs it reassuringly.

When we get there, my mouth drops open at the war party assembled. Row after row of bikes and pimped out cars wait for us, with assassins, guards, and scavs eagerly waiting to go. Major and Dray are there with Priest and Nan. I narrow my eyes at Priest, having realised he wasn't there when I made the announcement earlier. Striding up to them I try to control my glare.

"Finally heard the news I see?" I ask, my eyes still on the vehicles.

"Indeed, I was tending to my flock when a messenger reached us." I feel him looking at me, so I meet his eyes. Major steps between our staring match, making Priest turn back to the gate.

"You don't have to go, kid, The Summit needs you here," he says softly to not be overheard.

"I have to go, it's me they are looking for. Plus, The Summit can't go ahead without all the leaders here and Dray will be going no matter what."

"Don't you think that's what Ivar wants?" Major asks, making me look at him.

"I considered it, but it still doesn't change what has to be done. Make sure to keep the peace while I am gone." Blowing out a breath, I step closer. Thorn and Drax cover me so that no one watching can see what I am about to tell him.

"Watch your back Major," I warn, just in case anyone overhears us.

His eyes narrow as his gaze turns calculating. "You think someone..." He looks around before lowering his voice. "You could be right, but if so, the likelihood is they are going with you."

I nod as my eyes flicker to Priest. "Not necessarily." Priest meets my eyes and I turn back to Major.

"Promise me you will be careful?" I ask, done with pretending I still hate him.

"Promise, but you promise to come back." I nod with a silly grin, even as his face turns grave. "I mean it, come back and I promise to tell you anything you want to know."

His bribe works, and he knows it, shock courses through me and I nod. Blowing out a breath with a fresh determination I look at the cars again.

"Are we ready?" I ask in general.

Just then, Maxen jogs up, his chest bare with his white trousers clinging to his muscles. More weapons than I have ever seen line his body, and I raise my eyebrow as he reaches us.

"Gotta be prepared." He winks before turning serious. "Bikes are ready, Vasilisy has...commandeered one." I hold in my laugh as I nod at him.

"Let's get going then." He nods and turns to Thorn as I look at Priest, Nan, and Major.

"When we return, The Summit will continue, until then I suggest you think on what has been said." With that final warning I stride through the gate.

"Seeker land we go..." Drax mumbles, making me smile, it's just like old times, apart from the impending death and fight, oh wait...

CHAPTER TWENTY

SEEKER TERRITORY

The noise of so many engines rumbling as we race through the Wasteland is incredible, and the number of people here added an extra layer of protection. I agreed with Dray, he will ride first, and me and my men will ride at the back, protecting our rear. I love that even after we had sex, he doesn't think he can control me and trusts in my instincts, believing they are assets to protect myself and his men.

"It's a place of respect, you know?" I groan as a familiar annoyingly smug voice sounds. Looking to my left, I spot the assassin from before, I didn't see him there earlier and I don't know when the little sneaky bastard turned up.

"Sneaky fucking Seeker," I mumble, I don't know how he hears me over the engines, but he laughs. Louder, to be heard, I carry on, "What do you mean?"

Looking at me he starts to laugh. "You really are clueless about Seekers." Sobering up, he swerves around a rock before moving closer to me. "To ride at the back of a war party is the ultimate respect. It means they trust you with their lives and to protect them no matter what. Only one other person has ever been asked to ride at the back."

Blowing away some sand, I carry on our conversation, "Who was that?"

"Me," he answers before moving forward and riding in front of me, effectively cutting off our conversation.

Rolling my eyes, I pull up my bandanna to protect my mouth and nose as his bike kicks up dust. At this rate, with how fast we are riding, we should reach Seeker land before sundown. I just hope it's still there when we get there. With nothing else to concentrate on but watching the roads and land around us, I start to wonder what Dray's lands look like.

I know the Berserker stronghold is a castle, The Rim is a shanty city, The Ring a zoo, Worshippers a church and Paradise a bunker... so what about Seeker? I guess I never really asked, but I can imagine it dark and dreary, with lots of weapons and shady places for assassins to hide, or maybe that's just my imagination. The road we are on is twisting and we are using it rather than riding straight through the sand, it clogs up the bikes and isn't an easy ride.

Squinting, I spot something on the left, slowing my bike I leave a gap between me and the war party. I don't know why I noticed it, but something is pulling me to go and check it out. Maxen and Thorn glance back and when they spot me, they slow down too, signalling to Drax and Jax to do the same. When the rest of the bikes get a bit further away, I swerve towards the object and speed up until I stop a good few meters away. When I can finally make out the shapes, I want to vomit.

Tied to a post where the road twists are Dagny and Cherry. I can hear the other bikes roaring closer, but I don't move as I stare at their lifeless bodies.

Cherry is tied to a post, both arms and legs cut off and her clothing nowhere to be seen. Her body is covered in blood and her throat slit, her head is nailed so that her face is pointed towards the road, but it's the utter terror and despair carved into her lifeless face that is my undoing. Swinging my eyes, unable to help myself, I take in Dagny. Similar to Cherry he is tied for the world to see, but even in death his face is determined. His breasts, which I am guessing he covered up, are on display and when my eyes drop to the rest of him, I clench the handlebar desperately. Not only did those animals expose him, they nailed a cock in between his legs. My breathing is harsh and sawing out of my chest as I look for a sign of who could have done this monstrous thing. My eyes land on the Berserker brand drawn crudely in blood at their feet. Time slows down as my ears ring, guilt hunching my shoulders because this is my fault. I don't know how, but someone must have seen me with them and used them as a punishment because this type of killing is what it is...a punishment and a warning. To me, taunting me and daring me to find them, they are hoping to anger me until I lose control. I will, but not in the way they expect.

Standing in the darkened corner of my cell, my hair tangled and covered in blood, I wait for them to come, I know they will. The screaming will have alerted them if nothing else. I feel like a monster right now, but strong as well. A cold smile curves my lips as I look down at the dead man at my feet. One of the bastards who gutted Petal lays there, bleeding out like she did. Only he had no one to help him, no one to answer his cries or begs, instead, the last thing he saw was my face as I screamed and raged, and cut him up. I'm numb though, I should be scared at the pure, unfiltered rage running through me, but I am just a puppet. It's like I am here but I am not. Finally, something snapped in me, a force I have never felt before rose, and the next thing I knew I was leaping at the man taunting me. I should be scared, this is will have repercussions.

I will be punished. You don't just kill a Berserker and get away with it, but instead a twisted sort of joy fills my chest. It might be the last thing I ever do, but I will take some of those bastards with me. I can hear the footsteps as they stomp down the stairs, reacting to the scent of blood and sound of screams, like animals. When they round the cell's corner, they stop dead, two of them, gawking at the man before their eyes snap up to meet mine. I don't know how much they can see, my whole body must look like a shadow to them, the fire not reaching me.

"What tha fuck have ya done, slave?" shouts one of the guards as he bangs on the cell door. Grinning, I step forward and into the light, when they see me, they gasp and fall back, their eyes wide as they take in my blood-soaked body.

"Holy fuck," the one of the left whispers.

"She's fuckin' lost it!" the one on the right shouts, eyeing me warily like I might break through steel to get to him.

The fear in their eyes has my smile stretching, something powerful unfurling in my chest at the sight. All my life here I have felt powerless, nothing, just something to be used and ignored, but now they notice me. Now they fear me, and they will fucking pay for everything they ever did to me and my friends—even if it takes twenty years. I will kill them all.

"Worth?"

"I'm okay," I croak, before dismounting and moving to the bodies. I have to think of them as that. They aren't people anymore, they aren't my friends, they are just empty shells, hopefully they are together in the next life.

Kneeling at their feet, I bow my head, whispering a warrior's goodbye and bidding them peace for their journey. A tear drops to the sand, the heat soaking it up right away like it never existed, the only sign of my grief and pain. I might not have known them for long or that well, but I knew them with one look. The love they had, the fight and hope in their eyes. I knew their story, their past, and struggles. I will remember them like that, not like this...meat for the crows.

"I am sorry," I whisper before raising my head and looking at them. "I promise you, I will make them pay." With that I stand and square my shoulders, the deafening silence from behind only serving to help the screaming and anger flow through me.

"We bury them," I shout, my voice strong, even though I still face away just in case they can see the truth in my eyes. My blood is burning and my chest tight, my darkness clambering to get out, pushing me to burn this fucking world and all the evil in it down.

I hear movement behind me as I drop my bag to the ground, the least I can do is help them. I watch as both my men and the assassin get to work on getting the bodies down, following my orders without hesitation. A hand lands on my back and I know who it is without looking.

"We will get them all," he warns, his voice silky and filled with deadly intent.

"I know, but I wonder what they have left us at yours," I reply coolly, trying to tame the storm inside.

"As do I." I can hear the sadness in his voice, but when I look his eyes are still as cold and expressionless as ever, making me wonder if I imagined it. "I will burn this world down to get to them if they have destroyed what I worked so hard to protect," he vows, eerily echoing my own thoughts. As much as Dray scares me, he reminds me of my darkness and I know we are both made of the same blood and pain. I wonder how far he will go, how far I will go? Thinking back over all the people I have lost and how many lives have been ruined by Ivar and his twisted control, I realise I would do anything.

We step forward at the same time, reaching for Cherry's body as it falls. I wince when I catch her, the blood spraying everywhere and staining my hands. Breathing through my nose, I focus on the next step until there is nothing left to do, I am just standing above two unremarkable patches of sand covering their bodies. I can feel the blood drying and flaking on my skin, but I don't bother wiping it away. I will ride into the Seeker camp like a warrior and any

Berserkers that are there will know they have pushed me too far this time. It's time to finish this war, before the week is through, I want Ivar's head at my feet.

WE GET BACK on the road, the mood more somber as we all check our surroundings better. They know we are coming, and we can't be more prepared. Bloodlust coats every face as we ride hard and fast, like that might stop what has already happened.

I expected bloodshed and mayhem, but as I see a sign for Seeker territory all seems calm and quiet, too quiet. The terrain starts to get more uneven, hilly with the roads ending in dirt paths and eventually nothing but wasteland. Yet Dray navigates it easily, not even looking where he is going. It makes sense that they would hide their camp, sneaky little assassins. A town seems to appear out of nowhere, mismatched roofs and smoke billowing from the sands. At least twenty homes are scattered in a tight formation, with darkened paths winding between them. We don't bother stopping, but I look on curiously. No one appears or looks out of the town and that has me frowning, surely they have heard us coming.

We ride around the town and around a hill before I let out a whistle, this is not where I imagined Dray living—it's a fucking mansion.

CHAPTER TWENTY ONE

THE WARNING

Towering from the sands, in complete contrast with the new world, is a fucking mansion. We aren't talking a big house, we are talking about a house big enough to hold the whole clan. The windows are now brown and dusty, the outside, that obviously started as white, is dirty with more stains than I can count, but it still looks...good. Plants grow on each side of the stairs, which lead up to a wraparound porch and two large wooden front doors. Three stories tall with more windows than I can count, and spanning the whole of the clearing, it's an imposing bit of architecture. Bikes and cars span the left side of the patch of gravel in front of it, and a smaller building is shut up to the right. That's where Dray leads us, and I park up behind him before jumping off and looking around. Again, it's silent. No guards, no Berserkers...no people.

"Where is everyone?" Drax asks, and when I look at Dray, I can see he is thinking the same.

A Seeker slips up next to him. "I just checked the guard stations, they are all empty."

Frowning, I look back at the still house. How can something like a home send fear shooting through my body? I have a terrible feeling, so I draw a blade and I hear a few others do the same.

Dray doesn't bother talking but strides up the steps to the front doors, where he kicks them open. They bang against the wall and I slide up next to him, he goes in right and I go left only to stop and blink. I expected bodies and blood, but the inside is pristine, well, as clean as you can get when you live in a Wasteland. Paintings hang on the left canary yellow wall and on the right white wall. Looking up, I take in the room. High ceilings, running right to the roof, are covered in intricate paintings and even hosts a chandelier, squinting I hold in a laugh when I spot the weapons hanging from it. A staircase, split in two, runs from just in front of it, going up three stories. We seem to be in some sort of entrance. A door leads off the right and a hallway leads through the middle of the split staircase. I shake my head when I spot the decorations, that is more like it. Big suits of armour stand in attention and every weapon you could image decorates the wall like an armoury. Dray heads that way, us on his heels keeping an eye out for anyone. The hallway is dark when we reach the middle, the light barely penetrating back here, so I nearly yelp when I slip on something, grabbing an axe on the wall to keep myself upright. When I right myself, I crouch down and run my finger through the dark liquid pooling in spots on the floor, lifting my finger into the air I growl.

"Blood." I point out, tracing the spotting across the floor and where it leads to a closed door on my left. Standing, I grab my swords and head to the door. Dray meets me there. I put my back to the wall as he waits for me. When I nod, he kicks in the door and I quickly spin into the room, crouching lower just in case anyone is aiming a gun. When no shots go off, I slide to the left, putting my back to the wall once again and allowing Dray to follow me in. He doesn't hesitate like me, but stands in the open doorway, the light framing him as he searches for the source of the blood. When no one jumps out, I step away and go to search my half of the room. I have to squint, the room is that dark, but I can make out the shapes of objects. Mainly what looks like tables and chairs, maybe it's some kind of meeting place? Running my hand along the wall, I stop when I reach material. Feeling around I open the curtains, letting some light stream into the room. Carrying on, I freeze when my hand touches something wet. Pulling my hand back slowly I look down at the floor as my feet stick. There, laying in a drying pool of blood is a Seeker.

"Dray," I murmur in a hushed tone as I drop to a crouch and push the body over. When I do, the head rolls away until it meets Dray's boots as he stops in front of me.

"Berserkers," I confirm, looking up at him. He ignores the head, but anger crosses his face. Nodding, he offers me his hand and I take it, he helps me to my feet and we quickly search the rest of the room before joining the others back out in the hallway.

"Get ready, Berserkers have been here. That kill is no more than a day old. They will have taken out the guards before playing with the others." They all nod, their faces stark and filled with anger as we head back down the corridor. Maxen and Thorn come up the back and watch our rear.

We carry on, slower and more cautious this time. We pass doors and stop as each person takes a room until we have cleared them all. Stopping at the end, the hallway opens into a large circular room, a water fountain in one corner and a fucking garden growing in the other. Only one more door stands down here, a massive hand carved one waiting for us. When we sneak across, tiptoeing lightly, I spot the bloody handprints before the others and tighten my grip on my weapons.

As one, we throw open the doors and rush inside only to stop in horror. What looks like a banquet hall, complete with two long tables on either side, and one running along the back wall, make up the room. Game tables are set up in one corner and a bar is in the other. Large stained-glass windows are framed at the back, their red and yellow panes of glass refracting around the room. Large, elaborate light structures hang from the ceiling lighting the large room, but it's not the size of the room that has me freezing, but what has been left behind.

"Fuck me," comes a whisper from behind me and I can't do anything but nod.

The room is filled with dead Seekers, no, not dead—massacred Seekers. Body parts are littered everywhere, and it would take weeks to find out where they all belonged, but there must be over twenty bodies in here. Blood is splattered on the walls, like buckets of it were thrown against the bland white, standing out as it drips down. The marble floor is covered in red, splashes and slides of it everywhere your eyes look. I spot the odd dead Berserker but not nearly enough. They wiped through them, it's obvious by the room they weren't expecting them. They had set up for dinner, the flies now feast on the rotting food. Every time I run my eyes around the room, I notice something I didn't the last time, like my mind is trying to reject the horror before me and protect me. I couldn't even make out where the parts went at first or what the bits of bodies were, but now I can, and I have to swallow hard. On the floor near a table leg I spy a young girl's face, and over on the other side of the room I see the half cut up face of an older women. They didn't just kill the men, the warriors, they butchered everyone.

"This isn't everyone," Dray rumbles, his voice freezing cold.

"How can you be sure?" I ask, my voice even and numb.

"I know," is all he replies as he carefully walks further into the room.

I turn to see the anger and pain on the Seekers' faces behind me and I feel stupid for not thinking about the fact these people were probably their friends, their brothers or sisters, wives, children. They have lost nearly everything, yet they stand strong and proud looking at Dray to tell them what to do.

Most people faced with the sight before them would wither away, they would freeze in shock and be nothing but a numb shell. Dray is different. He pushes that all away and focuses on being a leader, a warrior. Pride fills my chest as he turns to face us, his strength is astounding even when met with the potential end of his people.

"We need to find the others. We will check upstairs before we check the basement. We stick together and watch each other's backs. They will not get the better of us again!" he screams the last and picks up a chair, throwing it at a wall where it smashes. His chest heaves as his face turns animalistic, his rage taking over.

"You heard him. Let's go and stay low, Berserkers love going for the throat." That makes me freeze and I quickly look back at the bodies, seeing the lack of heads I close my eyes. "Be on the lookout for the piked missing heads, they will be somewhere unless they took them back to Ivar as a trophy."

WE DO AS Dray ordered, we stick together and work our way slowly through both upper levels, but they are untouched, and we find no evidence of anyone. When we gather back in the entrance, Dray turns to a section of wall and I watch in rapt interest as he pushes on a panel that looks no different from any of the others. A section of the wall slides away to reveal a set of stairs going down.

Grabbing a lit torch from the stone wall, he starts descending to the bowels of the mansion and I quickly follow, unwilling to leave him to face whatever awaits us down there alone. All you can

hear as we stomp down the stone stairs is our breathing and footsteps, anyone down here listening hard enough will know we are
coming. Dray stops suddenly and holds his arm out to stop me. I
do so silently, tilting my head to the side to listen to whatever has
alerted him. When he lets out a laugh, I eye him worriedly. Has he
finally lost his mind?

I suppose the death of your people would do that to someone,
especially seeing as though he wasn't the most stable of people
before.

"They are safe," he declares and before I can caution him, he
reaches out and runs his fingers along a wire which was invisible
until he pointed it out.

"Boobytraps?" I ask. He nods and quickly ducks under the
wire, waiting he holds it for me and I slip under. He drops it again
and the Seeker behind me swears as he tries to find it again.

"How many are there?" Looking around I am extra careful.

"That tripwire, which drops blades from the ceiling, a mine at
the bottom of the stairs, and flamethrowers a couple of feet
down," Dray answers as he carries on, a renewed urgency in
his steps.

"Well aren't you fucking prepared," I mutter incredulously.
Who the hell boobytraps their home with mines and flamethrowers? Oh, that's right. The psychopath in front of me.

I like the idea of the blades though. I reckon I could rig something similar up for my room. There is no such thing as overkill
when you have a fucked-up Berserker King hunting you.

Once Dray knows the booby traps are still set, we move even
quicker, bypassing them until we reach the bottom of the steps
where he turns and, without asking, lifts me over a normal looking
stone tile and puts me down on the floor next to him. Turning to
the others I point out the mine, just in case they didn't see, and
follow after Dray as he strides down the hallway. When he reaches
a corner, he throws himself around it just as an arrow goes flying

by where his head would have been. He plucks it out of the wall and laughs.

"Too slow, I thought I taught you better," he jokes as a mammoth sized man lumbers around the corner, clutching a crossbow delicately. He's huge, his bald head shining in the light and his ridiculous arms bulging. His face is square and angry looking, only highlighted by his Seeker scar he wears.

"'Bout fookin time," he rumbles, shuffling to put his crossbow away over his back.

"What happened?" Dray demands, all signs of joking gone.

"Fookin' scraggly haired fucks attacked as we sat down for suppa. Started slaughtering everyone, I managed to grab as many as I could and get em locked down here. Bastards stayed for hours, sounded like they were searching the place for somethin." Looking at Dray seriously, he steps closer. "Why the fook are those pigs attacking us?"

"They want a war," Dray answers simply.

I grind my teeth, but something doesn't sit right with me. Why come all this way, kill half the Seekers then just up and leave? They didn't even leave anyone behind by the looks of it. So why?

"Did you see a man with a skull crown, a giant sword strapped to his back who was surrounded by a snake looking man, and a man the same size as you?" I question, trying to add up in my head why this feels so wrong.

The man turns towards me, throwing Dray a look that says 'who the fuck is this' but he answers anyway. "No, only those fookin rats." He jerks his head upstairs. So, that means Ivar and his closest men weren't here, so, where were they? And why did they send Berserkers to attack the Seekers? Questions pile up, but Dray distracts me as he speaks.

"Get everyone back upstairs, sweep the camp. Bring any of those bastards to me alive. Then we honour our dead." The man nods before slamming his fist to his chest. Dray returns the gesture and turns back to me as the man lumbers around the corner, his voice booming out to the remaining Seekers I am guessing.

"Something doesn't feel right," I spit out, a sick feeling forming in my stomach.

"I know, I feel it too. Let's get back upstairs, soulmate."

CHAPTER TWENTY TWO

Sex and Bubbles

My men and I join the Seekers in searching the camp. I stay near the house and within two hours a horn sounds to ring the all clear. My shoulders slump at that, even though I know I have to go back and help sort the bodies. My mind has been running a mile a minute trying to figure out why this attack doesn't sit right with me, but I just can't grasp why.

There were more Seekers who survived than I thought and I give added respect to the sneaky bastards. Men, woman, and children all came out of hiding and started working together to achieve Dray's goals. I watch the way they look at him, with reverence and respect. The men gather around him asking for advice and showing him things they have found. Whereas some of the women giggle and blush when he looks at them, some are hardened warriors like the men and don't even seem to bat an eye at the half naked man candy that is Dray.

I catch one of the female warriors watching Maxen though, and I debate killing her, especially when her eyes drop to his arse and she licks her lips.

"Such a jealous little thing, aren't you?" Maxen laughs, making me jump and my glare turns away from the woman to his face.

"Fuck yes. You better remember that, and I have violent tendencies and stab first, ask questions later," I growl out, narrowing my eyes at him. Smug bastard just winks at me.

Growling, I turn back to picking up a torn off arm and adding it to the wheelbarrow we are sharing. Maxen jokes and pokes at me as we work, trying to keep the mood light, and it works.

Three hours later and I am exhausted. My arms ache, my back is killing me, and my head is pounding, but the room is finally cleared of bodies. I follow the silent parade of Seekers outside to watch them honour their dead. I've only ever seen a normal burial and a Berserker honouring, so I am curious as Dray leaps up onto the hill out back where all the bodies are. Standing there like some avenging god, he takes in his people.

"Today we lost many. Those animals came onto our land, they broke the peace and shed blood in our home. They will pay, we will ensure that, but first we say goodbye to our fallen. Tonight we lay you to rest, may the next life be kinder to you and welcome you with open arms. To the fallen!" he shouts, thumping his chest.

A chanting starts up as the Seekers stomp their feet. Singing soon joins in as Dray leaps down and accepts a torch from the man next to him. Turning, he lets everyone see before tossing it onto the pile of bodies. It lights with a whoosh, and he steps back and watches the flames dance. The singing lasts until the last flame dies out, and nothing but char and the smell remains. It goes quiet, then and a soulful, heart-wrenching voice takes up the song. Blinking in shock, I look at Dray as he sings about loss and death until his voice tapers off. Only then do the Seekers start to break up and walk away, each with a look of peace on their face even as the scent of death and decay linger on the air, but I can't take my eyes away from Dray. Turning, he walks towards us, his eyes only for me.

"We rest now, today has been long. Pick any rooms on the third floor, they are reserved only for my generals and me. Tomorrow we figure out our plan." His eyes stay locked on me even as his words are meant for my men. "Champion, you are with me." I arch my eyebrow at that, but he walks away, striding towards the mansion's back door.

"He needs you tonight, angel," Jax says softly before kissing my lips and walking away. Drax kisses me and offers me a sad smile before running to catch up with his brother. I turn back to Maxen and Thorn.

"He's right, we will see you in the morning, Mi Alma. Try not to kill him." Maxen kisses me softly, setting my tired body alight and steps away to let Thorn move in and hug me. His arms wrap around me and I snuggle into his heat, wishing I could stay here, but they are right. I saw the look in Dray's eyes; this should be interesting. Thorn steps back and drops a kiss on my forehead before him and Maxen wanders away. When I look back towards the mansion, I see Dray's shadow at the window. Taking a deep breath, I set off to find out what he wants from me.

When I step through the back door, I see his back disappearing around the corner and I jog after him. I end up chasing him up some wooden back stairs that I didn't spot before. When I reach the third floor, I stop and look around, wondering where he went. The walls on this floor are a deep red, almost blood coloured, and there are six doors. A black leather couch sits under a window at the end of the corridor and the rest of the floor is bare. Only one door stands open, at the very end of the corridor and set back from the others. Rolling my eyes at his dramatics, I stride through it and stop, blinking into the darkness. The sound of running water has me tilting my head. Relying on my hearing, I follow the sound through the room, stumbling over furniture every now and again until I see the light peeking out of a door just ahead. When I push it open, I take in the bathroom before me.

Bigger than my room back at Nan's and double the size of the one at The Ring, the room screams money. It was probably some rich bastard banker's holiday home before everything went to shit. A tub, square and huge, sits on a raised area at the very back of the room. Big enough to fit at least three people, it spans the whole end of the bathroom. A toilet, two sinks and a mirror run down the left-hand side of the room. A marble table is to the right where Dray stands with his naked back to me, dried blood coating it and highlighting his scars.

Music fills the room and I look back at Dray as he steps away from the table to reveal an old style gramophone. Some old school jazz fills the room and I watch curiously as Dray strips off, laying his weapons on the table, until he is completely naked before me. Still not saying a word or looking at me, he climbs into the running bath and slides down the side. Finally, he tilts his head until his eyes reach me, they look haunted and downright sad, and I automatically take a step forward.

"Stay with me?" he asks, his voice quiet. I don't even bother to answer as I copy him. I strip off my weapons and lay them next to his before dropping my clothes and slipping into the tub to sit at the opposite end. His head turns again, his eyes tracking me, watching me without speaking.

I drink in the sight of him as we soak peacefully, the water turning red with the blood of his people. Without questioning, I pull the plug and run it again to get rid of the blood. Laying back once more, I watch him.

"Where did you get the scar?" I ask, the jazz music relaxing me and making me ask things I usually wouldn't. His scars are his business, sands below I have enough myself, but I find myself asking anyway.

"My father." Just when I think he won't say any more, he sighs and leans his head back. "The man was pure evil. He lived to torture my brother and me, his people also. They hated him but were too scared. When I was thirteen, he held a meal. Everyone knew that meant bad news. It was during the main course that he flipped. He just started attacking people, cutting them up. None of the guards knew what to do, they couldn't stop him—he was their leader. Blood was flying, and people were dying, and no one was doing anything...so I did." He blows out a breath and closes his eyes as if remembering. "I jumped in, weaponless and scared as hell, I deflected his blows. Using my body, I took the brunt of his bloodlust and anger, cut after cut until I stumbled and fell, my arms ripped open down to the bones. I couldn't even lift them to protect myself as he raised his blade once more. He ripped through my face and stood over me as reason came back to him. He cleaned his blade and turned his back on me, left me there bleeding to death, screaming as I held my face." He opens his eyes again and stares at the ceiling. "A woman saved me, her name was Maria. Her husband was one of the men I had jumped in to save. She stitched me back together and took care of me, even when I wouldn't let her."

"Why do your men wear one?" I ask, my body relaxing further into the warm water.

"Stories spread at what I had done, I had saved my people from my own father. They remembered that, so when I killed him and my brother, it became a sign of great honour to wear the scar."

Shrugging, he moves the water, causing it to lap at my skin. "It started with Maria's husband, he said it was the only way to honour my sacrifice and it caught on." His eyes land on me again. "Does it bother you, the scar?" His voice is vulnerable, and I can tell my response will hit him deep. For someone so scary and powerful, he sure does have a lot of emotions still, more than I ever imagined.

"No," I reply honestly. "I love it, it was the first thing I noticed about you. I don't know why but it made me feel better, I had so many scars and when I saw yours I thought to myself, there is someone who knows suffering and pain like me. Now every time I look at it, I will remember how brave you are."

He stops moving, his eyes locked on me, and he doesn't even breathe. I jerk back as he bursts into movement, flinging himself across the tub, the water splashing with him, until he stops right in front of me.

"That is because we are the same, we are survivors but more than that. We are warriors." I nod, and he moves between my legs. Turning around, he leans his back against my chest and I cup him with my thighs and wrap my arms around him, just holding him.

"Will you tell me about your brother and father?" I ask softly, I need to know. I have this insane urge to know everything about him, about all my men, and this is the first time he has shown me any weakness and really opened up, after coming to his home I feel like I know him better than ever.

"What do you want to know?" he replies.

"Anything, everything. What happened?" Leaving one of my hands on his chest I start to play with his hair.

"Me and my brother were never close. He was weak, always bending to my dad's will and he let him shape him until all that was left was a shell, a copy of my father." His hand lands on my thigh underwater as he strokes my skin and I shiver.

"You killed them," I say the statement casually as I grab the cloth from next to the bath and start washing the blood from every-where I can reach on him.

"Yes. I would do it over and over again if I could." He sighs as I run the cloth down his chest before wetting it again and washing his shoulders.

"You were really young to run a clan, did they not challenge you? I see the devotion they have now, but surely it wasn't always that way?"

"It was rough at first, constant fights for strength, but when the cannibals came down from the mountain and attacked us in force, I showed them I was exactly what they needed," he murmurs, relaxing into me, a soft peaceful look on his face, one I have never seen before. It sends a thrill through me and I falter before carrying on washing him.

"You're not who I thought you would be," I say conversationally, dropping the cloth on the side when I can't reach anymore.

"Don't stop," he demands, making me roll my eyes before he carries on. "What did you think I would be like?"

I smile remembering the first time I saw him at The Ring. "Terrifying. Don't get me wrong, you have your moments, but I know you would never hurt me. I thought you would be a cold, unforgiving bastard."

"And I am." He laughs, his body shuddering against me.

"True." I grin. "But you are also caring, brave, and your loyalty astounds me." He freezes up against me.

"Looks like you are finally starting to accept me, soulmate." I groan at the term and I know he has that cocky, crazy smile on his face.

"Don't get too ahead of yourself, I still might kill you," I warn, wrapping my arms around him and holding him to me even as I threaten him.

"Then I would die gladly," he admits, snuggling back.

Sands below, he is so crazy. The thought sends a burst of happiness through my chest and forms a smile on my face. I guess I am just as crazy.

We sit in silence for a bit before the water starts to cool. Dray pushes away and grabs the cloth, wetting it, and starts to clean me. I fidget but let him do it, fair is fair after all. When he is done, he throws the cloth away, unplugs the bath and grabs me under my thighs, scooping me up until I have to wrap my legs around his waist. Standing, he steps out of the bath and drops me onto the counter under the mirror.

Stepping back, he grabs two towels, throwing one to me that I catch, and he keeps the other. I guess some guys would try and be sweet and soft and dry me, but I'm not a fucking child. I can dry myself, thank you. I do just that and he waits for me before turning and leaving the room. I follow after him and he turns on a dimmed light this time, so I can see.

The bedroom is big, but also empty, with just one large bed and an open window leading out onto a balcony. He leaps onto the bed and lies back with one arm under his head and the other on his stomach as he arches one leg and keeps it bent. He watches me as I look around, following me with his eyes like he is tracking his prey. I find a hidden door and when I open it, I grin at the arsenal hiding in here. He has a fucking armoury in his room, I shouldn't expect less. Axes, knives, swords, maces, even a gun. I step back only to ram into a chest, I didn't even hear him move. His words move my hair, he is that close. "Do you like them?"

"I think I am jealous," I respond, running my eyes over the weapons again. I spot a particular weapon that has me nearly drooling.

"What's mine is yours," he adds, and I snort.

"We aren't married, you psycho."

He laughs and wraps his arms around my waist and drops his head on my shoulder, leaving a gentle kiss there. "Might as well be."

I grind my teeth and consider grabbing one of the weapons and murdering him. Although, I do debate his words as I eye the dagger again, it's beautiful. A copper handle inlaid with inscriptions, obviously hand carved, but it's the blade itself that has me unable to look away. Curving down but also up, the blade splits into two, with jagged teeth on each prong. It's amazing, I bet it cuts like butter and I can't help but keep looking back at it.

"You like it?" Dray asks, making me almost jump, I had forgotten he was there.

"Yes," I grit out, knowing he would only wait until I admitted it.

"Keep it." He steps away before sliding past me, standing in this room of weapons naked as the day he was born and looking like some kind of mad man, but it has me licking my lips as his peachy ass faces me. And when he grabs the blade, a sheathe as well, and turns to me with the blade balancing on his hand, I consider jumping him.

Most girls want pretty flowers or clothes—I can't think of anything more romantic than a weapon, and it doesn't escape my notice that this is the second time now he has given me one. I can see the look in his eye, taking this blade would mean more than just accepting a present, but I can't seem to care. My greedy hands grab it and I poke the end, pulling my finger away to see the blood welling at the end, making me grin. Before I can move, Dray cups my finger and pulls it to his mouth slowly. Watching me intently he sucks on the end, licking the blood away. My mouth drops open on a pant. Still looking deep in my eyes, he sucks on my finger, hard enough that it has its own heartbeat. My pussy throbs at the same time. He pulls away with a pop and I decide to throw everything out the window. I leap at him, the blade dropping to the floor with a bang. He catches me and spins in one move, smashing my back into the wall, pushing a grunt from me as the weapons dig into my back.

He moves in fast, licking up my neck before biting my ear, making me tighten my legs as my eyes flutter closed.

"Now, what weapons in here are we using this time, soulmate?" He grins before biting down on my neck, making me rub against him. Smiling at his dirty mind, because we always do seem to end up with weapons, I balance my feet on the wall and I kick off, we tumble to the ground, me on top of him. Grinning down at him, I watch the fire burning in his eyes. "How about none?" I ask before leaning down and slamming our lips together.

He grunts, his hands grabbing my hips as he thrusts up underneath me. When I need to breathe, I pull away and stare into his eyes. Using my hips, he lifts me up and I lean back, he grins at me and I narrow my eyes right before he throws me off of him. I start to scramble to my feet, but he pounces and pulls me down so my back is to his chest, then I find myself falling backwards with a yelp. I sit up and he allows me, until I am facing the wall of weapons.

"Dray—" I cut off on a moan as he nudges my clit with his cock, the metal cold against my skin.

"You were saying, soulmate?" I can hear the amusement in his voice, and I let out a little warning growl. His hand comes up and circles my throat, squeezing slightly in warning and my pulse skyrockets. I never thought I would appreciate a man having control over me, but I know he would never hurt me, and I love that for once I can let go without worrying about hurting anyone or being hurt in return.

He squeezes again as my pussy floods. "Fuck, I can feel how wet you are." He groans, thrusting up again and nudging that bundle of nerves. Moaning, I lean my head back until I see the ceiling.

"Like that? Then you will love this," he says before lining up and thrusting inside of me. I let out an embarrassingly long moan and try to move on him, needing him deeper, needing something. I gasp when his other hand reaches around and flicks my nipple, making me writhe on top of him. Then he really starts to play. With each thrust up, he squeezes my throat a little bit harder.

I'm like the wild animal I always accuse him of being, the noises coming from my mouth should embarrass me, but all I can do at this moment is feel. Feel Dray as he stretches me, hitting that sweet spot inside with each thrust. Hear his grunts and moans as he fucks me from behind. He surrounds me, fills me, and owns me, and I fucking love it. I explode with a grunt and he cuts off my breathing for a second which throws me straight into another orgasm. When I can see straight again, his hand slowly uncurls from my neck and it throbs in time with my pussy. I let out a little whimper when he lifts me and slips from my needy pussy.

"Dray." I don't even know what I am asking for at this point, but he obviously does. He pushes me forward with a hand on the middle of my back, none too gently, until I tumble onto my hands and knees.

"I've got you, I've always got you," he whispers into my ear before biting down my back until I arch and push back my ass, needing him inside of me again.

I hang my head as I feel him move behind me, he lines up, and with no warning, pushes inside me again. Reaching forward, he trails his hand across my arse and up my back before wrapping my hair around his fist and pulling until I am stretching my neck. He keeps me there on the edge of pain and pleasure as he starts to move. Slow at first, then speeding up until he is hammering into me with every thrust and I have to throw a hand out and grip the wall of weapons to stop from falling.

My nipples tighten painfully as that feeling starts to build again, and I push back until we find a hard and fast rhythm.

"Fuck." I hear him grunt out before a cold wet finger probes at my arse. I freeze a little and quick as a snake, he leans into me and bites my left shoulder, making me clench around him.

"Behave," he commands before running his finger back around my other hole. I can't stop the little whimper that escapes my lips and slowly he enters me, stretching me deliciously, still running that line of pain and pleasure. Like a knife's edge.

When he adds a second finger and slowly starts to pull them out before slamming them back in, I am lost. His hand in my hair, his cock buried deep in me, and his fingers fucking my ass, it's too much and I explode, crying out. I hear him roar before he thrusts into me twice more before stilling, his cum lashing inside me. My body is like jelly, well fucked and tired, so I tumble forward into the carpet, turning my head so I can breathe. He follows me down, laying on my back, his softening cock still inside of me.

We both lay there until we catch our breath. I can't help but shiver when he leaves a soft gentle kiss on my shoulder and groans before pulling out of me.

"Fucking hell, you are amazing soulmate," he says hoarsely.

I close my eyes with a soft smile, but they fly open when I am scooped up into his arms. I offer him an arched eyebrow look and he grins madly before striding out of the armoury and over to the bed. He throws me into the middle where I bounce once before settling in. Watching me with a soft look in his eyes, he crawls up the bed like an animal and settles in next to me, spooning me from behind until I am warm and so fucking tired.

Just as I start to fall asleep, I am sure I hear a whispered '*I love you, soulmate.*' But that must just be my imagination.

I DON'T KNOW what wakes me up, but when I do, I find myself curled up on Dray's chest as he holds me to him, snoring softly as he sleeps. I don't think I have ever seen him sleep. Unwilling to disturb him, I slip off his chest and out of the bed. I freeze when he turns over, cuddling his pillow, I figured he would wake up. Someone like him would be a light sleeper, but he doesn't, so I grab my clothes and weapons and slip from the room and into the hallways, quickly getting dressed. When I am there, I stop and stare at all the closed doors. I guess I should find my men, but I don't know where they are. I debate my options when a door opens and Maxen slips out, looking fully awake and still half dressed. I lean back against the wall and smile as I watch him. He doesn't even notice me, a frown on his face as he walks towards the end of the corridor where I am. His head snaps up and he stares at me, the frown disappearing and a smile flirting on his lips.

"Where were you going?" I tease.

He grins and stops in front of me, looking down. "To find you," he admits, looking sheepish.

"Why?" I ask, placing my hand on his chest, when I do, he closes his eyes before smiling again.

"I needed to see you were okay, I guess I am so used to being by your side that I don't know how not to be," he whispers.

"I know what you mean, I missed you too," I admit, and he opens his eyes.

"Will he mind if I steal you for the night? We don't know what will happen tomorrow, so tonight stay with us?" he asks, gripping my hand over his heart.

"Okay," I whisper back, and he quickly tugs on my hand, pulling me along to the door he came from before pulling me inside. When I get there, I see all my men—apart from Dray— lounging around, still fully awake.

"Let's go back to how it was. We will get you drunk until we pass out. Sound good?" Maxen asks from behind me.

"Sounds perfect," I say and they all look up from the table and grin when they spot me, various looks of happiness on their handsome faces. Sands below, what did I do without them?

CHAPTER TWENTY THREE

THE BRANDS

We are all seated around the table, more types of liquor than I can count are spread between us and we all have a drink in front of us. I watch as Drax says something to Thorn which makes him laugh, banging his fist on the table as his eyes scrunch up in amusement. It's the little things in this world, there is so much shit and hate, blood and death, that you have to appreciate the good when it comes.

"Okay, okay!" Thorn says through laughs before clearing his throat and getting everyone's attention. I lean back in my chair, kicking my feet up on the table. "I think it's time we showed her."

I arch my eyebrow, not understanding what they are talking about. I run my eyes around the table as they smile at each other. "Show me what?" I demand, narrowing my eyes when no one instantly tells me.

Dropping my feet from the table, I try to catch all of their eyes. "Tell me what?" I repeat louder, starting to get nervous.

As one, they nod and stand. Sitting back further in my chair, I dart my eyes around before Maxen moves closer. "Mi Alma, what we have is something so precious. Something deeper and stronger

than anything this world can throw at us. We can't always understand the fight you are going through, but we want you to know we
will also be there." Stepping back, they line up and take a deep
breath. My heart is racing and my chest is tight as I wait.

Maxen turns slightly, so I can see his neck, I don't know how I
didn't notice it before. Jax pulls off his shirt and points over his
chest. Drax drops his pants and turns so I can see his ass. Thorn is
last, and he turns so I can see his back. I squint as I look at the
black ink on their skin. Standing slowly, I move closer to inspect it.
When I see what they have done, I stumble back with a gasp,
shock coursing through my body. In a circle on their bodies is my
champion mark, but they added a heart in the middle. I look at
each of them, speechless. "I got mine done, because you always
watch my back," Thorn says and smiles at me.

"I got mine on my ass because you are always looking at it,"
Drax says with a wink and I choke on a laugh.

"I got mine over my heart, because you reminded me that I
have one again," Jax says softly.

I look at Maxen and he smiles at me, love shining in his eyes. "I
got mine in the very first place you touched me, where you bit and
kissed me."

"When did you–" I ask on a choked breath.

"Tonight, while you were with Dray. We have been planning
on it for a while," Jax answers.

Well, that explains why I never noticed them, but still. I don't
even know what to say, they marked their bodies for me, to show
me their love. I stand here like an idiot watching them.

"I love you, I love you all," I say eventually, forcing the words
out, but truly meaning them.

"You better, I didn't mark my pretty skin for nothing," Drax
says with a wink.

I snort out a laugh before standing to face them, needing them
all tonight. Feeling bold, I grab Drax and Maxen's hands because

they are the closest, and spotting the door in the corner, I drag them to the bedroom before letting go. Turning to face them where they are all crowded by the doorway with confused looks on their faces, I grin. Slowly, to tease them, I strip off my clothes. Dropping them to the floor until I stand naked before them.

"Your turn," I demand in a velvety voice, and watch as they jump to get undressed. So much skin and muscle on show I have to clench my thighs together. When they are done, I turn to face the bed before throwing them a grin over my shoulder. "This should be fun."

I crawl up onto the bed, swaying my ass, and I hear a groan behind me, making me smile. Turning over, I face them all where they stand at the edge of the bed, gripping the covers and end board as if to stop themselves from reaching for me. Watching them still, I run my hand slowly down my naked chest before running it around my breasts. I hear a gasp and I arch my back as I tweak at my nipple.

"Angel," Jax grunts out the warning.

My eyes open again and focus on them as I touch myself, I am so fucking wet for them already. I know they are mine, where Dray and I fought for control, and he dominated me, my guys are just that. Mine. They might be strong, they might be warriors, but I am their fucking leader and they wait to see what I want. It turns me on, and I spread my legs and drop my hand there, feeling how wet my pussy is.

"Want some help with that, baby?" Drax jokes, but when I look at him, I can see the strain in his muscles as he fights to keep himself there.

I make him wait, moaning as I rub my nub, letting them see how turned on I am. I hear a growl but still no one moves, and I love that power.

Finished torturing both them and myself, I look at Drax. I don't feel embarrassed or shy, fuck, I never was shy, but seeing the pure lust coating his face throws any more reservations out of the window. They want this too. "I want your mouth on my pussy," I order, and he grins.

Letting go of the bedding, he moves to the bed before crawling up on all fours and settling between my spread legs. He peers up with a cheeky grin before licking a long line on my needy pussy. My hand drops to his hair to anchor him there as I push him deeper. He lets out an appreciative hum before spreading my lips and circling my nub with his tongue. He teases me and I love it.

I peer at the others, and when my eyes land on Maxen, he grins before striding forward and without hesitating, wrapping his lips around my left nipple. Throwing my head back I moan, and when I feel another mouth wrap around the other one, I thrash my head before meeting Thorn's eyes. Drax takes that time to remind me he is there by slowly sliding one finger inside of me as he sucks on my clit.

Holding my hand out blindly, I reach for my other man. "Jax," I moan and he is by my side in an instant. I pull him down next to me before smashing our lips together, letting him drink down my moans. Drax adds another finger, curling them inside of me, and I have to pull my lips away from Jax as I come so hard I see stars, so hard that I can't stop shaking and every part of me feels sensitive. It's too much and when Drax sucks on my clit again, I don't know whether to push him away or pull him closer. Opening my eyes as my chest heaves, I meet his eyes as he rises from in between my legs. His chin is wet with my juices and his lips swollen, but his eyes are fucking wild. Maxen and Thorn move away, watching us with a grin as they lounge on the bed.

"On your knees, baby," Drax orders and I chafe at his control before he reaches down and flicks my clit. Fuck.

Jumping, I turn around to find Jax lounging against the head-board with his hand wrapped around his cock as he watches me. His eyes are dark and I don't hesitate as I crawl towards him. He lays his head back, still watching me as he runs his hand up and down his cock, pre-cum beading at the top. When I hover over him, I lower my head and lick a long line up his chest before biting his neck gently.

"Please, angel," he begs, and I grin against his skin where his pulse thunders.

"Please what?" I ask before licking back down and around his nipple.

"I need you," he pants, his eyes open and pleading.

I need him too, so I lean back and centre myself over his hips. He helps guide himself to my warm wet centre. Together we work until I am seated on him, his balls against my skin as we both adjust to the feeling. Then I start to move, slowly at first, just working my way up and down until I need more. It's like Drax hears my thoughts because he pushes me down until I lay on top of Jax and then his hands rub at my arse as I remember his promise from before.

I know what he is going to ask, so looking into his brother's eyes I answer him. "Yes." Then I slam my lips to Jax as we fight for control, him locked inside of me as his brother parts my ass cheeks. His cold hand runs down to my pussy, circling where his brother's cock is buried deep in me, and gathering the wetness before he runs his fingers back to my other hole. I push back and he takes it as permission, sinking not one, but two fingers in me, stretching me. I groan into Jax's mouth and shake between them at the feeling of being so full. Drax pulls out slowly before thrusting back in, this time with three fingers.

Pulling my mouth away from Jax I moan. "Drax, please, I need you inside of me."

I can almost feel his grin as he pulls out his fingers and lines up his cock. "As my woman asks," he says cockily before pushing in. Throwing my head back I pant as he keeps pushing until he is all the way in, his balls slapping against my ass cheeks. I don't move, I don't even breathe as I try and adjust to the feeling of them both buried so deep inside me.

When I drop my lips back to Jax, Drax starts to move. Thrusting shallowly as he and Jax figure out their rhythm, and when they do, I am fucking gone. I just lay there between them as they fuck me, my pussy and ass so full that my eyes flutter closed. It doesn't take long for that feeling to start up again and I clench my pussy around Jax making him grunt and thrust up harder. That's when they show me they were holding back. They fuck me for real.

"Fuck, angel. I love you," Jax moans as he closes his eyes in ecstasy and explodes inside of me. Drax groans and tightens his hands on my hips and follows his brother. Fuck, I need more. I need to come. So I nudge Drax and he groans before slipping out of me and falling on his back next to his brother, his eyes still closed and his mouth slack.

All I know is that I need to come and when I spot Maxen there waiting, I smirk. He leans back as I crawl up his body until I hover over his big, hard cock. We don't speak as he lowers me onto him, slowly working in every delicious inch until I am groaning again. Throwing my head back with my eyes closed, I yelp as the room spins. When I open my eyes again, Maxen is grinning above me and I can feel something soft beneath my head. Arching my neck, I realise I am laid on Jax's thigh. Not that he seems to care.

My eyes shoot back to Maxen as he pulls out before thrusting back in again. He does it again and again, teasing me as I glare at him.

"What is it, Mi Alma?" He winks and I wrap my legs around his waist and pull him to me.

"Fuck me, not play with me," I demand and he grins before pulling back and hammering into me. He doesn't stop, his cock bumping my cervix every time he buries deep. Panting, my head drops to the side where I see Thorn watching us as he touches himself. My eyes drop to his cock and I can't help but lick my lips. His eyes dart to mine before dropping to my mouth.

"Thorn, let me taste you," I pant and he groans before moving to my side, even as Maxen keeps fucking me. I am so close, I can feel it. He doesn't go gentle like I expect. Instead, he cups my jaw hard, making me open my lips and thrusts inside. When Maxen pulls out, Thorn thrusts in until I am a sweating, needy mess, moaning around Thorn's cock.

I can feel myself winding higher and higher and Maxen's thrusts stutter for a moment. "She's so fucking close, I can feel her," he groans to Thorn.

I have to hold in my gag as Thorn thrusts in deeper than ever, hollowing my cheeks as much as I can to accommodate his size. It's not pretty and refined, it's pure fucking lust as they both fuck me.

When Maxen reaches down and hoists one of my legs over his shoulder, I am done. The orgasm rips through me so fast that I scream, almost choking on Thorn's cock as I clench around Maxen. He comes with a groan, locked inside of my pussy. I have to slip Thorn out of my mouth to breath, but I wrap one hand around his cock, needing him to come with us. Two pumps later and he comes on my chest with a yell. Maxen collapses to my left and Thorn to my right, until we are just a jumble of bodies.

"Fucking hell," Maxen mumbles and I can't help but laugh, the others soon join in as we all snuggle into each other, ready to face tomorrow together.

DISTRACTIONS AND DEATH

D ray is talking to me, but I can't concentrate on a word he is
saying. Something is still bugging me and looking around
now at the people gathered, I can't help but wonder what. Last
night was a distraction, an amazing one, but a distraction nonetheless. My body is jittery and my mind is screaming at me. When
the first shout erupts, I am not surprised.

Dray and I burst into a sprint, following the gesturing Seeker
through the front door of the house and out onto the gravel. Once
there, I see a crowd gathered around the side of the house, I follow
after Dray and burst through the throng, only to stumble back.

'Missed me, pet? Meet me at The Summit.'

Is scrawled in blood across the side of the house, it's dry so I
know it must have been done at the same time as the attack, I can
only blame the panic and burial on not noticing it, but now that I
have... I think through his words, there has to be more to it than
that. Why come all this way to leave a vague threat... either way, I
need to get back to The Summit and warn them that Ivar is on
his way.

Dray turns to me as my mind finally clicks on... he would have already been on his way to The Summit for him to have left this message, which means us coming here was to get me out of the way so he would have access to the leaders.

"It was a fucking distraction!" I yell at him before taking off at a sprint. Luckily, I have all my weapons strapped on and I am dressed for riding, having planned to leave later in the day to carry on The Summit. Maxen bursts through the front door and when he sees my face he sprints to my side.

"What's wrong?" he asks, panic winding through his face as he searches my body for injuries.

"It was a distraction. He wanted us here, he wanted a head start. He could already be there, we have to warn them!" I shout, a panic like never before curling in my chest. Major, Nan, Priest, Reeves, Dr Perfect Face... all of them are in danger. If he gets there, he will kill them all, and then no one will be left to stop him.

With a growl, I jog through the house, grabbing my already packed bag before trying to leave the room. Maxen runs in with the others following closely behind, even Dray and Vasilisy are there, a hard look on their faces.

"Mi Alma, what are you doing?" Maxen asks, arms folded as he blocks the doorway.

"I can ride fast, I know shortcuts, I might be able to get there and warn them before he makes it," I shout, dropping my bag and staring him down, ready to fight through him if I need to. He looks at me as his face drops, making me feel like shit.

"You would go through me? I am only trying to help..." he whispers, before moving out of the way, his jaw clenching as he looks at the wall, ignoring me.

Fuck, I don't have time for this. I glance at the open doorway and back at him. "I have to ride fast, I need to warn the leaders. I gathered them there like a fucking offering for him. This is my responsibility, I have to stop this," I finish, hesitating as I pick up my bag and sling it over my shoulder. Dray steps forward.

"I need to reinforce my camp..." He hesitates, and I know the feeling. I offer him a small strained smile.

"I know, stay here, catch up when you can."

He growls before turning and punching the wall, his back heaving with his breaths.

"I will be okay," I say softly, and I watch as he hunches his shoulders.

"You shouldn't face him alone," he growls.

"He might not even be there yet, the quicker you finish, the quicker you can be at my side. In fact..." I turn to the guys. "Help him? Please, it could be a trap. Getting me to leave so they can attack again. I need someone here I can trust." I watch as their faces close down.

"No," Jax says, dismissing my idea instantly.

"Jax—"

"I said no!" he shouts, his face enraged. He steps forward and faces me. "You are not rushing back there, he could be waiting for all we know. We go together."

"Baby, please. I can't have any more blood on my hands, I have to warn them, but I need you here. I need you to help Dray, then you can follow me. We will only be apart for a couple of hours."

He stares me down and Drax steps up to his side, his face serious. Blowing out a breath he stares at me, his hand restraining his brother. "Are you sure about this?" he asks.

Swallowing hard I nod. "It's the best plan we have."

"Then that is what we do," Drax says, his voice hard before dropping me a wink, making me smile.

I see Thorn and Maxen start to argue and he shouts over them. "Shut the fuck up. The more we argue, the less time we have to catch up. Taz is right. She knows this man better than us and she has never steered us wrong yet. So, have a bit of fucking faith in our girl, brothers, or I will kick your ass for her." He winces at my dirty look, then he carries on. "Okay, I will help her kick your ass. So, pull up your panties and let's get this shit done."

"Well fuck," I murmur before leaning into Drax and dropping a kiss on his lips. "Thank you," I whisper only for him.

"Always baby," he whispers back before turning to the others with an expectant look in his eyes.

Thorn steps forward, his eyes sad and worried. "Stay safe babygirl, we will be right behind you." I nod and close my eyes as he leans in and presses a lingering kiss to my forehead, making my heart pound.

He turns and leaves the room without looking back, a determined Drax on his heels. Jax blows out a breath and turns to me. "Wait for us." Is all he says before leaving without a goodbye.

Maxen is last, still hesitating before stepping close to me. "Stay safe, Mi Alma. Remember, we are always with you." He covers my heart before yanking me close and smashing our lips together. He lets go as fast as he grabbed me, leaving me reeling from the desperate kiss. With a nod, he turns and leaves as well.

I turn to Dray and Vasilisy, who steps forward. "I will come with you, little queen." I don't even have time to argue before he too has left.

"Ride hard and ride fast, soulmate, I will be chasing you like always." I nod and Dray steps forward so we are toe to toe. "If he is there, you fucking kill that bastard, but save some for me." I grin at him and he grins back, his belief in me making my back harden. He doesn't kiss me or offer sweet words, instead he pulls the blade he gave me the night before and pushes it into my hands. "Keep this hidden, just in case." I nod again, like a broken doll, and he turns, striding away before stopping at the door with his back to me.

"Oh, and Worth? Don't you dare have too much fun without me, I want to make a Berserker coat before the day is through." With that, he leaves to sort his people and I am alone. Alone for the first time in months. It's cold and I feel paranoid, but I have managed all my life, I can manage for the few hours it will take them to sort out the Seekers. I know this is the best plan, but why do my bones ache and my heart hurt? My stomach churns and I feel as if every decision I am making is costing lives, I just hope it isn't my own.

Steeling my spine, I leave the room, descending the steps with my head high and my face blank. Vasilisy waits for me at the bottom of the steps, with our bikes. Swinging on, I don't look back before I gun it, I can't afford the weakness that it would show. Not now, not when I know I am going to face Ivar before the day is through. Today, I bring back the old Worth, with a few new perks. I grin at the thought and run my hand down my leg until I feel the knife Dray gave me.

Sands below, don't let me be too late.

Vasilisy and I ride hard, not stopping, pushing our bikes to the limit. I can hear mine rattling even as I press the gas. He follows me, leaning and swerving as we cross the back roads. Once we hit the main road out of Seeker territory, the land I know like the back of my hand comes into view and I go to town, hitting all the shortcuts I know. It's reckless and stupid, and if anyone attacks us now I wouldn't even see them coming, but my mind has narrowed to me getting back to The Ring in time to save them. I can hear my heartbeat as it crashes against my chest with every mile we travel, I can taste the sand as it kicks up and sprays my face. The air whistles past me, burning my ears, my eyes water from the speed and yet, I go faster still.

I don't even double check that Vasilisy is still with me as we hit a tunnel. Carved into a stone wall, buried under a mound of sand, is a tight old train tunnel. A passage from this side of the Wastes to The Ring. It's pitch black and there's a possibility it's filled with cannibals, but it will shave at least three hours off our ride, so I knuckle down and try to keep my breathing even.

I hear Vasilisy laugh as we gun it into the tunnel. He pulls up next to me as we flick on our bike lights. Groaning at the mess inside, I have to change gear and slow down so that I don't crash into the debris littering the passageway.

"I forgot how amazing it feels to be alive!" Vasilisy shouts as he dodges around a cement divider.

I glance over at him to see a crazy grin covering his face as he whoops and revs his bike. Shaking my head, I turn back to face the tunnel, only to swear and swerve as a body flies out of a hole in the tunnel wall. I swerve so fast the bike goes down and sends me skidding across the concrete, the bike following me. I smash into a sandbag and quickly roll as the bikes smashes, two seconds later, right where I was not a moment before. I don't have time to catch my breath, I grab a sword in one hand and my whip in the other.

Crouching, I wait. Vasilisy jumps from his bike as it is still moving and slides to my side, yanking his axe from his back and holding it with both hands. He roars into the tunnel, daring them to come at us.

A horrible noise sounds from the darkness, a mix of laughter and choking. Gritting my teeth, I wait. I don't have time for this shit.

"No playing with your food, I want to be back on the road in two minutes," I warn Vasilisy. I see his grin stretch from the corner of my eye.

"Aye, little queen. How about a friendly competition then?"

I tilt my head in consideration, even as I hear something dragging through the dark, echoing around the tunnel. "What kind?"

"Most kills?" he replies, tightening his grip on his axe and I do the same, hearing them get closer, scuttling in the dark like the vermin they are.

"You got it," I reply when the first one jumps into view, landing on all fours with its head tilted and its nose in the air. The bike's broken light shines a path and I can see that its eyes are white, fogged over, it's obvious it is blind. Makes sense if it lives down here, and when it sniffs again and lets out a coughing chuckle, I groan.

"It can smell you, I told you that you needed to shower," I taunt Vasilisy.

"You little fo–" He cuts off as one of them flies from a pile of debris and straight at him.

I grin and decide I am bored of waiting, plus, Berserkers take this shit seriously. Getting a running start, I leap into the air the same time the cannibal pushes off from the ground like an animal on all fours. We meet each other mid-air and twist as we fall to the floor. I roll and spin into a crouch to meet its teeth bearing down on me. An evil smirk crosses my face and I see its eyes widen too late, as I aim my sword from the floor and its own momentum propels it until it's skewered on my sword. Using the movement, I turn with it and pull my sword from its gaping mouth, its eyes open and empty.

"One!" I shout and I hear Vasilisy curse.

Grinning, I turn when I hear movement behind me. A cannibal comes sprinting around the corner, but instead of mindlessly flinging itself at me, it darts in and stops, trying to figure out where I am. Good, at least this won't be easy and I can work off some of my aggression.

I draw up my sword and stand silently, waiting. It stops moving and tilts its head to the side, crawling slowly around me in a circle. I don't move to keep it in my eyesight, instead, I stay staring forward, my ears trained on the little huffs it keeps releasing. I block out Vasilisy and wait.

It lets out a high-pitched scream and it grates on my nerves. When I don't make a noise, it starts to get mad and scratches at the ground, its unseeing eyes flickering back and forth. It stops in front of me, sniffing at the ground and I smile. I tap my chest lightly and it growls before pouncing, but I'm not there anymore. I slip behind it and using my whip, wrap it around its neck. It starts thrashing, more horrible inhuman noises emitting from its blood encrusted mouth.

"One!" Vasilisy shouts and I grunt, tightening my grip on the cannibal.

Gritting my teeth, I yank, a scuffling behind me has me looking over my shoulder to see two more coming my way. "Motherfuck–" Twisting and yanking with everything in me I hear its neck snap, and I drop it quickly with my whip still wrapped around it and grab my other sword and wait.

"Two," I yell breathlessly.

"Ya cheatin!" he hollers back, making me laugh even as a cannibal flies through the air. Ducking to the side, I spin so my back is facing the tunnel wall and they are both in my eye line.

"Come on, all you can eat buffet right here!" I yell, holding my arms out to my sides. Both cannibals turn to me and let out a scream.

"Yeah, yeah, come and get me. I taste better than that old bastard." I crouch as I talk, grinning at the curses flying from Vasilisy's mouth.

"I'll gi you old bastard, ya little shite," he yells back, grunting as he fights.

One flies at me and I grunt as it hits my chest, sending me back into the wall. I manage to get one of my swords between its head and mine, but it is using the weight of its body to pin the other to my chest. I can see the other one circling and know if I don't move soon, I could be cannibal fodder. No thanks, I only like to be eaten for fun.

I have to turn my head away as its face gets closer, its rancid breath hitting me as it chomps on air trying to reach me. When I spot Vasilisy's fallen flamethrower next to me, I let out a breathless laugh. Turning my head back, I blow a kiss at the cannibal before using the wall and pushing us. It tumbles back, not expecting it, and while it's on its two legs I kick out, hitting it in the chest until it flies back to the floor.

I drop my sword, a risky move, and turn and sprint to where I saw the flamethrower. I can almost feel their breath on my back and I jump, rolling over the hard cement and grabbing it as I go.

"Eat this, motherfucker!" I shout as I point the flamethrower. Pulling the trigger, I watch in rapt fascination as a column of flame shoots out and hits the cannibals mid-leap.

The noise they make burrows through my head and the smell has me sneezing, but I don't let up until they have stopped writhing and are nothing more than charcoal curled up on the floor. Letting go of the flamethrower, I lean back on the floor.

"Four!" I shout.

"Ah, ya fuckin' won," Vasilisy says as he walks over, kicking through the bodies and making the ashes float away, he offers me his hand and I grab it, hauling myself to my feet. Looking around I spot the dead cannibals and our bikes.

"Time to go," I say and he nods. I pass back the flamethrower and he cradles it like a baby, glaring at me. Backing away with my hands up, I laugh.

"You dropped it!" Turning, I right my bike and kick the gas to make sure it still works. When it roars to life, I jump on.

"Forget something?" Vasilisy asks, holding up my sword and whip, and I gape at him. He passes them over and it's my turn to cradle my weapons like a baby before sheathing the blade and wrapping my whip back up.

He jumps on his bike and spins in a circle, showing off, and I roll my eyes before setting off through the empty tunnel, the smell of barbequed cannibal following us.

WE GET BACK on track, anxiety nudging me again and making me remember why we were rushing, although not nearly as bad as before. I think the fight helped me think clearer and I know hurrying and getting myself killed won't change anything, even if I hate being patient.

I slow down to a pace that won't kill us if we crash, not by much though, and we ride silently, both our minds locked on what we will find when we get there.

About twenty minutes later, we see the top of the building as The Ring comes into view. I look back at Vasilisy before speeding up slightly. We pull into the car park, and park at the very back, just in case. Turning off my bike, I look around for any vehicles I might recognise. Frowning, I smack my bike. I forgot how busy it was because of The Summit, any of them could be Berserker rides and I wouldn't know. We are walking in blind and I hate it.

Taking a deep breath, I swing my leg off the bike and stand next to it.

"Ya ready, little queen?" Whenever Vasilisy's emotions run high his accent gets more pronounced, to the point I can barely understand him, like right now.

"Let's do it." I nod and we walk side by side towards the closed gate of The Ring.

Chapter Twenty Five

THE DECISION

I know something is wrong when I reach the gates and no guards greet me. "Fuck," I mutter, my heart slamming into my rib cage as I take a deep breath. He's here, isn't he? I always thought I would be filled with rage, an avenging warrior woman, screaming as I fling myself at him... but I find terror racing through my veins, fighting with anger at the thought of seeing him. One day I knew I would, and I know I will kill him or die trying, but I also know that man is responsible for some of the darkest, most painful times of my life. He played my strings like a puppet, ripped out my soul and rebuilt it. So, yes, anger is there, but so is terror. Terror that I might freeze, that I might retreat back into myself. Nothing more than his pet...

"You think you will ever be free of me, pet?" he pants. "You think I will ever let you go? You. Are. Mine!" he screams the last, spittle flying from his bust lip and raining blood and spit down onto my upturned face.

I just stare back, my face blank and my eyes dead. What more can he do to me? He took my only friend, broke my body, and stole my innocence. All that is left is death, and I would welcome that with open arms. The thought makes my lips stretch in a smile.

He watches it form on my face and lets out a wordless scream, his eyes crazed and his crown titling with his movement. I stare at him impassively, waiting for the next hit, but instead, he steps back, his control returning as an evil glint enters his eyes.

"You aren't bothered about me hurting you, but what about hurting the people you care about, pet?" he taunts, and I launch myself from the chair as he laughs.

Stepping closer, pushing past the memories, I spy the writing through the gates. No doubt Ivar's pet torturer's handy work.

"Are you ready to play, pet?" Scrawled in blood.

"We could wait here for the others," Vasilisy adds, his voice hard like he doesn't want to wait.

"Wouldn't make a difference, we both know they are watching us. They knew the minute we pulled up; if we try and wait they will only come and get us. Better we go in on our own terms," I say, blowing out a breath.

"Aye, least ya can protect your men," he adds, both of us just staring at the gates.

Gritting my teeth, I unlock the gate and push, when it doesn't budge I start to get angry, all the worry and panic at seeing Ivar again spirals into pure, red-hot fury. I let it out with a cry, kicking out and smashing the gates back into the posts at the side. I look at Vasilisy and he grins.

"Now, *that* is how you make an entrance, little queen." We share a grin before turning back to face The Ring.

I might die as soon as I get in there, but sands below, I will die on my own two feet, free.

As soon as we step through the gates, I hear the whispers of the Berserkers obviously watching us. I decide to ignore them, they won't attack. Not without orders, and they are probably waiting to see what I will do.

Holding my head up high, I walk down the same dirt path I have a million times. I just hope it won't be my last. I feel like I am walking to my death, and it makes me look around with a new light. I once thought of this place as my cage, but glancing around now, I can smile at all the beauty and happiness I had here. I met Major, the man, in his own words, is an asshole. But an asshole who saved me, trusted in me, loved me when no one else did. He fought for me when my own father wouldn't. I finally gave into my men here, I let them in, I trusted them. The Ring is an important place for me, it's a place of change, so it makes sense I would meet my end here.

We walk past the empty ring, a feat by itself. I wonder what they did with all the clan's warriors, I think idly, eyeing the silent fighting ring which was full the other day when we came. When the house comes into view, I spot the Berserkers waiting on the steps.

"No matter wha happens, little queen, I will be by your side and we will go down fighting." Vasilisy reaches across the small space between us as we stand and stare at the steps. When his hand touches mine, I allow myself a second of comfort.

"Thank you, for fighting by my side, you didn't have to," I say softly, just for us.

"It wa a pleasure, I get to say I finally saw a true queen." I grin over at the crazy bastard and he grins back. Who knew I would grow to care for a Berserker so much? Ivar jaded my view of them, and if Vasilisy is anything to go by, they can't all be bad. Maybe I can use that to my advantage, I just don't know how.

When the door to the house opens, we split apart, our stances turning ready, just in case. Ivar's pet torturer steps out, shielding his eyes from the light as he looks around, before his eyes land on us. I can see the evil grin from here and I have to grit my teeth. Looking at him now, no longer a child, I can see that he is not the big monster I made him out to be in my head. In fact, I am probably the same size as him, he just has more muscle, but it's his sick mind that is the worst. He is so twisted and cruel, and I know what it is like to be on the receiving end of that.

Strengthening my back, I refuse to cower. He might have seen me at my darkest, but he will also see me at my strongest. Striding across the sand, I meet him on the steps, stepping up each one until we are equal and mere meters apart. Vasilisy's heat moves behind me, watching my back as I stare down the monster in front of me.

"He is waiting for you," is all he says, his eyes sparkling with delight and madness as his lips curl up into a big smile. His cheeks crinkle and the lines around his eyes show that time has not been kind to him. I should be filled with terror, but I know whatever they do to me will not matter. They have done it before and I will die knowing the taste of freedom and love, and they can't take that away from me. So instead, I stare right back, waiting for him to lead the way.

"Looks like the kitten finally got her claws," he mocks and the two warriors flanking the door laugh. I cut them a look and they snap their mouths shut, making me smile.

"You have no idea. Now, unless you want me to use them on you, I suggest you show us inside." I arch my eyebrow and wait like I have all the time in the world.

"I hope he lets me play with you first," he sneers, his eyes lighting up with lust, but not just for my body, for my screams and pain. He gets off on it, I remember that like it was yesterday.

"In your dreams, now move the fuck out of my way," I demand, tilting my head and showing him how serious I am. I am tired of this dick measuring contest.

He stares me down for a second before something flashes in his eyes and he steps back, still locked with my gaze. When I arch my eyebrow and roll my eyes, he turns and opens the door. Stepping inside I get a sense of déjà vu. It feels like it was weeks ago when I turned up here for The Summit, although it was only a matter of days, so filled with hope that we could come together and defeat Ivar. So much has happened, so much blood has been spilled in that short amount of time, all reminding me exactly who I was dealing with. It was a child's dream that The Summit would work, and we could all rally together and defeat Ivar. He is always one step ahead, and it only shows now more than ever.

Where I followed rules and sat and fought through the political bullshit, he was breaking treaties and slaughtering people, making his moves on the chessboard, playing dirty. I guess it's my turn, fuck the rules. Fuck the politics; I was always better at fighting than talking.

The blood from Priest's punishment is dried in a puddle on the floor, but there are also new splashes spread around the hallway. The red is bright against the white paint, a warning.

"Looks like you had some fun," I say dryly, trying not to think of whose blood it might be.

"Not as much as I would have liked," he replies with a wink, which sends a cold shiver through my body. I try to think logically, he wouldn't have killed any of the leaders, including Major and Nan. It would be a stupid ploy, I just hope they didn't piss him off at all... they are not exactly discreet with their thoughts and if they sent him into a rage...

I even hope Doc and the Paradise people are okay.

When we reach the doors to The Summit meeting room, I ignore the two scav bodies propped up next to it like honour guards. Blood covers the walls and I have to breathe in shallow breaths from the stench of piss and shit. People died here, quite a few from the smell of it.

Vasilisy has been quiet throughout, following my lead, but I hear him mutter under his breath when the smell hits him. I wish I could say it is like those movies I watched when I was younger, all dramatic and shit. The person died, their eyes slowly closing as a peaceful expression crossed their faces. Instead, death is just an end, and not a pretty one. It's not dignified and peaceful, especially like this. Your body shuts down, expelling the waste, and it's painful, their eyes hold their terror of their own demise, and they will be frozen that way forever. I notice their clothes have been removed too, not even death allows them peace. That's Ivar's way. Even now they are humiliated and paraded about, smeared in shit and blood. Another reminder. When I spot what they have done to their genitals, I have to hold in the bile that wants to rise from my stomach. Gritting my teeth and pulling my lips shut tight, I try to look away, but when I do I meet his eyes and see the delight there. He was waiting for my reaction.

His eyes meet mine as he touches her. The ferals were dragged away by some Berserkers while I was tied to the wall outside, my hands chained to the top, and my feet spread and chained to a boulder next to it. The freezing wind up here chills me to my bone, even as the sun shines down on us. I don't want to look, I don't want to see but I know if I don't, Ivar will only make it worse, do something worse. So my eyes lock with his, Ivar's pet torturer, as he plays with the remnants of Petal's... no I can't think of her like that otherwise my mind will break, her...her body.

Crouched on the other side of her body so I can see him clearly, and him me, he drops his hand into the hole the ferals made in her stomach and rummages around. Bile rises and I have to swallow repeatedly, I will not be sick. I will not be sick. I repeat it until the need disappears. I try to think of other things but when his hand raises from her half-eaten body, covered in blood and other things, I can't keep the horrified gasp from escaping. He grins, knowing he is getting to me. When his hand opens, I see the lump of a red bloody organ and my face pales. He raises it slowly, and still with his eyes locked on me, takes a bite. Blood smears around his face and when the scent of it hits me, I can't keep the contents of my stomach down. He laughs hard, throwing his head back, showing me the half-eaten organ and the blood coating his teeth. I retch again and my vomit splashes down the front of my clothing as tears are squeezed out of the corners of my eyes.

"Do you like my handiwork? I think they are some of my best yet." His voice brings me back and I meet his eyes. We stare each other down as the door behind him opens.

My eyes flick up automatically and my heart stops at the man who stands there.

"Hello, pet." Ivar's smile is wide and cheerful as he looks at me, his crown sitting on his head and his wide, scar-filled chest covered in weapons. His tight leather pants are the ones that he always wears, and his hair has grown. After all these years, I am finally facing my demons. The man who twisted and carved me, Ivar The Destroyer.

I can't help but drop my hand to grab my blade and he sees me do it, his head throws back and that familiar laugh booms out, running across my skin and raising memories.

"Now, now, pet. Is that any way to greet me? Why don't you come and have a seat, it seems we have things to talk about and everyone is waiting." He steps aside, and I glance around him to see Major, Nan, Reeves, and Priest all sitting ramrod straight in their seats around the table. Doc stands at the back, as do some of the other Paradise guards. Berserkers are everywhere, covering every surface, some even asleep on the floor and it's obvious why none of the leaders tried to make a break for it. They are quite literally trapped with the devil.

UNDER THE CAREFUL scrutiny of everyone, I make my way

inside and to the chair left free for me, the one to the left of the head of the table, where Major sat last time.

I don't want to sit down, I don't want to be at that disadvantage, but I know I have to. Gritting my teeth, I sit slowly, at the edge of my chair, ready to move if anything happens. I jump when a hand lands on my leg under the table and squeezes. Looking to my right, I nod at Major. He looks like he doesn't have a worry in the world even though one of his eyes is black and blue, and his lip is split. His hair is out of place and his suit ripped, yet he sits there like he is still the leader here and I respect the hell out of him for it. I watch as Vasilisy gets manhandled to stand with his back to the wall next to Doc. I nod at him and he relaxes slightly before glaring at the two Berserkers tugging him. They back away quickly which makes him grin.

I run my eyes over the rest of the leaders. Priest's face is blank, but I can see the quiet fury burning in his eyes. Reeves looks pissed, there is no other word for it, his face is an ugly purple shade and his nostrils are flaring as he glares at every Berserker in here. I look at Nan last. She looks calm, way too calm, the type where she usually just starts shooting people. Her nose is obviously broken, and dried blood has dripped down her face, and onto her pearls, then finally to stain her pink cardigan. One of her eyes is sealing shut with bruising and I can't see her handy shotgun anywhere.

A Berserker stands nearly straight behind her, his face covered in blood with a massive cut marring his neck, his eyes are locked on the back of Nan's head with a searing intensity and I am betting she did that to him, you gotta love her.

Ivar walks around the table, strutting as everyone watches him. When he reaches the free chair at the head of the table, he looks around before dropping into the seat, casually and leaning back, watching us.

"A little birdie told me a Summit had been called, but that can't be correct or I would have been invited." He points out, grabbing some food from a plate, which is put in front of him, and eating casually. With his mouth full he carries on, spitting half chewed food with each word. "So, why don't you tell me why you are all here... it wouldn't have anything to do with me, would it?" He finishes the food and stares around.

Major clears his throat and Ivar's eyes snap to him. I want to take the heat away, draw his gaze to protect Major from the murder and hate darting around in the madness that is Ivar, but I can't. Major would never let me. "A Summit was called, to discuss the borders of the clans."

Ivar snorts, obviously smelling the bullshit, and his eyes flicker to me for a second, but it's enough of a warning for me to shift in my seat, sliding sideways to protect Major as much as I can without looking obvious.

"Don't lie to me ring maker," he warns, his voice low and deadly. I know he takes in my stance because a smile curves his lips, pulling up at the scarred side of his face. "I know why you are gathered, you think you can overthrow me. You think you can start a war!" he screams the last, the spittle flying from his mouth and hitting me, but I don't bother wiping it away, not daring to move in case he snaps.

"Can ya blame us, eh? You have lost it!" Nan shouts, leaning forward with a defiant look in her eyes. I freeze when Ivar lets out a chuckle. I know he will remember that and what Major said. He will make them pay and the thought chills me to my bones.

"I called it," I say, sitting back in my chair, and when his eyes land on me I don't even flinch.

"Oh, little pet, you don't think I know that? I have eyes and ears everywhere. It was so funny watching you run around and play hero, trying to save everyone, trying to convince these fucking cowards to join you. What would you have done, eh? Marched up to my castle, demanded my head on a pike? I don't think so, you are still that broken little slave girl." Laughter starts from the Berserkers in the room.

"That's where you are wrong," I say, silencing the room. "I wouldn't have asked for your head, I would have gotten it myself." I smile, my mask clearly in place and his face wipes clean, nothing but anger there. Good, get mad, forget the insult Major and Nan threw your way. I can take it.

"Is that right, pet? Think you can take me? I think you would freeze, you would hesitate. You are still soft. Still weak." He leans forward, spitting the words in my face. I don't lean away even as his hand darts out and grabs my chin, twisting and putting pressure painfully on it. "You are nothing but what I want you to be, you've had your fun and now it's time to come home. Don't make me kill them all to do it." He warns, the truth in his eyes. He would, he would kill every single person in the Waste to get to me.

"Why?" I ask, the question haunting me since I was little, I search his eyes for the answer, holding in my wince as he puts more pressure on my chin.

"You are mine and I wasn't finished with you yet," he says, like I am stupid for asking.

Looking into his face I debate his words. He really would start a war because of one slave, because he didn't get to break me and kill me? He would really jeopardise everything for me? Yes, yes he would. He really is crazy, Major was right. He has lost it.

"No, I will never come with you. I will slit my own throat first," I admit and he grins before leaning in, his lips touching mine.

"I was hoping you would say that, pet." He kisses me hard, biting my lip as he goes, and blood explodes in my mouth. I yank my head away, ripping from his grip, and pant as blood drops down my bruised chin onto my chest.

With his eyes on me, he talks to his men. "Bring me the dishonoured."

I freeze when I hear the Berserkers jumping to do his bidding. He smiles at the anger running through me, and carries on, "Kill those insects at the Seeker compound."

My heart stops as I stare at him in shock, he can't mean my men...

How? We checked the whole compound for Berserkers, but I see the glee in his eyes. He can get to them, I know it from that look alone. I have to do something, I have to stop them, I have to protect them. What will make him hesitate, what can I use against him? I rack my brain, and when I finally form a plan, a peace settles in my chest like this was what was supposed to happen all along.

Grabbing my knife, I ignore the Berserkers as they all move to intercept me, obviously thinking I am going for Ivar. "Do that and I will kill myself right now." Holding the knife to my own throat I stare at him, showing him how serious I am. I would slit my throat, I would do anything to protect them. "Hmm, then what would you do. Your little pet would be bleeding out and it wouldn't be by your hand. You want me, you need me, so kill them and I will take that all away from you."

I can feel everyone holding their breath as I challenge Ivar, playing his own game. I let him decide what he wants to do, it's in his hands now. Finally, his face turns red and he looks away. "Ignore that order," he spits out at his men and turns to me again. "You are going to pay for that," he says, and I nod, dropping the knife. As soon as I do, he snaps his arm out and grabbing my head, smashes my face into the desk. I hear my nose crunch and I can taste the copper tang of my own blood. My ears ring and my head spins. I don't even notice he has let go of my head until I push back and I raise my head. Major is out of his seat and Nan is squaring up to a Berserker. Doc and Vasilisy have weapons to two Berserkers and everyone is waiting to see what I will do. It would be suicide to attack them now, and no matter what I said, I don't want to die.

"I'm fine, sit down." Major searches my face before sliding back into his seat. Nan grumbles but does the same, only Doc and Vasilisy ignore me. "Now!" I shout, noticing the other Berserkers inching their way over. Vasilisy sighs but does as he is told, but Doc tightens his grip on the Berserker.

"Doc," I warn, and he flinches but doesn't drop it. "Evan!" I shout and I think it's the shock of hearing his name that makes him step back and look at me. "I'm okay, let him go." I gesture at the Berserker and he releases him. Turning back to Ivar, I ignore the agony ripping through my head and face him.

"Finished?" I ask, licking the blood trickling from my lips. He follows the movement, lust blooming in his eyes.

"For now." He nods before looking back at the others. "Now, where were we?"

"Being mental, as usual," Nan mutters, making me chuckle before I choke on my own blood.

I cough and sputter and only when Major leans across and smashes my back, do I spit out the blood on the once pristine table. "Thanks," I mutter hoarsely.

"You okay, kid?" he asks quietly.

I nod and look at him from under my lashes. "Stay quiet, don't antagonise him. We both know how this ends. You can always come after me, but we need you alive," I mutter and stop when a large fist smashes into the table under my face.

"What are we whispering about, pet?" Ivar asks.

"Nothin'," I reply, reaching up and grimacing when I feel my bent nose. Fucking great. It took weeks to heal last time, and it never set straight after it. Taking a deep breath I grab both side and twist, I have to hold in a scream as it clicks back into place, but when it does it feels ten times better.

"Good, so I will get straight to the point. You know what I

want, but I obviously need to remind the others who I am." He taps his chin and I go cold, I know that look. "So, I think I can do both at the same time."

He gets to his feet, his leather creaking as he moves and holds his hand out to the side. He doesn't even look, just expects it to happen, and it does. A gun lands in the palm of his hand and he quickly checks it before flicking off the safety. I rise slowly, and the others do the same. Stepping back from the table we move in closer until we create a circle. Rolling his eyes, Ivar rounds the table so there is nothing but air between us.

"Like I said, they must be reminded. I think killing one of them is fair enough, the others will soon scatter like the bugs they are and run back to their own little shit holes they call camps. I know who I want to kill, but the decision is yours pet." He raises the gun and points it to Major, then swings it to Nan. "Which one do I kill? They both offered me insult."

I freeze and turn my eyes from him to them. Nan stands up straight, ready for whatever happens, and Major takes a deep breath, resignation settling in his gaze. No, no this can't be happening. I can stop this. Grabbing the knife, I fumble with it to raise it to my throat.

"I don't think so pet, that might have worked once, but not again. You try to kill yourself and I will shoot them both then I will have my fun with your men." The threat is real and I quickly drop the blade to the floor. "Good girl," he purrs and I swallow hard, trying to think my way out of this.

"Decide, or I will. Who do I shoot?" he asks, his gun wavering between them both.

I shake my head, staring from it to them.

He gets tired "Fine. I will." When the shot goes off, I jerk like it hit me, and I turn as if in slow motion. I watch in dawning horror as a red patch blooms on Major's chest. He blinks before looking down. Chaos erupts, but all I do is stare as Ivar laughs. Major's mouth opens and closes before he stumbles forward. Automatically, I dart towards him, just in time to catch him as he crumples to his knees. Still numb, I lay him on his back and just stare.

"I'm sorry," he gasps, blood bubbling on his lips as his breathing turns erratic and his face pales. I panic, fluttering my hands over him, not knowing what to do, my emotions coming back with a bang.

"I'm sorry," I wheeze, turning to the room. "HELP HIM! I WILL DO ANYTHING!" I scream desperately until a cold hand lands on my arm, then I turn back to Major.

"It's okay, you will be okay." His voice is getting weaker, so I have to lean closer so no one else can hear us. "I love you, Tazanna Worth, make them pay. Be the woman I know—know you can." I sob as his breathing stops for a second. His eyes unfocused and he looks over my shoulder like he doesn't even see me. "I'm coming baby, I'm coming, Cara."

His body jerks a few times before he stops breathing, that horrible death rattle in his chest, until he is still, his eyes locked over my shoulder even as a smile twists his blood covered lips.

"No," I whisper, before I let out a heartbroken scream, ragged and wordless. It pours out of me and I can't seem to stop even as my arms are pulled back and I am dragged away. I fight them to get back to him. "I need to save him, I can save him. I have to!" I punch, kick and claw until they release me and then I scramble back to him, no not him, his body, one that is already cooling. His lips are blue and his face blank.

"No!" I cry. "I need to...I have to..."

I am pulled away again and I sag in their arms as they drag me from Major's body, roughly handling me, one thought ringing in my head. I have to bury him, I have to offer him rights or he won't cross and see his daughter again. It's what gets me fighting until I am nothing but an animal, biting, clawing, and attacking everything. My eyes widen too late as I see the pommel of the sword descending to my face. Something crunches, and I fall backwards as the room begins to darken. I fight with everything in me to keep myself here, there are things I need to do. Things I have to do. *Major...* It's my last thought as I succumb to the blackness edging my vision and I welcome it, anything to get away from the crippling agony of losing the man I loved as a father.

"*Little queen!*" comes a scream, but it's so far away and I am so cold, I am so tired.

CHAPTER TWENTY SIX

Don't Say Goodbye

"No, again," Major shouts from the side of the sand, watching me with a hard expression. He looks out of place here, with his perfect suit and well-mannered looks, but he obviously knows what he is doing. So, I pick myself up and go again, and again, until my body is one big aching muscle and I can hold the sword properly. When I get a hit on the guard and defeat him, I can't help but grin, looking towards Major. The look of pride he beams at me makes all the pain and effort worth it.

"Good, tomorrow we will teach you two swords," he calls, walking towards me, ignoring the dirt gathering on his pristine black shoes.

Swinging the practice sword casually in an arc, I grin. "Two swords, huh? I like the idea of that." We share a smile before we are interrupted by a ring guard running onto the sand.

When he reaches us, he hesitates before whispering in Major's ear, I see his face shut down. All trace of emotions wiped away. He nods and looks at me, instantly my back straightens and I know it is bad news.

"He is back. Best go and get ready." His face is calm, but his voice wavers with anger and before I can question him on it, he spins on his heel and leaves the fighting pit. All my excitement drops away and my shoulders hunch. I had three days, three whole fucking days of not seeing him. I wonder if this is what it feels like to be free?

"Little queen," comes a desperate whisper. I know that voice. I start to swim up from the memory but as soon as I do, I can feel it. The pain, the pure unfiltered agony rolling through my body. My heart feels like it's being pulled from my chest and my lungs are tight. My face feels like someone took a hammer to it, but it's the bone deep sadness that has me flinching away, back into the safe and almost happy place of my memories. I hesitate, not wanting to abandon whoever is whispering to me, but as I float there in blissful torment I slip away again, with nothing or no one to hold on to. It's just me.

Looking into the tiny dirty mirror, I stare at the creature I have become. I was in his care for two hours, although they felt like a century, and this is what happened. For the last three days I had become more, the bruises had faded and I had forgotten to flinch when people came near me. Yet two hours with him and I am nothing more than a shell again. My face is bruised, broken. My left eye will be black and my cheekbone hurts so much he might have broken it. My bottom lip is double its normal size and a gash runs across my entire forehead from his cane. I know I won't be able to sit down and my back will have more scars. I think the only thing he didn't touch were my legs. Lucky me.

Then I start to get angry, this defeated looking creature can't be me. I hate it. I hate the weakness and fear in her eyes. I hate the sunken, dead acceptance. My fist cocks back before I can stop it and smashes into the mirror, shattering it. My reflection still stares back at me, but from a million tiny pieces. Shattered, like me. It helped, so I do it again and again, screaming as my knuckles are cut open, yet I can't stop. The anger has to go somewhere and what is one more pain?

I don't even hear him until he catches my fist mid swing, gently turning it over to show me the destroyed knuckles. Blood is running freely and dropping to the floor, I can see the inside of my muscle and, I am pretty sure, some bone. I look up from his perfectly manicured hand holding my destroyed one, until I meet his eyes. There I see the anger I feel, the heartbreak and utter desperation, but why does he care? I am no one, I am just a slave.

"No, never," he mutters hoarsely, making me realise I spoke out loud. "You are so much more than that, you are a fighter. You are a survivor." Looking down, he rubs some of the blood away from the edge of my fingers "You will heal, and you will thrive, I can see it in your eyes... you are like me."

"Why do you care?" I ask, not giving a shit if it gets me punished. He's too kind to me, it's too much. He must want something, he wouldn't teach me to fight, teach me to protect myself, feed me, clothe me, and spend his nights telling me stories if he did not. It's just how the world works.

He blows out a breath, his eyes searching mine. "Because, kid, what kind of world do we live in where I can watch a young girl be destroyed right in front of me and not care? You take each shot and keep moving, that's why I care. I care because I can save you... no that's not right. You can save yourself, but I want to help." The honesty in his expression and words stagger me, and he watches me as hope blooms to life in his eyes, mirroring what I am feeling in my chest. I stare at him with stars in my eyes; can he really mean what he says? It's stupid, but I trust him. He spent three weeks earning that trust, so why don't I give him the benefit of the doubt.

"Are you okay?" he asks softly, still holding my hand.

Three simple words, but something no one has asked me for a long time, because no one cares. Three simple words and Major has my heart. I throw myself into his arms, sobbing all my pain and fear *away. He holds me here in the locker room of the pit, his arms wrapped around me like he will let no one ever hurt me again as I bloody his perfect white shirt.*

"I've got you, kid, I've got you," he whispers, squeezing me tighter as I curl my fists into his shirt and hold on tight, like I might be snatched away from him at any minute. "We will get through this, I have a plan. I'll get you out, you can come and live here, and we can work through all the books you eyed up in my library when you didn't think I noticed." I snort out a desperate laugh and tilt my head back to look into his sincere eyes. His hand comes up and cups my face. "You're going to be okay kid, you can get through anything, just remember to fight with everything you have in you..."

The memory starts to fade, and I can feel my body again, with an anguished cry I try to hold on, try to bury myself back in his arms, but it's no good. I can feel it fading around me, and the last thing I see is that fucking soft smile and eyes so full of love and pride for me.

"I love you," I whisper as he fades away and I am left looking at the ceiling of a moving car. Blinking, I groan before I remember to be quiet, my whole body hurts. I forgot what it felt like to be in constant pain. I don't want to, but looking won't make it less real, so I slowly turn my head, having to close my eyes for a second when my vision spins. Fuck, I couldn't even fight my way out of a scav den at the moment. I spot Vasilisy first, I must be laid on his legs, my head propped up because he is staring, no glaring, at the other people in the car, his back is ramrod straight and his hands are clenched in anger. He glances down when he feels my gaze and shakes his head slightly. I get the idea and flutter my lashes shut so I can only see through the slits, if anyone glances my way they will think I am still passed out. Slowly, to not draw attention to myself, I turn again, until I can see the rest of the car. I have to stop halfway again, when my head feels like it will explode, but keeping my breathing even and shallow, I finally have my head turned to face the rest of the car. I count three Berserkers in the back and there must be two in the front. It looks like we are in one of the war cars, as Ivar calls them, basically an old modded army truck.

I don't want to talk, but I am curious how long we have been on the road and when we are going to make our move. Thinking through my options, I work through my body at the same time, testing to see if anything is broken. When it doesn't seem to be, I let the pain consume me for a moment before pushing it away. Sands below, I can't fight off an army right now. I just need to bide my time, allow my body some time to heal so that I can fight. With that thought in mind, I close my eyes again, keeping my breathing nice and even, and lose myself while still being aware of my surroundings, which is harder than it sounds with my heart breaking in my chest as I remember what happened.

God, Major.

His name sends a throb of pain and grief through my chest like a knife. I thought he was unkillable, so strong and sure, logic backing him up and the laws keeping him safe. At least now I am breaking no treaty by killing Ivar, he did that when he killed the leader of the safe zone. No blood will be shed in The Ring, outside of the fighting pit, or they forfeit their life. It's something drilled into me by Major and I thank him for that now.

I guess most people would skirt around the pain, trying to forget it, but I do the opposite. I let it consume me. I let it grow inside of me until I am nothing but the rage he created. I think of all the people I have lost: my brother, my father, Petal, Noah, and now Major. I let the hate and fury twist inside until I don't know where I end and it begins. It is what will get me through this.

I GUESS I must doze off, my head wound worse than I expected, because I am awoken when the truck jolts to a stop. "We are here, little queen."

I nod and groan at my own stupidity, at least the pain isn't as bad as the last time I woke up. *Yay for little things.* We jerk to a full stop and I sit up slowly, facing the blank faced Berserkers opposite us on the bench. I think the only reason I woke up with all my clothes on is that Vasilisy worked as a watchdog. Even now his eyes follow their every movement, the sweet, funny man I met disappearing, and the true Berserker peeking out. Sitting up straight, I keep my eyes dead, not freaking out like they are obviously expecting me to.

I watch them nudge each other before they lick their lips. Morons, don't they realise I could kill them without even moving? A part of me wants them to try and come at me, I would love to let some of this rage out.

With a disappointed frown, I watch them decide against it and slip out the back of the truck. I am surprised they didn't chain us, but I am betting they know we aren't stupid enough to try and get away. It's not like we would get far with a whole army on us.

The flap is held back and an impatient looking Berserker grunts at me, and gestures for us to leave the truck. Gritting my teeth against the pain rocking through my body, I stand up and hunch over to make my way out of the truck. When I reach the end, before I can even step down, the Berserker grabs me and throws me to the ground. Pushing up from the sand, I hold in my pained moan and get stiffly back to my feet to see the Berserker grinning now. Fucker.

Cocking back my arm, I let loose. I hear his nose crunch as he howls and falls back into the truck. A grinning Vasilisy hops down next to me and faces the crowd of Berserkers as they all come to see what the commotion is. Standing tall I face them all, it's time they realise I am not a slave anymore. No, I am the fucking Champion.

"Anyone that touches me will end up like him, or with my knife buried in his gut!" I yell and I hear a few nervous laughs even as some take a step back, realising how serious I am. I guess if you kill enough people, word starts to get around that you aren't to be fucked with. Turning, I face my once prison with fresh eyes. The last time I left here I was a trodden down slave, now I am the exact opposite, even if I can taste the metal of the shackles.

The castle—yes, you heard me right, castle—sits on top of the hill, okay it is probably more of a small mountain. Two tall towers reach into the scorching sky and the grey brick only reflects the merciless heat. Sand, dead trees, and plants litter the dirt paths up to the only entrance to the castle. At the bottom of the hill sits little houses for the Berserkers who are in the inner circle. Looking to the left of the castle, I spot the dungeon built into the side of the mountain, I spent more time there than I care to admit. It looks taller than I remember, but not nearly as scary. There are Berserkers patrolling everywhere, with weapons strapped to every inch of skin. The dirt tracks to the castle and to the road are lined with skulls on pikes and the Berserker symbol is flying high on the flags, but it somehow seems...less impressive.

"Get moving," comes a hard voice from behind me, right before I am shoved with a weapon sticking into my back. I stumble forward and start walking. Everything here is built for a purpose. The roads allow the guards on patrol to see who is coming, and booby traps line all the other ways in and out of this land. I remember it all like the back of my hand and I hate myself for it when my feet carry me automatically up the tracks towards the huge metal gate and guardhouse.

"Hasn't changed, has it? I guess it's just us," Vasilisy says from my side, and it's strange how in sync we are.

I look over to see him eyeing a house sadly. "Was that where you lived?" I ask and he snaps his gaze back around.

He doesn't answer and I leave him to it, everyone has a past in the Wastes, everyone has horrors they would rather forget. I won't push him to remember or rip open his pain just to distract me from the looming castle.

We reach it quicker than I would like and the metal gate pulls up automatically, the gears and chains cranking loudly in the quiet. It seems to take forever for it to rise but when it does, I am pushed through and into the training courtyard. Everyone stops and turns when they realise that Ivar must be back. I spot two Berserkers flirting and they straighten instantly, their eyes alert and all signs of flirtation disappearing. In fact, all the happiness seems to be sucked away and everyone turns cold and determined. Looking around the gathered faces, I realise something else... they are scared.

They might not all support Ivar, but they are all terrified of him. It's in their body language, the way they hold their eyes and the submissiveness rolling off them. Maybe Vasilisy is right, maybe it's time for a new leader. I just plan on it not being me, in fact, he would make a great one. I look at him from the side of my eye. First, I need to overthrow the throne, then put him in place. Time to get to work.

Welcome Back, Slave

I don't get time to gawk at my revelation, I am hustled inside the castle. Past the throne room and straight to the dungeon. Three flights of stairs, three locked doors, and six cells later, I am tossed inside by two impatient Berserkers. I turn back around and glare at them as the metal barred door slides shut, locking me in. When the guards step back, I step up to the bars and holding on, peer through. Vasilisy is thrown in the cell opposite me, and Evan to the left of him. I can't see anyone else and when the guards walk away, I turn back around.

"They only took us?" I demand.

Vasilisy leans against the stone wall and turns his head to face me. "Aye, little queen, too many guards a think. So they grabbed what they could and got out of there."

I nod, it makes sense. Plus, the others would have been on their way, and they wouldn't want to be there when backup turned up, would they. Fuck, the guys are going to lose their shit when they get there and find out I am gone. I hope they don't do anything stupid.

I mimic Vasilisy's position but slump on the cold hard floor instead. With nothing else to do but wait, I look around my cell and with a gasp I realise, it is actually *my* cell. The one from when I was younger... fucking asshole. I run my eyes around the room... it feels smaller. Or maybe I am just bigger, no longer half-starved and crazy. The metal bed frame stands next to me, pushed to the wall of the cell with only a mouldy, soggy mattress and pillow on top. A small window sits high up on the back wall, with claw marks on the wall underneath from when I tried to reach it. On the wall opposite me and hidden after the barred door is a pot and another stone wall. This one marked up with chalk. Line after line, each one representing a day I survived. My head hits the wall as I stare at the ceiling. It's just another head game, another way to remind me of what I am, but this time it won't work.

"Doc, you okay?" I ask eventually, needing to fill the quiet.

"Fucking peachy," he grumbles, and I snort.

"Why did they take you?" I ask, confused. Vasilisy makes sense, but Doc?

Vasilisy starts laughing and I look over at him with an arched eyebrow look. "What?" I ask when he just chuckles. I glance at Doc to see his face is bright red and he is looking at everything but me.

"Your Doc here, he decided to tag along. Some shit about protecting ya, keeping ya alive," Vasilisy says through chuckles and I look back at Evan with a wide-eyed look.

"Doc, why?" I ask eventually, truly shocked. Why the hell would he volunteer to come with me?

"Someone has to keep your crazy ass alive. You think those boyfriends of yours won't kill me if you die? Nope, I like my cock where it is, thank you. So, you better keep your crazy ass in this world." With that, he shuffles away, and I hear him slide down the wall in his cell.

A grin stretches my face even as I call out, "I knew you liked me, Doc."

"Fuck off," comes the muttered reply.

I laugh and let the conversation die.

Ivar leaves us down here for hours, trying to make us panic and do something stupid. It doesn't work, so I wait patiently. Knowing with each hour I am down here is another hour my men are out there looking for me.

"WALK FASTER," SAYS the Berserker guard. He grabbed me about ten minutes ago, leaving a screaming, angry Vasilisy behind, and a narrow-eyed Doc. I glare at the guy before speeding up. He stops me at a familiar room and knocks on the door before stepping back and leaning against the wall. When it opens, I throw one last glare at the guard.

"Welcome back, slave," he says with a grin.

I don't reply before stepping into the sitting room, or as Ivar calls it, his play chamber. The room is dark, the curtain pulled shut tight, so the only light is the fire roaring in the corner of the cold room. I shiver but don't try to cover any more of my skin, it won't make a difference, he keeps it cold as another form of punishment. I don't know where he is, but I run my eyes around the room. It's the same, and not, all at the same time. Two sofas face each other near the fire, and that's where the cozy part of the room ends. A rack of weapons runs the length of the wall on the other end of the room with tables underneath filled with his torture equipment, or toys as he calls them. The last time I was here, there was a creepy statue I used to lock my eyes on in the corner of the room, but it now lays in pieces on the floor, like he broke it and wouldn't let anyone fix it. The massive painting of the castle surrounded by flames has knife marks through it and hangs at a wonky angle. It looks like someone went on a rampage.

"I missed you, pet," comes his voice from somewhere in the darkness. I squint as I look for him.

He steps out of the shadows and the fire lights up his face. The flames twisting and dancing across the burn scars. I don't bother replying, not willing to play his games.

"You know I don't like it when you ignore me," he growls, the anger in his voice rising. "What do you say to that, pet?" he growls the last and steps closer again. I know what he wants me to say, but I seal my lips shut and instead, offer him a fuck off smile.

I watch the moment he snaps and, in a detached sort of way, wonder why I decided to push him. The lock clicks loudly in the room as he turns away from the door and walks to his toys. I wait there, like a statue, for whatever he will do. As long as he doesn't kill me, I can survive it.

When he decides on his toy, he turns back to me, his eyes alight with the need for pain and suffering. I offer him nothing, my face blank and my mind already drifting away to happier times.

I must have drifted more than I thought because he appears in front of me at the same time something digs into my arm. Looking down, I stare at the pliers clipped onto my skin—interesting choice. He only usually goes for those when he wants to take his time. He pulls back, leaving two cuts that slowly trickle blood down my skin.

"We are going to have some fun, pet. How I missed you," he mutters, caressing my face with the pliers before he runs them across my lips, cheek, and finally to my ear. I stumble when he clips the skin there, but I swallow the scream and straighten my stance. When I don't react he throws his toy away.

"I want you to scream for me," he threatens, his voice low.

I smile at him again. "Not a chance. Cut me, hit me, bite me, break me, but I will never scream. Not ever again."

He lets out a horrible yell and goes mad, full Berserker, nothing but insanity in his eyes. I don't even try and protect myself as punches and kicks rain down on me. I revel in the pain, letting it consume me.

Minutes blur together, and I find myself in a gasping heap on the floor as his booted foot smashes into my ribs. I hear them crack and I bite my lip to hold in my howl. It goes on and on, him screaming at me the whole way through. Telling me he missed me, he hates me. That I am his. When he has purged his system, he stumbles away as if drunk, and lands on one of the sofas and stares at me as I lay on the floor on my side. I watch in disgust as he buries his hand in his pants, gasping and groaning at my blood coating his cock. I push myself to my knees and then to my feet. Not looking at him as I hear him jerk himself off. He comes with a pathetic sounding groan and seems to forget about me for five minutes. When he remembers I am there, he walks over and kisses my cheek before slipping out of the door. Once he has gone, I let out a sigh, my body screaming at me. At this point I don't know how I am still standing.

The guard from outside comes back in, he takes one look at me and sighs, his eyes turning sad for a moment before he covers it up. "Come on, slave." He doesn't touch me, but I follow him as he leads me back down to the cells. I nearly fall down the stairs, my legs hurt that much but he catches me, and without a word, helps me walk the rest of the way. At this point, I can feel myself shutting down, I lean on him even more and he basically carries me. Opening the cell door, he walks me towards the bed and lays me down gently even as Vasilisy and Evan scream questions and insults at him.

I look into his face as he arranges my body, wincing when he looks at me, he looks defeated. "Thank you," I mutter, and he jerks before his eyes meet mine.

"Don't–don't ever thank me. Not for this, god not for this." He stumbles away and runs away like the hounds of hell are on his tail, only just remembering to lock my cell before he leaves.

I breathe through the pain, I can hear them calling me but I can't answer just yet. I feel like if I open my mouth, the scream I held in will come out and might never stop.

"Please, little queen, talk to me," Vasilisy begs, and it's the desperation in his voice that gets me going.

"I'm okay," I say as loud as I can before I start hacking out coughs, each one jarring my bruised ribs, searing my insides.

"Like the hell you are," Evan yells, making me smile as I close my eyes and settle back.

"I've had worse, don't worry about it. Try and get some rest, they will be planning something tomorrow."

Evan grumbles but I hear him shuffle and then get on his creaky bed. Vasilisy's breathing is so loud I can hear it from here, and it's surprisingly comforting.

"Sing to me?" I ask, allowing my weakness to show for one second.

He doesn't answer but a soft, loving song pours from his mouth, wrapping me up in the story about a woman and a man who run away to be together and build a house on a lake. As my eyes are fluttering shut, I get a few more words out. "Thank you, Vassy."

His song stutters to a stop. "Anytime, little queen, anything for you," he replies vehemently, sounding choked up. He's quiet for a few minutes before his song starts up again and I find myself lost in his words.

Chapter Twenty Eight

MISSED YOU, PET

The days blur in a mixture of pain and anger. My body is getting accustomed to the pain, but the humiliation is the worst. I forgot what it felt like to be treated like nothing but a slave... a pet. The comments and barbs, the wandering hands. All meant to break me, but it won't.

Every day Ivar plays his games. Sometimes just him and me, and sometimes with the others. Every night Vasilisy, Evan, and I sit and talk. We tell each other stories, sing, even joke. Just to show each other that we are there. On the nights where my body is broken, and it hurts to move and I don't want to talk, I curl up in my bed and they sing to me. Transporting me to magical places. Yet, the whole time I am thinking. I am scheming, planning my way to kill him and his men. Because I will. I will do it with my last fucking breath if I have to.

Today was no different than the other days. Ivar took us outside and made us fight his men. I was weak, slower than ever before. Half starved and body hurting, but I still managed to kick some ass. Afterwards, Ivar was so angry that we won the fights, he threw a hissy fit and locked us back up, taking his rage out on his men. Better them than us.

It means we have more time than normal down here in what Evan is calling our party house—don't ask. Somewhere along the line, we became friends, and he let go of his attitude. Even Vassy likes him.

Tonight's topic of conversation is the past. A stupid subject if you ask me, but Vassy brought it up and it's not like we have anything better to do.

"Might as well tell us, Doc. We might not make it till morning. You don't seem the type to want adventure, and you sure as shit don't like people, so why the fuck did you come?" I ask casually as I lean back on the cell wall. My head tilted to see the other cells.

"True. It was over a girl. We were... well we were sort of together. She was three years younger. When you turn eighteen, they make you decide what you want to do. She picked patrol. First year she was fine, I hated watching her go out, not that she would ever know. Then one day she didn't come back. After that, I volunteered for every patrol just to try and find her. But I never did. People said she left, people said she died. But I have to keep looking... when you came. You gave me hope, if you could survive for so long when people thought you were dead... then maybe she could." He takes a deep breath and I see the tears glistening on his cheeks. "But then I came here, saw what the world was like, saw what it cost you to survive. She wasn't like you. She wasn't a fighter. She could shoot a gun but not much else. If a warrior like you struggles to survive, then there isn't a chance she would have." He turns to me then, his eyes heartbroken. I know the look; I saw it for years in my own eyes. "It made me hate you, made me resent you. That wasn't fair, and I am sorry."

Well, fuck. I nod my head and offer him a smile. "We didn't get off on the best foot. I resented you as well. I hated that you got to live down there, all safe and protected while I was stuck out here. I compared my own pain and past to yours without even knowing you. That wasn't fair either, I am sorry. Sometimes pain can be found even in paradise." He nods, his eyes still glistening, and offers me an understanding smile. Now, we might never be best friends but we sure as shit aren't enemies. If it's one thing I know, pain has a strange way of bringing people together.

"What about you Vassy, anything you want to get off your chest before we meet the grim reaper?" I joke. Depending on my Berserker stalker to lighten the mood like always.

"If we are sharing it seems only right. I had a wife." I gasp, I had no clue. "She was a warrior, much like you, little queen. In fact, you remind me of her so much. She wasn't beautiful, not in the way you are. But her strength and courage gave her beauty and I loved her for it. I fell in love the day she held a knife to my throat and called me a cock-loving bitch. It took me years to wear her down, and when I did, I felt like the happiest man. I didn't know of Ivar's madness then, ya see. I was only a lowly patrol, living on the outskirts. We moved in together, she fell pregnant. A big no-no in our world. So, we were going to leave, to run and make a life of it, but then I heard my Noah was in trouble. She told me we were staying, family is family and we take care of our own. We were going to take him with us. I got into the castle, working with the guards. Only then did I see what had become of us. When I got there, it was too late. Noah was dead and his da was heartbroken, screaming of revenge. Treasonous words of killing our King. So we stayed, to make sure he didn't do anything stupid. One day, I got home to find her dead. They had found out about the movement and took what was most precious to me as a reminder of what they were capable of. She went down fighting, took four bastards with her, but there were too many. She died with ma unborn babe in her belly and a knife in her hand." He takes a deep breath before carrying on. "Death comes to everyone eventually, all that you can ask for is that you go out on your own terms and in your own way."

"Shit," is the only response I can think of, but Vassy doesn't mind, he smiles at me. Understanding everything I wish I could say to him.

"It is okay, little queen, we will be together again."

We go quiet after that, each lost in our own thoughts of those we love. I haven't let myself think of the guys in days, it's too painful. I wonder what they are doing right now. Are they searching for me? Fuck, of course they are. I bet those crazy bastards have cut a path through the Wastes with bodies trailing behind them. I just hope they laid Major to rest, it's the one thing I wish I could have done before I die.

"I have a plan," I say eventually, breaking through the silence. I hear them both shuffling as they turn to me.

"Yeah?" Doc asks.

"Yeah," I mimic and smile at his grunt. "Kill Ivar, clear up the clan and put Vassy here on the throne. Then I'll get my guys, move to the middle of fucking nowhere. Where no one knows my name, my story... I'll just live," I finish, imaging it in my head, finally giving life to the thought I barely let myself think.

"I am no King," Vassy says eventually. I shake my head and he carries on, "No, little queen, I'm no King. Never will be. I don't have tha strength nor tha instincts. I will stand by your side, but you must become Queen."

I snort at that, and wince when it shakes my body. "I'm no fucking Queen, I can barely keep myself alive."

"Not true. You are a fookin Queen if I ever did see one. Ya are stronger than all tha bastards up there, smarter too. Ya would earn their loyalty, ya would bring the clans back together. I have already seen it start to happen. Nah, little queen, I am no King, but I will be your right-hand man."

I ignore him, rolling my eyes. I don't want to be Queen, hell, I don't want to be a Berserker. I just want to be left alone.

The sound of boots stomping down the stairs and keys jangling has us all jumping to our feet. They haven't come for us at this time before——something is wrong.

Five guards stop between our cells, torches held in the air as they look at us. The big bastard in the middle is the one to speak. "Time to go, slaves."

"Where are you taking us?" I ask, stepping back into the middle of my cell to have room if need be, old habits die hard after all.

"Ivar is throwing a party, to celebrate his pet's return. You are the guest of honour," he sneers and the others laugh.

"What about those two?" I ask, jerking my head to Evan and Vasilisy.

"They are insurance," he grunts out.

I blow out a breath and hold my hands in front of me. Fucking bastard, using them against me.

I let them shackle me without a fight, as does Vasilisy and Evan, all of us not wanting to fuck anything up in case it gets taken out on the rest of us. One wrong move and it would be the end.

We are dragged up the steps and paraded through the castle, music and laughter fill the air as the sound of men cheering reaches us, but something is screaming at me, pulling at me to get the hell out of here. A feeling in the pit of my stomach that tonight is going to be terrible.

THE PARTY IS in full swing when we are dragged inside and paraded around like fucking cattle. The place is jammed, every Berserker in the clan must be in here. Cushions line the floor where Berserkers lounge, both men and women, laughing and drinking as they rip into a massive feast. The only table with chairs is at the head of the throne room, where Ivar and his circle sit. The fucking prick lounges in his blood-covered throne, with his crown on his head, and watches it all with an evil smile. He is planning something, that I can tell. He's too happy, too focused. It can only mean trouble.

A drunk Berserker falls into me, sloshing his beer from his metal goblet all over my clothes and making me grimace. Usually I would have backed away, whimpering out an apology, but I remind myself that I am not here like that again. So, taking the beer, I jerk my head forward, headbutting the drunk bastard so he falls back howling. Keeping my eyes on the downed man who is struggling to get back to his feet, slurs coming from his sloppy mouth, I down the beer. Once I am done, I wipe my mouth with the back of my hand and throw the goblet at him.

"Get another drink, you clearly need it." Then I turn away, showing him my back. The Berserkers around us roar with laughter as the man screams at me. I feel pretty good until the metal shackles around my wrist clang and I am dragged into Ivar's pet torturer's waiting grasp.

I grimace and dig my feet in. I freeze when Ivar holds his hand out and the chains are handed over, the metal slithering across the floor like a snake. My hands are bound together and tied to the chain, controlled by Ivar himself. Vassy is chained to his chair like a dog, not that he cares, or shows he does. He lounges there, pretending to be asleep but I can see his hands twitching and his eyes following Ivar's every move. Evan is tied in the corner to a chair, forgotten about because they don't see him as a threat. I find myself getting angrier and angrier all night as women play with him, touching him, teasing him, hurting him, all the while laughing as he bites against the gag and kills them with his eyes. It's not just the women though, the men are just as bad. I saw one of them shove their hands down his pants and I found my eyes memorising that man before I looked at Evan, telling him with my eyes I would kill him for him. He didn't look away, instead, we suffered through it together before I was passed to the next Berserker like a fucking trophy. All night, passed around the room until now. Ivar is obviously tired of others playing with his pet. The room quiets a bit as he tugs gently on the chain, making me stumble forward. If I had been at full strength, he wouldn't have budged me, but as weak as I am, I find myself falling forward. He laughs, and a few others join in, sounding nervous. The women pawing at Evan even leave him alone to come and watch the show they all know Ivar is going to put on. Looking around the crowd, I see some uncomfortable, and even angry faces, aimed at Ivar. Maybe there is more to the rebellion inside the camp than I thought.

He tugs again, harder this time, but I am ready. I dig in my feet and fight against the chain, pulling it back towards me until he is pulled forward slightly. It's a small victory, but one nonetheless. Glaring now, he stands from his throne and the room goes silent. The music stops, the clinking of goblets, even the laughter and joking of the Berserkers all stops.

He slowly winds the chain around his wrist, watching me the whole time and I take a deep breath before I am yanked to him like a wild animal. Stumbling, trying to keep upright, I fight against him but it's no good. I land at his feet with a groan, my knees hitting the stone floor of the dais hard, jarring my body.

Once there, I raise my head and glare at him, my eyes flicker to Vasilisy for a second as he slowly gets to his knees, his eyes locked on Ivar with a deadly intensity, the hate shining for everyone to see.

"Now, isn't that better pet, on the floor at my feet where you belong?" his voice booms out before he lets out a laugh. A few others join in, but not as many as I was expecting.

Ignoring them, I slowly get to my feet, even as he yanks on the chain to try and make me get back on my knees. His face turns red and some chuckles sound from the crowd.

"On your knees, slave," he demands, his nostrils flaring as he starts to get angry. He looks the part of a mad king tonight. Laced up at the side, leather pants hugging his massive thighs, his hair pulled back in straggly honour braids with his crown woven in. The scars on his face highlighted in the harsh lighting. His chest is bare, his Berserker branding a massive tattoo in the middle of his chest, scars scattered around it like a declaration of how strong he is. His body almost vibrates with malice, and his eyes show nothing but hate and anger.

"I'd rather stand," I drawl casually, and I notice the vein in his forehead bulge. His little torturer steps forward, glee lining his face as he stares at me.

"Want me to teach her a lesson, my King?" There is so much anticipation in his voice.

Ivar taps his chin before shaking his head, his eyes still on me, running up and down my body, making bile rise in my throat. "No, it seems our little pet doesn't care what we do to her..." He trails off and looks at me again, his eyes lighting up. "But she does care what we do to other people. Tell me, pet. When you found your little boyfriend hanging from the ceiling, did you cry?" He steps forward, dropping the chain he is holding, and his words finally registered. Out of the corner of my eyes, I see Vasilisy get to his feet, his hands clenched so tightly I bet his nails are cutting his palms.

"I bet you did. Did you hold him? Touch his dead body? Were you angry at him?" His words are like a blow to my heart, because yes, I was so fucking angry and the fact he knows that kills me. He steps down until we are meters apart. "Do you know what happened to him?" he asks causally. When I don't answer he picks up his gun casually and aims it at Vasilisy without looking.

Grinding my teeth, I force the words out. "He killed himself." I choke on them, the words so heinous and filled with pain.

He laughs, before looking back at me, the gun dropping to point at the floor. "Did he?" he asks, winking at me and I go cold, the memory of Noah swinging from the ceiling at The Ring flashing before my eyes...the fight...the pain...the softness in him. My mind whirs as I think it all through before I gasp, looking back at Ivar. I should have known, but I thought... God, I am so stupid.

"Ah, I see you have finally worked it out, I did wonder when you would. It was my last gift to you." He looks at Vasilisy with a grin before looking back at me, his words rubbing salt into the wound and ripping that heartache back open again. "He cried, you know, he begged and screamed. He was so weak, so fucking pathetic. He said your name like it was a prayer." Each word is like a blow, and the inferno inside of me starts bubbling until all I see is red. The need to kill him, to make him pay, overwhelms me until I can't think clearly. I know it's exactly what he wants, but I can't seem to care. I let myself go, I let the darkness take over. As he steps closer again I slowly wind in the chain shackled to my wrist like he did. I hear Vasilisy move, obviously seeing what I am doing. I can almost taste his panic. He knows what this will cost me, but I don't care. "At the end, he pissed himself as we all stood and watched, crying like a fucking baby as he choked." I let out a scream, raising my hand, ready to unleash the chain. I see the panic flash in Ivar's eyes, he wanted a reaction, but he didn't expect me to have the balls to kill him.

As if in slow motion, I hear the scream from Vasilisy before I see him. He throws himself at Ivar. Knocking him out of my path. I stare, not able to do anything else as they both fall to the floor with Vasilisy on top, but he doesn't stop there. His eyes are wild and filled to the brim with hate and death. He lets out a heartbroken yell before raining his meaty fists down at Ivar's face. Panic like no other winds through my body, I don't care what they do to me, but they won't let a dishonoured Berserker attack the King. They will kill him.

The thought gets me moving and I tackle Vassy off Ivar and pin him to the floor, my eyes searching his. When he looks at me, I see the determination there. "Why?" I ask, my heart smashing into my chest as I hear the Berserkers closing in and the roar of anger from Ivar. "Why!" I scream in his face, smashing my fists into his shoulder. He lets me, he just lays there and lets me, a serene look on his face.

"Because it wasn't time. Not here, not now. You would have never made it."

I gasp, my eyes filling with tears as I realise he did it to protect me. He gave his life for me.

"No." I shake my head, even as I feel them bearing down on us. "You fool," I scream.

"Kill him, little queen. Be smarter than he is, then take your crown. Save the Wastes." With that he pushes me from him and I roll to the side to see him sweep out his arm and take down a Berserker before grabbing his weapon. Crouching on the floor he looks at me. "I will die the way I lived, but remember why you are here." With that he turns to the encroaching Berserkers.

"Vassy! No!" I yell and try to scramble to my feet, only to be held back by arms winding around my waist.

I watch in horror as he holds out his arms and lets out a war yell. "Come on then, you traitors. I'll see ya in the next fucking life!" I can't look away. I can't blink.

He would have probably managed to kill more if he wasn't chained to the chairs. A fact I think he chose to ignore as he flings himself into the awaiting mass of warriors. Hacking, cleaving, and screaming, as he takes as many down with him as he can.

I have to help. Looking around I spot the torch next to us, placed near the chairs. Darting forward, dragging the man holding me, I grab it and without hesitating thrust it back into his face. I smell the burning first before the scream of pain hits my ears, almost deafening me. The arms fall away, and I pick up a forgotten sword.

Letting out a yell, I jump into the fray. Bodies are everywhere, and I can barely see in front of me to figure out who is friend and foe, so I just swing. I swing until I can't feel my arms, until blood covers my face and I have to blink it away. Climbing over dying men, I leap and swing. When there is nothing but bodies scattered at my feet and blood dripping from my sword, I finally look up. Vasilisy glances back at me from where he stands, yanking his stolen sword from a dead Berserker's chest. He offers me a grin and I grin back, it costs me. I don't see the arrow until it is too late. It hits him in the shoulder, twisting him as he is knocked back, the sword forgotten.

Another flies through the air and hits his other shoulder. He falls back again, letting out a scream as he does. I try to get to him, but the bodies in the way are slowing me down and my legs are aching. I throw myself across the distance as he drops to his knees, his eyes on mine. In them I see acceptance, but I won't let him die. He can't. I fall to my knees in front of him with a scream as his body jerks from the impact of another arrow. He doesn't cry, he doesn't beg, he just stares at me.

"I need my right-hand man," I cry, grabbing his shoulders.

"You have five others," he gasps out.

"No." Not again. Standing, I jump over him and stand with my arms spread, facing the crowd. Ivar stands in the very centre, a bow held in his hands with another arrow nocked while the Berserkers hold their weapons, ready to jump in if need be.

"No," I say loudly and he arches his eyebrow at me. His face is already bruising, which makes me wince.

"Take her," he orders, and I scream, raising the sword as I rush towards him, ignoring Vasilisy's advice to bide my time. If I can reach him, if I can kill him, I can save Vassy.

I don't make it two steps before something hits my arm, making it go dead and my fingers automatically drop the sword. Then bodies are thrown at me, pushing me to the floor as they create a Berserker pile.

"No!" I kick and thrash, but it is no good.

"Bring her and the traitor, let's remind them why I am King," Ivar's voice roars, even reaching me under the pile of warriors, and my blood turns cold. Vasilisy...

We are dragged outside, excited hoots following us as Ivar leads the party. There is only one reason why he is bringing us out here. The thought has me fighting again and it takes three Berserkers to hold me, even though Vasilisy doesn't fight the two who are leading him to the raised wooden stage in the middle of the castle courtyard.

I am dragged to the post opposite and tied up as I kick and growl like an animal. I take a chunk out of one the Berserkers and he backhands me before walking away, leaving the two others to it. One leans closer, dangerous on his part really, and I dart forward and bite into his neck. Like a feral, I dig in and hold on tight, cutting through skin, and with the feeling of a balloon bursting, copper fills my mouth. He is punching my stomach and screaming but I hold on, I only let go because I have to swallow or choke. He stumbles back, his face pale as his hands come up and slip in his own blood as he tries to hold his neck where blood is pumping from him. I grin, blood filling my mouth and no doubt coating my teeth and face. He falls to his knees and all the other Berserkers ignore him as he faints then and there, I hope the bastard dies.

Spitting out the mouthful of blood, I turn to the other Berserker who seems to have forgotten about me and is staring at the man with a strange look on his face, he almost seems...relieved? It makes me falter and before I can bite him as well, he turns back to me and frowns when he sees my reaction. Slowly, as if not to startle me he holds his hands up, not touching me.

"Calm down, Champion."

I stop and stare at him and he blows out a breath when I don't attack him. Leaning closer, he looks around before messing with the chains and whispering. "Sorry 'bout this. Gotta make it look good or they will kill me. I am sorry, I wish I could stop this."

"Then do it," I mutter and look around to notice a few other Berserkers looking my way and winking before turning back to the show. What the fuck?

"I can't. If I do, it will blow everything we have planned, and it's so much bigger than one man's life."

I growl again and he glares at me. "Vasilisy is my friend too, Champion. But he knew the cost when he did that stunt earlier. Do not disrespect his choices and bravery now. This is much bigger than you and him."

I blink as I stare at him. "You are part of the rebellion?"

He nods and steps closer, lowering his voice. "There are a lot here who are. They tire of Ivar, but until there is a good option to replace him, they follow out of fear. Vasilisy convinced us it was you. After tonight, I can see where he was coming from." Ivar's laugh booms across the clearing and the man closes his eyes painfully. "Don't look away, to do so would dishonour him." With that he turns and takes up guard next to me, ignoring me completely.

Looking ahead, I see Vasilisy with his hands now bound in front of him and a noose around his neck. It's one of Ivar's favourite ways to kill people, something about if their neck doesn't break. All I know is, the only time I saw it happen haunted me, and this will be so much worse, but the guard is right. To look away would dishonour him, he made his sacrifice for me. I must accept that, even if my heart screams for the man I was coming to care for like family.

He meets my eyes as the Berserkers leave the platform and he smiles softly. I can't return it, that would mean I would have to move my mouth and if I do, I might scream and never stop. There has been so much death; I have lost more people I care about recently than most do in a lifetime. Pain has been my constant friend since Ivar stole me, but this is a different kind and I can already feel it consuming me, the darkness fighting in me, trying to get free, and I might just let it. It has to be better than feeling...this...

Vasilisy holds my gaze as Ivar starts to talk and I don't even allow myself to blink, even when my eyes burn and start to water.

"Traitor!" someone screams, and I tune them out. I can see Ivar talking out of the corner of my eye, but I don't want to hear it. He steps towards Vasilisy, a knife flashing in the light. I swallow deep and harden my eyes, warning Vasilisy as much as I can. I see him ready himself and the knife descends on his Berserker branding on his chest. It's where everyone who is voluntarily a Berserker gets them, I am the only person to have it on my shoulder and it was done as a slur to me being a slave.

Most men scream, most men pass out or beg, but Vasilisy just takes it as the tattoo is hacked away, taking half of the left side of his pec with it until you can see muscle. Blood gushes down his chest, colouring his stomach, and into his trousers.

Ivar steps away and holds up the flap of skin, some of the crowd cheers and Ivar frowns. I make sure to take a quick look at the crowd to see who didn't join in—they can live.

I look back when I hear Ivar moving on the wooden boards again, he walks to the lever and stares at me. I avert my eyes, staring at Vasilisy as he mouths at me, 'Goodbye, little queen.' I hold in my cry as I hear the leaver fall and the board under his feet drops out.

I let out a short sharp gasp as he drops through. His neck doesn't break and Ivar cheers again. I have to watch as he chokes to death, his feet and arms twitching as his face turns purple and he gasps out, trying to breathe. Those three minutes are the longest of my life, I still don't look away until he stops moving, his body swaying in the breeze. He's dead. They killed him.

I look to Ivar, he grins at me and I let go, I lose all humanity. I embrace the darkness, I welcome it like an old friend and hide in it so I don't have to feel. I am a true Berserker and they will feel my wrath before the night is through.

Chapter Twenty Nine

You Can't Keep a Champion Down

I don't remember much after that, apart from when I find myself facing my cell, I am covered in blood and the side of my face feels funny. Blinking, I am shoved into the cell and I spin instantly to see the two hesitant Berserkers there. They quickly smash the door shut and retreat, keeping their eyes on me the whole way.

Hours pass, and I walk the tight confines of my cell. Evan tries to talk to me but I ignore him, instead I pace. I hear boots on the stairs and know it is time. Time they pay.

Nothing but pure instinct and hate fuel me now. I move back into the middle of the cell and wait. When the guard comes to do his check, he squints into the dark, clearly not seeing me. When he steps close to the bars, I spring forward. He doesn't have a chance to get away, grabbing his neck with one hand, I search him for the keys. When I find them belted to his hip, I snap the cord holding them and, with his face still smashed to the bars, hand them over. He takes them slowly and I grab his sword from his other hip and hold it to his dick. "Open the cell," I growl. He swallows hard and fumbles with the keys, almost dropping them before he gets it open. As soon as I hear the lock click, I let him go and yank open the door. He stumbles back, wide-eyed as I grin at him. Tossing the sword in my hand to get a feel for the weight I saunter towards him.

"You should have listened to my warning, I swore I would kill you all," I say before throwing the sword. It imbeds in his neck, pinning him to the wall behind him. Stepping closer, I pull out the sword and he falls to the stone floor, his hands holding his neck as if he can stop the blood from flowing freely. I hold his eyes as he dies and then I search his body for anything useful.

Evan's face is pressed against the cell door and his mouth is moving but I turn and, ignoring him, slowly ascend the steps, listening for any more Berserkers. When I don't hear anyone, I peek out of the wooden door and check the corridor. I check left and right before stepping out. The bloody sword held in my left hand, I saunter down the corridor, not rushing, not caring if anyone finds me. Let them come at me right now, with how I am feeling, they wouldn't stand a chance. I walk past a familiar door and hesitate. With an evil smile, I turn back around and face it. Ivar's little pet torturer's room, I forgot how close to the dungeon he was. It's time for some payback.

I don't knock and quietly slip inside. The room is dark, but I can hear water running in the attached bathroom. Luckily, I know my way about the room and I tiptoe through silently until I stand at the doorway, watching him. He is lounging back in the tub, the water mucky with blood and dirt, and I grin as I step inside. He put me through hell and back and it seems only right I do the same. I notice his weapons on the side, too far away for him to easily reach. His eyes are closed, and I stop when I tower over the tub. When he still doesn't notice, I watch him for a moment. He groans and when I see his hand moving on his tiny cock in the water I smirk.

Bored of waiting, using the tip of the sword I nudge his chin.

He jerks upright, his eyes wide and his chest heaving as he faces me. When he gets a good look at me, he pales and I know I must look like a monster.

His eyes narrow with arrogance. "If you wanted to play, pet, all you had to do was ask."

I grin at him, making him falter for a second. "That's not how it's going to be, pet." Then I flip the sword and smash the pommel into his face. He falls back into the water and I grab his hair and force his head under. His hands reach up and grip at me, smacking and fighting as he chokes on his own dirty bath water. I look around the room as he chokes to death, and only when he starts to slow do I bring him back up. He sputters and gasps as water flows from his lips. I allow him a second to breathe before I dunk him back under again. I do it again and again until he is begging, his voice raw and scraped as he pleads with me. I thought it would make me feel good, to get back at the bastard who hurt me so much, but all I feel is empty. I let go and he scrambles from the bath, slipping on the floor in front of it and ending up on his arse.

"You won't get to him," he says from the floor, looking at me, and I know he sees the death in my eyes. His eyes dart to his weapons and I laugh.

"Yes I will, and then I will kill him and wear his fucking skin as a coat." Darting forward, I slip Dray's knife from my boot, grinning at the fact the Berserker who searched me was more bothered about feeling me up than looking for actual weapons, he got the obvious ones but missed this little knife a fact I am grateful for right now. Crouching before him I grin. "This might hurt, pet," I mock.

His eyes widen, and he starts screaming as I hack through his flesh, cutting away the Berserker brand, dishonouring him. He passes out halfway through, making it easier. Ripping the skin away, I hold the brand as I hack off his hair and shove them both in my pocket. "You are not a warrior, you are a sick son of bitch."

With that, I grab the decorative pot next to us on the counter and slam it down on his head, again and again until his face is bashed in and he isn't breathing. Standing, I drop the pot and let it shatter on the floor. I leave him there, naked and dishonoured for all to see, and go in search of my next target.

I NOW HAVE four Berserker brands and braids in my pocket. I made true on my promise to myself to kill the bastards who cheered, sweeping my way through the castle and hunting them down. I crouch next to the open doorway and poke my head around before rushing in. I don't wait as I leap at a Berserker and cut his throat before spinning and gutting the next. Raising my sword, I go to kill the third before I notice it is the man from before, the one who told me about the rebellion. I drop my sword and turn my back on him, ignoring his questioning look. He doesn't seem bothered I just slaughtered two of his friends. When I crouch and start to cut off their brands, I hear him gag. Eyeing my handiwork, I smile. I am getting good at this.

"What are you doing?" he asks and I notice he looks a little pale. I glance back down before moving on to the next and then I stand and face him.

"You are part of the rebellion, correct?" When he nods I carry on. "Good, gather the others. Either you help or you get the fuck out of my way. Tonight is the night that Ivar dies." With that, I walk away and I hear him scramble to keep up.

"Shit, okay." I hear him pant and I speed up. "He's in the throne room, so are some guards." I nod my understanding and I hear him stop. "I will get the others and meet you there." I wave my hand and his footsteps sound, going the other way. That's fine, he can get the others, but I am not waiting.

I make my way to the throne room, only running into three patrols who now all decorate the hallways of the castle. I know I have been hurt, but I can't feel it at the moment and I just can't seem to care.

When I reach the double doors of the throne room, I take a deep breath and square my shoulders. Ready, I kick open the door and stride down the middle of the room. Ivar squints from where he sits on the throne with a woman's head bobbing up and down on his cock as he holds her there.

When he spots me, he grins and purposely starts moaning loudly. The guards in the room step forward but hesitate when Ivar doesn't panic. He will regret that. When I stop before him, he moans long and loud before pushing the woman away. She scrambles to her feet, panting and wiping her mouth before covering her chest. She eyes me, and her eyes light up with knowing. She nods before stepping away, and marching back down the room, leaving me with Ivar and his men.

Grinning, I grab my stash and throw all the bits of skin and hair at him. He catches them automatically, and when he notices what they are, he pales and jumps to his feet. His face turns beet red and he thunders towards me. When he gets close, he raises his fist, but I dodge the punch and sweep my leg out, then kick back so he falls back down on his throne. He eyes me slowly before climbing to his feet, more cautious this time. It will be his weakness, he doesn't want to die. I don't care, not in the darkness like I am.

"What do you think will happen here, pet?" He starts to circle me and I keep him in my eyesight. "That you will march in here and kill me?"

I shrug. "Pretty much."

He throws back his head and laughs before stopping in front of me. "You forget one thing, pet."

I tilt my head and eye him. "What's that?"

He grins evilly. "I am King." He snaps his fingers at his guards. "Take her weapon and bring her to my room." He carries on grinning, but when no one moves, it's my turn to smile. I eye the guards to watch as they nod at me and step back so their backs are to the wall.

He growls and turns on them. "Did you hear me? I said get her!" When no one moves he screams, throwing a tantrum. "You fucking traitors, I will kill you all..." he carries on, his back to me, and I use the opening.

Slipping behind him, I drop down and cut the backs of his knees. He lets out a pained yell, choking off his rant mid-word, and falls forward. I stand slowly and walk around him until I am positioned at his front. He looks up at me, his face murderous.

"You are nothing. You are a fucking slave. A fucking toy, you won't kill me!" he screams as blood starts to puddle beneath him. I hear the throne room doors open and spare it a short look to see the rest of the clan making their way in. I see some familiar eyes, but I don't know everyone so I need to do this fast. He turns and screams at them to stop me, but not one person steps forward. Some are probably wondering what I will do, some don't care, and the others want his death. I can see it in their eyes.

Turning back to Ivar, I see the moment he realises the truth. "They don't care. You lost their respect, you lost your right as King, and I am going to make you pay for everything you did."

He turns back to me, his face turning purple in his anger. "Even if you kill me, you will still be a broken slave girl," he spits, and I grin again.

"That's where you are wrong. I was never broken, but you are." With that, I get bored of talking and I grip my sword tighter.

He starts to rant, insult after insult pouring out of his mouth as I bring my sword up.

"Ivar The Destroyer, traitor to the Berserker clan, I sentence you to death," I say casually, and I drop the sword, aiming for his neck. I hack and yell, letting everything out. All the years of pain and suffering, all the heartache and loss, I let it guide my blade as I chop through his neck. Like this, I can see how weak he is, relying on other's strengths to protect him, but when it came down to it... he was nothing more than a man. Blood splatters, and still I keep going until his head rolls away from his body. His eyes staring at me, still filled with dimming anger and his mouth formed in a silent yell, it still isn't enough. He deserved so much more. Reaching down I grab his head and turn to face the silent crowd. They are all waiting to see what I will do now.

Severed head and crown in one hand, bloody sword in the other, I stand on the raised platform with my chest heaving and blood dripping from my many wounds. I let out a wordless triumphant shout as I raise the head of their leader. I watch as they drop their weapons, confusion on their faces as they try to decide what to do now. They look to each other, and the brands and braids littering the steps to the throne, testaments to my kills. I wait for them to come, ready to take them all on, when the door bursts open and Dray storms in with an army of Seekers and scavs behind him.

He looks like the devil incarnate, a snarl twisting his lips, madness shining in his eyes, an axe in one hand and a sword in the other. He stops at the door, scanning the room until his gaze lands on me. He lets out a crazed laugh and saunters to me, even as I see the relief bloom in his cold eyes.

I look behind him, glad to see him but confused, he stops close to me, eyeing me like a cornered animal.

"Where are they?" I ask, knowing they wouldn't have let him come alone. They would have been right there with him, ready to fight to the death through a sea of Berserkers to get to me, it's the thought that got me through it. Seeing them again, holding them.

I watch his eye twitch for only a moment before his face turns blank and cold, but it doesn't scare me anymore. "Dray," I growl, stepping into his space, forgetting I am still holding the severed head of Ivar.

"Gone," he says, clenching his jaw. I blink stupidly; I must have heard him wrong...

"Gone?" I question.

"The city took them, guards stormed The Summit with guns. Took one look at the bloodbath left behind and panicked. We had only just got there. The guards recognised them and took them, not without a fight, but I couldn't stop them."

"Why?" I scream in his face, panic exploding in my chest.

He gets in my face, a snarl on his lips. "Because they would have killed me, then I couldn't have come for you. I'm not fucking sorry; I would have done much worse to get here. Even if it means you hate me." I can see the truth in his eyes, he's not sorry. He let them take them, didn't even fight it, because he knew they would kill him and he wanted to save me.

"I didn't need you to save me," I point out numbly, my whole body frozen.

"I can see that, never doubted you," he says, losing the snarl. His eyes are cold still and glittering with something, something that should scare me, but I feel anything but at the moment. Let them come, let them try, I will kill them all. "We will get them back," he promises, the threat clear.

I nod, a plan forming. "We will, but we will need an army." I grin grimly at him and he cocks his eyebrow, waiting for whatever I will do. With that look, he promises he will stand by me, and I nod back. Turning to face the amassed Seekers and Berserkers, I see some have taken my threat seriously and have left, the others are waiting, searching for leadership.

"They came to the north, they invaded our lands, they broke the treaty and they took our people!" I scream, the crowd cheers, raising their weapons, delight and anger staring back at me from every face. They are raring for a fight and I am going to give them one. "We will make them pay. We will head south and we will decimate the cities."

There is only one thing left to do... The Berserkers must have a leader, and only one thing will remind them of the pain and blood I shed to get that. Lifting Ivar's head dramatically, the room goes silent, anticipation thrumming through them. Half have waited a long time for a new leader, the other half have never dared even dream about it, but one thing is for sure, I need them and they need me.

I let go slightly and Ivar's head drops to the floor with a splatter before rolling down the steps and landing at the feet of the assassin——of course that slimy bastard is here. I lift the crown, and uncaring about the blood coating it, lay it on my head. It's heavy and I hate the feeling, but I jerk my chin up and raise my sword. Chanting starts in the crowd as I run my eyes across them once more. When I face the assassin, he winks before dropping to one knee, respect clear on his face as he mouths one word to me—— 'Archel.'

I take a deep breath... his name. He gave me his name. With that, the spell is broken, Seekers and Berserkers alike drop to their knees, their head bowed as Dray steps to my side.

Side by side, we face the two clans, a Berserker Queen and a Seeker King. Together, we will teach them the north is not to be messed with——we will make them fear us and regret ever coming here.

The north will win, and blood will flow. If my men have been harmed, then god save them all for what I will do. The clans roar for me, I am no longer just Worth, nor am I Taz... now I am Queen.

ALSO BY K.A KNIGHT

THEIR CHAMPION SERIES

- The Wasteland
- The Summit
- *The Cities (Coming 2019)*

- *The Forgotten: A Their Champion Companion Novella (Coming 2019) - turn the page for a sneak peek!*

DAWNBREAKER SERIES

- Voyage to Ayama
- *Dreaming of Ayama (Coming 2019)*

THE LOST COVEN SERIES

- Aurora's Coven
- *Aurora's Betrayal (Coming 2019)*

CO-AUTHOR PROJECTS

- Circus Save Me
- Circus Saves Christmas
- *One Night Only (Coming February 2019 in the Valentine's Between The Sheets Anthology)*
- *The Wild Interview (Coming 2019)*

ABOUT THE AUTHOR

K.A Knight is an indie author trying to get all of the stories and characters out of her head. She loves reading and devours every book she can get her hands on, she also has a worrying caffeine addiction.

She leads her double life in a sleepy English town, where she spends her days at the evil day job and comes home to her fur babies.

Read more at K.A Knights website or join her Facebook Reader Group.

THE FORGOTTEN

The Forgotten

A Their Champion Companion Novella

(Coming 2019)

ABOUT THE FORGOTTEN

The rules of Paradise are simple:
Everyone must work, Everyone must contribute, and If you leave,
you may never come back. They have been drilled into us since the
world ended and those bunker doors shut.

So why can't I stop dreaming of more?

With my eighteenth birthday and the selection approaching, I
must decide what role I will take within our community. But when
I am betrayed by the very people I was brought up to trust and left
for dead in The Wasteland this world has become, I decide to
leave for good. Decide to leave the only man I've ever loved and
the only home I've ever known.

Everyday will be a fight for survival, but for once in my life, I
finally feel free...if only my heart would accept that.

RULES OF PARADISE

ALL MUST WORK

ALL MUST CONTRIBUTE

IF YOU LEAVE, YOU MAY NEVER COME BACK

PARADISE IS THE NEW WORLD, TO QUESTION THAT
IS TO QUESTION THE LAW.

JUST FRIENDS

SNEAK PEEK FROM THE FORGOTTEN

With a mischievous grin, I spin away from the incoming guards and into the med bay. I should be in class, but I hate water systems. Learning it is so boring. So, I snuck out to come and meet Evan. Looking around his usual place of hiding, my grin stretches when I spot him bent over reading some boring medical book. For as long as we have been friends, he has been trying to convince me to join him in medicine, but it never appealed to me, being locked away down here and dependent on so much. I dream of bigger things, things he tells me to keep quiet. The type of things that make him roll his eyes and get that look on his face that reminds me of the age gap between us. Three years isn't a lot, but down here it probably feels like a lifetime.

He is so structured and ruled, liking his own peace and quiet and the boringness of everyday. Whereas I am the total opposite, he tells me I have my head in the clouds dreaming of a world that doesn't exist, but how can he not want to know what's outside? To see for himself, explore. The world might have died, but I am betting the human race survived, it's just who we are. I asked him once why he hung around me if he thought my dreams were stupid, he told me my hope was the light in the grey. I never asked again.

Rolling my eyes when he doesn't even turn around to see who it is, I decide to sneak up on him. That's the one thing I have going for me, I am quiet when I need to be, a trait hard earned from sneaking around down here. When I am close enough to smell his mint body wash, I lean down close to his ear. "Boo!"

He jumps, fumbling with his book and letting out a girly scream that sends me into hysterics. Falling back to lean on the medical bed I watch him through tear filled eyes. He turns to me, his short sweepy messy brown hair moving with him as his emerald green eyes lock on mine with anger. "Damn it Pip, you scared the shit out of me!"

Groaning at the nickname, I hop up on the bed and stare at him with my innocent smile. It makes him grunt as he bends down to pick up the book, which has to be thicker than both of his arms put together and that is saying something because Evan is shredded. I don't know why, it's not like he has to fight or go on patrol but he likes to keep fit.

His wide muscly arms are covered in half-finished tribal sleeves on each arm, and the ink continues up over his chest and around his neck. His eyebrow piercing glints in the light and I freeze when I spot the new addition to his lip. He has his usual black army boots on, tucked into black cargo pants, his white t-shirt sticks to his chest and I have to wipe my mouth to check for drool. Not that he would notice, I don't think he even knows I am a girl.

Evan and I grew up in the same section of Paradise, the orphanage, which was basically a forgotten room cleared for him and me. My parents were patrollers who were killed out there, something that was explained to me in excruciating detail to try and squish the longing I have to see the outside world growing in my chest. Evan's mum and dad left Paradise so long ago I can barely remember them, they told him they would carve out a better life for him out there. That it was wrong living down here, just surviving, they wanted to live.

So they left, faced the Wastes even though they knew they might never come back. All he has left of them is the rose tattoos covering the back of each hand, a promise that they will come back for him. They never did. I guess our screwed up past made us fast friends. I was new to the orphanage section, which was basically a massive room with beds shoved so close together you can almost touch. Only one bathroom is attached, so a hovel. A place to leave the kids that don't matter, but Evan sure proved them wrong. I knew he would. Ever since he was young, he wanted to be a doctor, to help people. I never understood why, it's not like he's a people person, but all he would say is that he did it for the people he loved, whatever that meant. Anyway, we have been inseparable ever since. Only, we both grew up. My feelings for him turned deeper, and I started noticing things a best friend shouldn't. But to him, I will always be Pip, the little girl he used to sing and cuddle to sleep when she cried for her dead parents. Shaking my head and the depressing thoughts away I point at his lip.

"New?"

He dusts off the book before setting it gently down on the workstation behind him and swivelling to face me. "Yeah, I was bored last night and decided to see if I could."

I giggle at that, I asked him to pierce my ears once and I have never seen such outrage in somebody's eyes before he snatched away his gun and walked away like Misty was chasing him.

Swinging my legs back and forth on the bed I look at the floor. My long brown hair falls into my face and with a puff I blow it away. Freezing, I hold my breath as a tattooed hand appears in front of my face. With the utmost care, Evan brushes away my hair and puts it behind my ear, smiling at me softly. I return it as his hand lingers against my cheek. Gulping, I beg myself not to lean into his touch. His green eyes change and my heart stutters as I see desire burning in them, but as quick as it came, it disappears and he drops his hand and turns away like I am diseased. He has been doing that a lot lately.

Gritting my teeth, I twist my mum's wedding ring on my finger nervously. "So, what we doing today Doc? Dissecting cannibals, stitching patrols who shot themselves in the foot?"

Without looking at me he turns on his computer and wiggles the mouse. "Nope, you are going to class."

Groaning, I fall back dramatically on the bed and stare at the boring white ceiling, just like every other ceiling down here. "C'mon Evvie, don't be so boring. I only have three months left and we both know I am not going into the water systems engineering." I shiver at the last, seriously? Who would pick cleaning out shit as their job for the rest of their lives?

"Exactly Piper, so stop being such a brat and just go to your classes and stop bugging me at work," he snaps and I sit bolt upright glaring at his hunched form. Brat? Bugging? Ugh, Mr. Mardy is obviously in one of his lovely moods today.

Hopping down from the bed I throw a glare at him as I talk, which can I just say is lost on him...it was a good glare too. All narrowed eyed with deep intensity, boy would have shit a brick but sadly he remains staring intently at his scans ignoring my strop. "Sorry for bothering you with my bratty ways your dickness," I say before turning to leave.

"Dickness, really?" he calls and I glance over my shoulder to see he hasn't even looked away from the screen, even if I can hear the smile in his voice. What a cum bucket.

"Yep, it's like your highness 'cos you are super stuck up, but also a dick. So dickness, maybe you should get that tattooed on you next," I fume, spinning around again.

"Where are you going Pip?" he asks and I don't stop this time, unwilling to let him see the hurt in my expression. He has been pushing me away more and more, and it doesn't get any easier.

"To hang out with someone who actually appreciates me and doesn't treat me like I am shit on the bottom of his shoe." Stomping out the door I hear him swear as he tries to come after me, it makes me smile a little. We can never stay mad at each other long, and sometimes it takes me spelling it out for him to realise what he has done.

"Come on, Pip. I didn't mean—oh hello General Kertol." I spin and see the Paradise guard's general standing with his arms behind his back and his expectant expression on his hard is face, which is swinging between me and Evan before he ignores me completely and turns to face Evan.

"Doctor Sencal, we need your assistance."

"Of course general. I will be right there," Evan says smoothly.

With a nod the general walks away, not even uttering a hello at me. I flip him the bird with both hands, immature but it makes me feel better. I look at Evan to see him glaring at me even as his lips twitch.

"We can carry on this argument later Pip."

Huffing, I turn around. "Sure, whatever you say your royal dickness."

Happy I got the last word, I flounce away in search of something fun to do, screw Evan and his attitude. I can't keep letting him get to me, and one of these days he will push too hard or say something he can't take back.

I GROAN as Todd fumbles against my chest, his clumsy hands looking for my breasts as he kisses me without breathing. Okay, so he's not the best kisser, or the smartest semen in the stream, but he sure is good looking and he does take my mind off Evan for a little bit. Plus, he sure can wear that guard uniform. Turning my head to the side, I roll my eyes as he pants into my neck and moans like a porn star. Really dude, I haven't even touched his junk and he sounds like he is going to explode like a shaken can of coke.

Looking around him while he fondles my breast and dry humps me like a dog on speed, I soon get bored. The room we are in is—you guessed it—all white! Gasp! It was probably a water storage plant at one point, but they never use it anymore and all the teenagers sneak down here to hang out. I am regretting that decision as Todd, the numbnuts of Paradise, dribbles down my neck. Okay, time to go.

"Todd, I have a meeting with my selection adviser," I say and push him away. He groans and moves back, looking disappointed.

"Fine, you want to meet later?" he asks hopefully, cupping his crotch as if I couldn't understand the implication.

"We'll see." Reaching down I grab my jacket and leave before he can corner me.

Sauntering to the classroom where I am supposed to meet the uptight adviser, I just turn a corner when I freeze in shock. My heart stops and I feel like I might faint. They don't notice me, too busy feeling each other up in the corridor, but I can see from the tattooed hands and arms who it is. Evan and some skank. He leans his head back against the wall and stops her with one hand, but I have seen enough. Spinning so they don't see me I flee, the tears start to fall. It's stupid and only makes me angrier at myself. I mean I was just doing the same thing, but Evan doesn't fuck around. Never has, hell I've never even seen him with a woman. Something about him always being too busy. He must care about her. The thought stops me, and I lean against the wall before sliding down to sit on my arse. All my hopes and stupid dreams of him finally noticing me and giving us a go evaporate. God, I am so stupid. Of course he would never notice me.

I sit there for a while, throwing myself a pity party before I wipe my eyes and drag myself to my feet. Fuck him, I have survived a lot in this bloody life, I can survive losing him to.

The thought drives me, but it also makes me realise I have been waiting. Just lingering like I knew something was coming, tugging on his doctor's coat the whole time like a child with a comfort blanket. Never making a real decision for myself. Well fuck that, it's time I decided how I imagine my future. I just hope I can be grown up enough to keep him in it, just as a friend.

Printed in Poland
by Amazon Fulfillment
Poland Sp. z o.o., Wrocław